A Sleeping Lion

Barbara Jago

Out of suffering have emerged the strongest souls; the most massive characters are seared with scars.
Khalil Gibran

For my son,
Karl Jago
Thank you for insisting I write this

Chapter 1

UGANDA 1995

A thousand flapping wings darkened the sky as birds took to the air, alarming the Colobus monkeys that screeched in fear as they scrambled through the treetops. The hackles rose on the necks of a pride of powerful cats, who preferred to hunt at dawn, knowing their prey was less alert, their young vulnerable. Alarmed, they sniffed the air, their manes bristling with apprehension. Reluctant to abandon their meal, after a hungry three days, they dragged the carcass of the young antelope with them as they ran from the smell of smoke being carried on the wind, and the sound of gunfire ripping through screams.

In the distance, a fierce orange glow of flames danced across the hellish scene of slaughter and mayhem being wreaked upon the people of Cobo village, by murderous rebel soldiers hell-bent on stealing their children.

***

Held at gunpoint and paralysed with terror, thirteen-year-old Joseph Amaru watched his father, Jacob, die in a barrage of bullets that tore through his head and torso. His father, simply trying to protect him and his sister. The impact spattered blood and brains on the walls of the thatch-roofed hut and sent Jacob's body crashing against his wife, Dembe, knocking her to the ground. Ignoring her howls of outrage and horror, a rebel, one of many, straddled her. Joseph averted his eyes, knowing his mother would not want him to witness her degradation, and, choking on anger, fear and helplessness, clenched his hands so hard he did not feel his nails draw blood as they dug into his palms. He pulled his terrified sister closer, blocking her view of their father's lifeless body and the gross sexual assault being inflicted on his mother, who, less than an hour before, he had helped to carry water in plastic containers from the river, in preparation for the day ahead. His heart splintered as the last of the armed rebels – a boy no older than fifteen – violated Dembe, and displaying icy disdain, riddled her with bullets.

Scared witless, five-year-old Mimi, her face pressed into Joseph's chest, babbled over and over, 'Twinkle, twinkle little star …' taught to her by her mother to chase away the bogeyman. Joseph had often told her there were no bogeymen. He was wrong.

***

Dragged into the clearing where village meetings were conducted and where, just the day before, he had taken part in school lessons taught by his mother (and ironically, celebrations to welcome a new life) Joseph gasped, his senses assaulted by smoke-filled air permeated by the rancid stench of burning bodies and the metallic smell of blood. He shuddered at the sight of the terror-stricken village children he had known all his life being herded together at gunpoint.

Recognisable as the rebels' leader from the grubby white uniform jacket he wore instead of the khaki worn by his men,

Odango Lusaka stood six feet five inches tall – a monstrous size for a monstrous man. Sweating in the humidity, he opened his arms as if to embrace the newly orphaned children before him, his voice booming: 'I am your father, now. I am Papa Odango. Who am I?' he demanded.

The children whimpered, prodded by the barrels of guns.

'Who am I?' Odango roared.

Terrified, all but Joseph answered, 'Papa Odango.'

His smile, displaying wolfish teeth the colour of aged tombstones, didn't reach his eyes, which narrowed on hearing the screams of protest from a woman nearby.

Ariya, a villager clutching her new-born son whom Joseph's mother had helped deliver the day before, was frantically trying to stop a soldier from taking her screaming daughter, Kizza.

At just twelve years old, Kizza was small for her age. Her skinny arms and legs protruded from a worn cotton dress, its once-vibrant colours now faded from constant washing. Despite her young age, Kizza was respected in the village as an assistant to her mother, a traditional healer much relied on to cure illness.

The soldier knocked Ariya to the ground and kicked her before slapping Kizza hard, making her head snap back. The second blow was delivered with such force, it lifted her off her feet and sent her flying into the midst of the cowering children.

The stifled rage simmering inside Joseph ignited. He lunged at the soldier, landing a punch that sent the man reeling. The rebels jeered and bustled around. A skinny man with no front teeth, grabbed Joseph in a firm grip, calling out, 'Commander, we have a fighter here!'

Odango watched Joseph kick and struggle to free himself from the man's grasp, as he was pushed towards him. 'What's your name, boy?' he demanded.

Joseph looked into Odango's soulless eyes, one of which was filmed with white caused by onchocerciasis, known in Uganda as river blindness. He shuddered.

'Joseph Amaru,' he replied.

'You like to fight? I like that in a man,' he smiled, taking a Kalashnikov AK-47 from a soldier standing close by and hanging it around Joseph's skinny shoulders. The weight of it almost made his legs buckle.

With the reek of gun oil catching in his throat, Joseph could feel the power of the weapon; it frightened him.

'Let's see how much of a man you are,' Odango said, his arms encircling him from behind. Joseph recoiled from the stench of his breath as the huge man leant close. Forcibly guiding Joseph's finger onto the trigger, Odango pointed the weapon at Ariya, who had fought like a lioness when they snatched her baby from her arms.

A belief prevailed among the ignorant that the blood and body parts of a newborn would bring wealth and long life, and cure diseases like SLIM, which was just becoming known in the Western world as AIDS. It was considered more potent if the victim was less than a year old, its body parts chopped up, and the blood drunk by diabolical shamans claiming to be healers.

Her husband struck down in front of her, and unable to save her children from the horrors they were facing, Ariya – blood running from her broken nose – turned burning, hate-filled eyes on the man responsible. The force of her glare made Odango spasm with fear. 'Kill her,' he ordered Joseph. 'Kill the woman.'

Joseph recoiled in horror, shook his head. Odango's eyes narrowed dangerously. 'I said, kill her.' Odango's tone, cold and emphatic, sent shivers of fear down Joseph's spine.

Taking the life of another human being was unimaginable to Joseph. His father had taught him to love his neighbour as he loved himself and to respect the poor creatures that were needed for food. Despite fearing for his own life, he pulled his finger away from the trigger.

With an exaggerated sigh, Odango ran his eyes over the petrified children and settled on the smallest, the one of least value. Too young for the brothels and too small to fight. He roared, 'Chop her!'

A soldier swung a panga, a type of African machete, slicing clean through Mimi's thin neck. She died instantly, falling like a broken doll in the dirt.

Joseph shuddered with shock, screams choking in his throat. Like his parents, his adoring little sister with her annoying, persistent questions and hunger for knowledge, was no more. The children were stunned into silence.

Odango roared again at Joseph, 'Kill the woman, or they all die!' There was no mercy in Odango Lusaka, who, once indoctrinated into the Lord's Resistance Army, had found the perfect outlet for his psychopathic rage.

Ariya had grown calm, accepting her fate. 'Do it Joseph. Save the children. Save my Kizza. Take care of her. Promise me."

Having failed to protect Mimi and not sure that he could even protect himself, Joseph hesitated.

'Say it! Say you promise! A life for a life,' Ariya urged, pain and desperation etched on her face.

His heart pounding, Joseph nodded. 'I promise.'

'You hear that?' Odango called out with a smirk on his face. The soldiers joined in his mirth. The grin turned to a sneer as he viciously slapped Joseph. 'Promises are not yours to make, boy.'

Ariya snarled and forked two fingers at Odango: 'God damn you! I curse you, Odango Lusaka. The demons will get you and you will burn in hell for all eternity.'

'Kill her now! Kill the witch!' roared Odango, who still believed in the power of witch doctors, despite claiming allegiance to Jesus.

'Be strong, daughter!' Ariya shouted to Kizza, then spoke gently to Joseph. 'I forgive you.'

Helpless against the evil force surrounding him and the threat to murder the remaining children, Joseph pulled the trigger.

The bullets from the automatic weapon raked through Ariya's body. A gasp of stunned disbelief left his lips and he staggered back in horror, watching Ariya fall to the earth with blood pooling around her. A mix of desolation and rage overwhelmed him, and he felt emotions he had never before experienced, as tendrils of revenge crept into his heart and mind.

Odango removed the gun from Joseph's trembling hands and passed it to a nearby soldier. The children shrank back as he lifted his panga and brought the knife down, slicing a stinging one-inch gash in Joseph's cheek – a fate they would all suffer in due course.

'The mark of Odango. Now you are mine,' he said, grinning like a proud father. *I will never be yours*, Joseph silently vowed.

Chapter 2

20 YEARS LATER - NAPLES. ITALY.

In Naples, once described as a vibrant city of threadbare beauty with a malevolent underbelly, fifty women and men sat at electric sewing machines, daily turning out hundreds of garments and other products. Huge rolls of colourful fabric and leather lined the walls. Clothing, handbags, scarves and hats, all bearing the fake logo of one famous brand or another, were being boxed by a team of industrious women for delivery across Europe.

A skinny man, polluting the air with his chain-smoking, held out a garment to a young woman who had sewn a crooked seam. He threw the garment into a bin, warning that the cost would be docked from her pay: 'One more mistake and you will be out of a job.' The woman, like most of the workers, would be glad to do anything but this, but she knew she had little hope of it happening. Outside of the syndicate, there was scant work in the city, and they all had families to feed. Deafened by the noise of the machines, which gave her a permanent headache, she sighed, her eyes going to a large photo on one wall. The hard-faced, bird-eyed man with sparse, black-dyed hair – Sergio Gianelli, the detested capo of the Gianelli family, for whom they all worked.

She would like to spit in his face, but knew there was no chance of doing so and living to tell the tale.

High in the ceiling above her, sturdy glass tiles cemented into the marble walkway of the magnificent Galleria Umberto tried without success to bring natural light into the cavernous space. Through them she could discern the shadows of people passing overhead. She wished she had the time to idle around her city, like the tourists who ambled through the galleria in awe of the many impressive shops and the magnificent construction of glass and iron that towered above them.

Impressed by the grandeur, sightseers were unaware of the illegal factories below their feet as they walked past hard-faced old men who sat in the galleria cafés drinking coffee and eating cannoli, wearing custom-made suits like badges of honour and talking about the 'good old days,' when they had been far from good. If anyone dared to challenge them about their violent past, they would shrug and tell them, 'It was the way it was. You did what you had to do if you wanted to survive.' The fact that they had survived was warning enough to be extremely wary of them.

Beyond the enclosed atmosphere of the elegant Umberto, Naples was – is – a world of chaos.

The city, never noted for its cleanliness, pulsates with life. Scooters and motorbikes dart noisily and dangerously in and out of the crazy traffic. Italians are reputed for their love of speed; Naples is no exception. The death toll on its roads is the highest after Rome, and many pedestrians add to that number. Neapolitans step into speeding traffic without blinking, while tourists hover nervously on pavements, hoping a friendly native will walk them across a busy road. On backstreet corners, men sell cheap jewellery, underwear and faux football shirts from rickety street stalls, ignoring the teenage boys who carry out business in the shadowy alleyways, pubescent girls in faux leather miniskirts and exaggerated eye make-up acting as lookouts for their narcotic-dealing boyfriends.

It was the way of life, each to his own, and a man's business was his own. But the angry roar of a crowd coming from the Piazza del Plebiscito, a magnificent square built of volcanic rock taken from Vesuvius and home to the city's most emblematic buildings, caught everyone's attention.

From his chauffeur-driven Rolls-Royce, Sergio Gianelli watched as the Piazza vibrated with tension and uproar. A heckling crowd railed against a speaker using a megaphone, trying to inflame anger against the town's growing number of illegal African immigrants, whom he blamed for the loss of jobs and the high cost of living. It was a cheap, blatant attempt to garner votes. Despite resenting the immigrants, the people of Naples resented the Northern League political party even more, never forgetting that they had fiercely criticised the poorer southern city for receiving tax-funded benefits from Rome. It took little effort for paid agitators to incite the crowd to action, and the whey-faced politician was soon pelted with rotten fruit and fish heads, forcing him and his assistant to make a hasty retreat to their vehicle. The mob jeered and cheered as the car made its swift departure, plastered in garbage.

Gianelli nodded and gave a satisfied grunt, seeing that his money had been well spent.

Chapter 3

On Lampedusa Island off the west coast of Italy, a storm raged. Thunder boomed with earth-shaking intensity. Lightning skittered across the sky, illuminating a group of terrified African men desperately clinging to the sides of a small fishing boat as it lurched around in turbulent seas. The rain, lashing against Joseph Amaru's face, went unnoticed as six-foot waves washed over them.

'Jesus! Help us!' one man pleaded aloud.

'Life jackets! Now!' Joseph yelled to the man at the helm.

The captain, a weasel-faced North African with a mouth full of gold teeth – his earnings made ferrying refugees from Tunis to Italy – struggled to keep control of the vessel. Fearing the worst, he cried out to a crew member to release the life jackets, previously only available if the immigrants he was smuggling into Europe paid extra. Too late. An immense wave enveloped the boat, which splintered under its might, throwing all on board into the raging sea. Screams for help went unheard as the refugees struggled against the onslaught of nature and their inevitable deaths.

Gasping for air as he surfaced, Joseph made a frantic grab for a yellow vest riding the surface. But the crashing surf tossed him around like a cork, hell-bent on separating him from the one thing that could keep him alive. Thinking this was no way to die after all he had endured, Joseph battled the waves and the elements until the slippery surface of the life jacket was within his grasp. With the deluge continually slamming against him, he struggled to inflate and lift the vest over his head. Unable to tie it around his body, he grasped the cord in his hands.

Lungs on fire and limbs numbed by the icy coldness, he let the force of the sea carry him, until he reached the point where he wondered if the peace he had so long sought was just a matter of closing his eyes and letting go. But his hands, frozen into claws, refused to release him from his grip on the cord. Energy spent, he drifted into a semi-conscious state, tempting nature and fate to do their work.

It was some time before he felt his feet drag against the seabed and his knees scrape against pebbles washed up in the storm.

The muscles in his legs screamed in protest as he staggered from the sea, retching up the salty mess from his protesting stomach and gulping oxygen into his starved lungs. Relieved to be on land, he pulled off the yellow jacket and turned to look back at the raging deluge. When angered, the ocean was merciless, yet it had spat him out, and he was grateful to it. He caught sight of something, and rubbed the water from his eyes, not sure what he was seeing through the sheets of rain. With a gasp of shock, he realised it was another man, clinging to a piece of the doomed boat, struggling to make it to land. With adrenaline pumping through his veins and obliterating the pain in his limbs, Joseph turned back into the maelstrom and fought his way towards the floundering man. Using the last vestiges of his strength, he helped him to safety before collapsing onto the stony shore.

Surrounded by life jackets that had washed up onto the beach, each containing the ghost of a man, the two lay prostrate in silent exhaustion, lacking the strength to find shelter, or even to speak. Rain continued to lash their drenched bodies as the crash of waves pounded the coast, mixing with the rumble of thunder to create a powerful symphony, partnered with lightning as it danced gleefully to nature's tune across the night sky.

Relief flooded through Joseph as the storm abated and all grew calm, his breathing and the pounding of his heart slowing with it. He looked up at the heavens and a deep sigh escaped him.

Europe. Freedom. Peace at last.

Wiping the rain from his face, the younger man reached into his shirt and pulled out a Bible wrapped in a plastic bag. Pleased it was still safe, he waved it at the sky, shouting, 'Thank you, Jesus!'

Joseph didn't believe Jesus had much to do with it. If there was a God – and he had every reason to doubt it – there was no evidence of Him this night, letting good men rot in the ocean when all they had craved was a kinder way of life.

'I'm Big Moses. Who are you, old man?' his companion asked.

It didn't surprise Joseph that the man thought he was old. His struggle for survival had taken its toll: lines etched his thirty-two-year-old face, and his cropped hair was prematurely grey.

'Joseph Amaru.'

Big Moses pulled off his sodden shirt, exposing a scarred body.

'Where are you from, Joseph?'

Recognising his native language, he answered, 'The same place as you.' *Hell.*

***

UGANDA 1995

Joseph and Kizza, tied in a human chain of misery, trudged for a day and a half through forests and across open bush to the northern border of Uganda, where Odango and the rebels were based. Once there, they gulped down water and devoured the meagre ration of food that was on offer.

The encampment housed at least two hundred people. The men, including boys younger than Joseph, carried AK-47 rifles strapped to their young bodies. Joseph was later to learn that to lose your gun was to lose your life. Young women, babies strapped to their backs, tended a field of vegetables big enough to feed a small army.

There was no welcome from the people in the camp; to Joseph, most appeared to be as unforgiving and cruel as the soldiers who had kidnapped them. He flinched, watching a small boy being beaten to a pulp for wanting to go home. Kizza, traumatised by the brutality that had invaded her life, was too terrified to look, and despite harbouring a grudge against Joseph for killing her mother, she clung to him.

The days ran into one another as soldiers repeatedly used all forms of violence on the children to ensure their obedience. Despite such brutality, they often had to attend an open-air Mass held by a man calling himself a priest. This man preached that their leader, sent by God and known as 'The Messiah', was fighting a rebel war against the government for the benefit of the people. Joseph felt the pain from the blows but mentally armed himself against the psychological brainwashing they had to endure each day, remembering his father's words: 'Don't let another man's words or deeds poison your soul. Think for yourself.' He soon realised that weakness here was a passport to death and urged Kizza, who had withdrawn into herself and hardly spoke, that if she didn't want to be whipped, chained for days without food and water, or die by the panga, it was best to play the game and follow orders. *Until the chance comes.*

Thoughts of Mimi and of his parents made his heart ache, and the tendrils of revenge grew stronger by the day. He seethed with frustration when they moved Kizza to the far side of the camp where girls, young as eleven, worked as servants, cooks, prostitutes and wives – gifts to loyal soldiers who would pick a name written on a scrap of paper from a sweat-stained hat. That girl was then theirs to do with as they wanted.

Jesus, please keep Kizza safe,' he murmured. It would be the last prayer to leave his lips.

Chapter 4

NAPLES 2018

Opposite the Napoli Centrale train station on Plaza Garibaldi, selling fake designer handbags from the pavement alongside other African men, Joseph smiled, watching Jacob, Benjamin and Bollo joke with tourists as they haggled about the prices of their fake goods. Big Moses called out, 'Looky! Looky! Designer bags. Thirty euros. Cheap as chips,' making the British tourists laugh. Abdi, a slight Angolan man with buck teeth and a permanent frown, looked sullen. Joseph had seen that look on many who had arrived in Naples expecting something better, only to find that work papers were impossible to obtain, and the only employer available to them was Sergio Gianelli. Joseph had accepted that if he wanted to remain and survive in Naples, he had to conform to the demands made on him whether he liked them or not. The job was less than desirable, but it was a chance to earn the money needed to serve his purpose, and he took it with both hands.

'Ten. I'll give you ten euros,' said a woman with tattooed arms, holding out a bag with the fake Channel logo imprinted on it to Big Moses.

'Did you say ten? Lady, ten wouldn't pay for the zip on that bag.'

'Okay, fifteen. I'll give you fifteen,' she persisted.

'Twenty-five, and we've got a deal.' He turned away, a sign he would no longer barter with her.

Disappointed that her attempt at haggling had failed, the woman made a show of examining the bag. It was a good copy with no obvious flaws, so she begrudgingly paid the price.

It impressed Joseph to see kind-hearted Moses for once not beaten down by a persistent customer. They could only earn a small margin on each product, requiring them to work long hours to make a living. The smile on his face froze as water suddenly splashed on the pavement near him and his bags.

Maria Rinaldi, the owner of the Café Borolo, a verbose seventy-year-old Italian widow with a commanding presence, had never forgiven her husband for dying of lung cancer twelve years before at the age of sixty-five. Smoking yourself to death was not something Maria could comprehend, no more than she understood why, to her mind, her city was full of African men. Sweeping the water into the gutter, she glared at Joseph.

He had intruded a few inches onto the pavement space outside of her café; now he edged the blanket displaying his fake designer bags, a few inches away until she was satisfied.

Tall and elegant, with long silver grey hair tied back in a loose bun, Maria ranted to herself, Italian style, loud enough for Joseph to hear.

'Coming here from God-knows-where, taking business away from good Italian people who pay rent and city taxes.'

He ignored her because, despite her obvious bigotry, he thought she was right.

However, she was complaining to the wrong person. He wasn't the Gianelli clan who blocked Africans from obtaining work permits, forcing them to work for them on the streets. He was just a man doing the only job he could do.

A black Mercedes with tinted windows pulled up in front of the café. The driver jumped out to open the back passenger door for a beautiful young woman who religiously visited Maria twice a week, sometimes with a child, and would often sit outside the café to smoke a cigarette. Never once in a year had she even glanced his way.

Seeing her, Maria smiled. *'Carla, luce della mia vita.'* The smile froze into a glare as she laid eyes on the driver, Mario. 'How many times do I have to tell you not to park in front of my door?' Maria said, with hands on hips and a look that dared him to ignore her.

Disgruntled, Mario moved the car a few parking spaces away, making Joseph smile. *I'm not the only one she terrifies.*

Maria turned, smiling at Carla. 'Come inside. I'll get you something to eat.' She gave Joseph another disapproving glance as she ushered the younger woman indoors.

'Please, how much for the black one?'

Turning his attention to the inquiring blonde teenager, he smiled wider. In the time he had lived in Naples, he had learned to differentiate between Europeans by their different attitudes when buying his bags. The Scandinavians were always polite when bartering, unlike the Germans, who were brusque, embarrassed by the haggling. The French scorned the fakes despite wanting them, often claiming the purchase was not for them, but for someone they knew. Brits overall were easy to deal with because they responded to humour, loved the fakes, and spoke the same language. English had been Uganda's official language since its independence from the British in 1962.

Eager to look and buy, a group of friends joined the Swedish girl. Joseph sighed with satisfaction, knowing he would sell his self-imposed quota today. The money was essential, not just for his spartan way of living, but for more important things, which if all went to plan would alleviate the deep sense of loneliness he had felt since leaving Uganda.

***

Glossy brown hair rippling down her back, Carla entered the café, noticing the sign in Maria's window advertising ROOMS TO LET.

The café's interior had remained unchanged since Maria's grandparents had first opened it in the 'fifties, making the Formica tables almost antique. Photos of famous Italian film stars covered the walls, especially Maria's favourites – Sophia Loren and Marcello Mastroianni.

The images were all yellow with age, much like the people they portrayed. It cloaked the café in a nostalgic ambience, where Maria and her customers were comfortable.

Carla slipped off her pink and cream Chanel jacket, hitched her knee-length skirt a little and sat near the window. After the death of her parents, she had spent her teenage years living in the café with Maria, doing her homework at the same table. She sighed with relief. Here with Maria for a few hours a week, she felt safe.

Working the ancient machine, which hissed and spluttered like an aged dragon, Maria produced an aromatic espresso.

'Nothing to eat, Nonna. I had breakfast.'

Maria placed coffee and a pastry on the table in front of her. 'So, you can't eat a small morsel from your grandmother?'

Knowing it was useless to argue, Carla picked up the cake and took a bite. As the sugary pastry awakened her taste buds, she grinned, glad she had relented.

'This is delicious. If I still lived here, I would be the size of a house.'

Sitting with her, Maria protested. 'There could never be too much of you, child.'

Carla frowned. 'Nonna, why the sign in the window? Have you got money troubles?'

With a shrug of her shoulders, Maria huffed, 'Of course I have money troubles. The entire world has money troubles, except the animals who run this city and that pig, Berlusconi, who still lives and breathes.'

Carla took her grandmother's hand and begged, 'Please let me help you, Nonna. You shouldn't have to work, wear Nonno's old shirts, or rent out rooms. I can make your life easier.'

'I enjoy wearing your grandfather's shirts.' Maria smiled, running a hand down the front of the shirt she was wearing with the sleeves rolled up, over her linen pants, 'Enrico loved his tailor-made shirts. They were the only luxury he allowed himself. And if I didn't work, what would I do? Sit around waiting to die, like all the gossiping old crones who gather in Arturo's café, because they have nothing better to do?' She reached out and touched Carla tenderly on her cheek. 'Don't worry about me. Just seeing you and my great-grandson makes my life easier.'

'Yes, but – ' protested Carla.

'No buts. I've told you many times I would rather die than accept *his* money.' Maria sounded adamant. 'But enough of that. How is my beautiful Giancarlo?'

'Growing every day. The school says he has above-average intelligence for his age.'

'Of course he has. He takes after his mother.'

Carla smiled, knowing that even if her son were the slowest pupil in the class, her grandmother would still think he was a genius.

'So, when will I see him?'

'You could always come to the apartment and see him

whenever you like, Nonna.'

Maria shook her head, frowning. 'You know I won't do that.'

Carla put her hand over hers. 'I know and I understand. It is what it is. But I promise you will see Giancarlo soon. He grows to look more like Pappa every day.'

'Ahhh…my beautiful Gianni.' Sadness clouded Maria's face at the thought of her dead son.

***

Gianni Rinaldi – Maria's son, Carla's father – had fought crime and corruption. He was involved in organising protests against companies owned by the Camorra, who were dumping millions of tons of toxic waste north-east of Naples in illegal landfills. Gianni, a lawyer, went head-on against political and police collusion with the syndicates. Maria rightly had feared for his life, but he was as stubborn as his father when it came to taking advice. To stop the dumping and to force politicians into action, he organised a massive demonstration that resulted in the toxic industrial complex facing closure. Not long after, Gianni and his wife, Francesca, died when their car was run off the road. Heartbroken at losing her only child, but knowing the Camorra was responsible for their deaths, Maria was powerless to react if she was to keep the then fourteen-year-old Carla safe.

***

The sound of a whistle drew Carla and Maria's attention to what was going on outside. From the window, they watched Joseph and other Africans wrap their goods in blankets and run. The police, on motor scooters, followed without enthusiasm.

'Every day is the same thing,' Maria grumbled. 'The cops make a show of chasing them, and they're back again in five minutes selling that fake rubbish. They should ship them back to where they come from.'

'It's not the Africans who make the fake rubbish and bribe the police, Nonna.'

Maria nodded in agreement. 'True. But better the devils you know...'

Chapter 5

The large warehouses owned by the Gianelli clan stood in an arid area on the outskirts of the city. Massive trailer trucks loaded with illicit fakes kicked up dust storms as they left to distribute their loads across Europe.

Joseph and Big Moses, waiting to pick up stock from the warehouse, surveyed the African men lined up in the relentless August sun. Europeans and Americans often lumped all African people together when they were in fact as diverse in nationality, language and culture as the people of any other continent. But they all had one thing in common: in escaping war or abject poverty, they now sought a better way of life. Like the men he shared a living space with, all the men appeared much younger than Joseph. Being an idealist, he had stayed in Uganda, believing – wrongly – that the conflict in his country would one day be resolved. But it never ceased, and the day came when he was left with no choice but to leave if he was to protect his loved ones.

Swigging from a plastic bottle of water, which was now lukewarm with the heat, Joseph cast his eyes over the nearby line of Italian drug couriers, some as young as fourteen (the legal age to ride a motor scooter), waiting their turn to be handed supplies to be sold on the streets. A cry caught his attention when an angry youth pushed another in the chest, accusing him of jumping the queue. A fight began. Punches were thrown. Others circled around like hyenas, jeering them on. *Cruelty in the young is easily aroused.* Memories assailed his mind.

UGANDA 1995

Joseph flinched, watching a boy who'd been caught trying to desert, being beaten to death by a group of children using sticks made from hardy teak wood Their survival relied on carrying out the gruesome order. The humidity in the rebel camp was oppressive; mosquitoes plagued everyone. As there was not enough room to house them all, Joseph slept outdoors on the ground. It was hard on his body, but he didn't want to be at ease, not here. The pain he felt created a barrier against the army's mantras: false promises of riches when they defeated the government and the illusory promise of continued life. Kids as young as ten, lugging AK-47s, would leave to carry out an attack but never return, despite having been told they were doing the work of the Messiah and that God would protect them. He didn't doubt that they had died in battle and their bodies left somewhere to rot; their guns, having more value, were always returned. The unfortunate ones chosen for latrine duty were also lucky to survive, often contracting malaria or typhoid, which were common in the camp; anyone showing symptoms was cast into the bush to die. It was the way of the rebel army. Child soldiers were expendable.

The supplies were meagre, but enough to keep them alive. After daily indoctrination and lining up for a small portion of plantains and vegetables, prepared and cooked by captive females, Joseph's eyes would search for Kizza without success.

After three weeks of indoctrination, he was chosen for night duty as a lookout. As ordered, and feeling the weight of the gun strapped to his back, he scaled a hundred-foot-high teak tree and lodged himself between the thick branches. In the fading light of dusk, he scanned the terrain, taking in the mountains to the north, the gushing river alongside the camp that stretched as far as the eye could see, and the densely wooded forests. He estimated it to be a few day's march to open-land savanna. Apart from the smoke coming from the women's cooking fires, the camp was undetectable from the air because of the dense foliage covering the roof of each hut. Not that Odango was worried about an air attack. Joseph had seen the anti-air missiles they possessed, provided by the Sudanese Intelligence, which, for a price, supplied arms and logistical support.

Inhaling the scent of the dense jungle mingled with the musty smell of woody undergrowth, and hearing the hollow knocking sound of a nightjar bird, he felt pangs of homesickness for his village. Soon he was overcome with misery, knowing that no one he loved and nothing of what he loved, remained. Night dropped like a black curtain, enveloping him in its intense darkness and sleep was soon tugging at his eyelids, when the roar of a lion startled him awake. He knew from a childhood experience that a lion's roar could be heard for miles, and they preferred the open bush to the forests, but it sounded close enough to keep him alert.

As the light of dawn eventually filtered through the branches, he recalled how he and Kizza would often sneak away from the village and climb a tree to welcome the sunrise. Her face, bathed in golden light, would light up with a big smile as the sun peeped over the horizon. *Where are you, Kizza?*

In search of something to eat after a long, tedious night, he saw a raiding party leave the camp. One of the group he recognised as boy from his village; Tombe, a stupid oaf who liked to bully others. This had led to many spats between them. It was clear to Joseph that he had accepted all they had beaten into him as he carried his automatic weapon with a dumb, proud look on his face, impatient to kill. *Marching off to die. Soon it will be my turn*, he thought, touching the automatic weapon hanging around his neck.

***

They gave me a gun to kill. They give the Italian kids drugs. The only difference is that drugs take longer.

Inside the vast, musty-smelling warehouse stacked with copies of designer bags, scarves, hats, sunglasses and trainers all made in the Gianelli underground factories, Joseph found respite from the searing sun. Fat Guido, his bulging silk shirt stained with underarm sweat, took the money from Joseph, counted it and called out to a worker. 'Nine Michael Kors.'

'I paid for ten,' said Joseph.

'You paid for nine,' Guido sneered. 'Are you calling me stupid?'

Joseph didn't doubt for one moment that Guido was stupid, but replied in a calm voice: 'I paid for ten. Count the money again, please.'

Big Moses shuffled nervously behind him. 'He paid for ten. We counted it twice. Five for me and five for him.'

'If I say it was nine, it was fucking nine. *Capisce?*' Guido spat the words through clenched teeth, blackened from smoking and too much cocaine. He jabbed Joseph in the chest as he spoke, but surprised by the hard wall of muscle beneath the shirt, took a step back.

Guido's voice grew louder, alerting a couple of Camorrista – armed thugs who worked for the gangster families, protecting their assets.

'You should have respect for people,' Big Moses protested.

Guido scoffed, 'Respect? For a bunch of *mulignanas*? Hey everyone, did you hear that? A fucking mulignana.'

Hearing the derogatory word meaning 'egg-plant head,' the Italian workers were amused, but one man stepped forward, his hand on the gun under his jacket. Aware of this, Joseph laid a hand on Big Moses' arm. 'Forget it.'

A worker delivered the nine handbags.

Joseph took them, giving Big Moses another warning look. 'Let's go.'

But his words fell on deaf ears. 'It's not right, treating someone like that. Jesus wouldn't like it,' Moses complained.

The Camorrista with the gun, stepped closer. 'Yeah? And how would Jesus like it if I blew your fucking head off?'

Joseph, five inches shorter than Big Moses, kept his head down and pulled his friend away.

Guido sniggered, looking around at the others. 'Fucking respect. Can you believe it?'

Walking away, Big Moses chewed on his lip, agitated. 'We get no respect. Why don't we get respect?'

'We don't need respect from them. Calm yourself.' Joseph glanced back over his shoulder with a slight tightening of his jaw. *Different skin, different language, but men like them are all the same*, he thought.

'Let's eat something.' He knew the mention of food would distract Big Moses from his agitation.

***

It was hard for immigrants in Naples to find a decent place to live, as prejudice and undeserved mistrust of them ran high. Many of them, escaping from their poor and cramped living quarters, would meet up at Jamal's café-shop, where they were always welcome, to socialise, eat, or use one of the four computers that sat on old tables serving as desks. For some, it was their only form of entertainment. Across a small countertop, Jamal took food and money orders – money to be sent home via Western Union to help support families. An old fridge, with a boisterous compressor, added to the chattering noise and held cold drinks and essential groceries.

Content with his lot, Jamal smiled at his plump baby boy playing happily in his pram, as his wife Saba served up food cooked on a one-ring gas cooker.

Joseph had known Saba throughout her pregnancy and had commiserated with Jamal when her hormones were running amok and he'd had to carry the blame for everything – even the state of the weather – but then he rejoiced with them when Sami was born.

The smell of spices emanating from the tiny kitchen in Jamal's café made Big Moses smile in anticipation. He paid Saba for a can of orange soda and a spicy kebab wrap topped with delicious sauce – a recipe from Saba's mother – which he tucked into with an enormous smile of satisfaction.

Joseph ordered the same. A kebab here was an occasional pleasure he indulged in. He pushed some money across the counter, which Jamal took and counted.

'Same destination?'

Joseph nodded. He had visited this shop tucked away in a side street every week for a year, sending home what he could to his wife and child.

'Business good, Joseph?'

'Up and down. I take each day as it comes.'

Jamal smiled and shrugged. 'The same here. I work sixteen hours a day to make a living. But at least it puts a roof over our heads and feeds us.'

Saba patted Jamal's stomach. 'Feeds him too much sometimes.'

'She's too good a cook, Joseph,' Jamal said, a big grin on his face.

Joseph nodded in agreement as he took a bite, savouring the spicy kebab stuffed into a freshly made pitta bread envelope with crispy salad. 'You're a lucky man, Jamal.'

***

Jamal Abbas felt like a lucky man, but his life had not always been easy. His father, Fariq Abbas, had been a successful business executive in Iraq and provided well for his family. They lived in a middle-class neighbourhood and life was comfortable. Jamal and his sister were privately educated , and Fariq's wife worked as a radiologist. Like so many of his countrymen, he tolerated the thought of Saddam Hussein, believing from experience that one leader was much like another.

Despite his methods, Saddam had brought a certain stability to the country, something which had been lacking for many years, and business thrived. Aware that politics was a dangerous game to get involved in, Fariq steered clear of anyone with strong opinions about the government. When the US attacked, he despaired, believing it would not end well and the Americans would rape his country. If things had been hard under Saddam, they soon became worse. Thousands of people perished. Commerce died, and so did his business. He became angry about the attack based on lies and turned that anger against the invaders. Because his anti-American stance was a threat to his family's safety, Fariq was left with no option but to leave Iraq. He salvaged enough money from his ruined business to seek refuge in Italy, where the welcome was far from warm. Working on the railways, a far cry from what he was used to, he was nonetheless thankful for the job. His wife, Farah, cleaned houses with her fifteen-year-old daughter, who studied at night. Jamal attended a local school to learn the language and the ways of the people. Uprooted to a place that at first seemed hostile, Jamal's world as a ten-year-old refugee was in chaos. Naples was not the easiest place for a foreign child to assimilate into. He took a few beatings and had to learn how to make the sign of the cross before the Italian kids accepted him.

***

Abdi, waiting to buy a can of Coke, snorted his derision. 'At least you don't have the Gianelli clan on your back. It's not right what they charge us. The tourists never want to pay the price we ask. How are we expected to live?' he grumbled.

Playing on a computer, Jacob responded, 'Complain to Gianelli, not to us.'

'And get killed for it? No thanks. But I spit on Sergio Gianelli.' Hearing this, everyone in the shop stopped talking. Jamal looked around, fearing the wrong person may have overheard as a motor scooter went past, carrying two youths who chucked their empty soda cans into his shop, a common-enough occurrence.

'I wouldn't say that too loud, Abdi, if I were you,' said Joseph, knowing how ruthless the Gianelli clan could be. 'Unless you want to stir up a pit of snakes.'

Chapter 6

The sleek white Rolls-Royce convertible with tinted windows arrived at the tall iron gates of a country estate. Surrounded by eight-foot walls and a mass of rain-starved vegetation, the complex stood in the shadow of Mount Vesuvius, a volcano waiting to erupt. The well-oiled gates swung open to reveal extensive landscaped gardens. The lush greenness and flowering bushes were in stark contrast to the dry red earth surrounding the complex and the bordering forest of trees wilting in the heat. An armed guard patrolling the grounds banged against the rails of a large cage to quieten the dogs, alerted by the sound of the arriving car. It pulled into the forecourt past two more muscular guards. Frankie Esposito closed the gates as his brother Toni, the younger of the two, opened the car door.

'Signora Gianelli, welcome home.'

Lucia Gianelli, clad in Italian haute couture, didn't even acknowledge his presence. Her shoulder length hair was a magnificent, shining curtain, as perfectly cut as the cream dress she was wearing. She would have been the epitome of style if it wasn't for the ostentatious excess of diamonds on her fingers, wrists and throat, glistening in the sun. As she entered the mock ancient Roman villa with marble columns at the entrance, she issued a curt order to the guards to unload her luggage.

The five-inch heels of her custom made, black patent-leather Louboutins made a sharp clacking noise on the blue-grey Carrara marble floor, as she made her way through the house. Priceless artwork hung on the walls. She didn't like any of it. Her taste, developed when she was a young art student, ran to modern, but her husband Sergio liked traditional Italian painters; his collection even boasted a Caravaggio. Lucia didn't doubt that he had stolen or swindled someone out of it. She could not think of one redeeming quality in her husband's nature – what Sergio wanted, he got by taking. She recalled their first anniversary nine years earlier, when she had invested in a gift for him, a canvas by American abstract expressionist Mark Rothko. When he saw it, he laughed and told her she had been had, 'Like the dumb bitch you are.' He refused to hang it, and when she complained, he burnt it – a two-million-dollar bonfire. At first, she despaired at the destruction and his ignorance, but it now gave her pleasure knowing a similar piece had recently sold for ten million. Every time there was a price rise on Rothko's work, she would casually mention it over a meal, hoping it would choke him.

Lucia was an exceptional beauty. She was just twenty years old when Sergio first saw her sitting in a pavement café flirting with a young man sporting shoulder length hair and a cute dimple. Both were talking avidly about their day spent at the local art academy. Determined to have her, Sergio donated a sizable chunk of money to the Academia and requested a tour of the premises. Stopping at Lucia's easel, where she was working, he pretended to be impressed by her work. Flattered by his attention, she accepted his invitation to see his art collection. Finding his way to Lucia's heart was easy. She was a magpie for anything that sparkled, especially the diamonds he showered her with.

He was fifty when she married him, a man who exuded power and had a certain charm, when it suited him. Blinded by the glamour of his wealth, at first Lucia didn't see the cruelty that went with the thin lips, Roman nose and emotionless eyes. Nor did she know of the long list of widows he had created.

In ten years, there had been no children from their union – a failure on her part, in Sergio's eyes. But Lucia knew better. She was Sergio's second wife. His previous one of twenty years, also childless, conveniently died in a car accident, leaving behind a seemingly distraught husband free to marry her. It didn't take her long to realise grief was an alien feeling for Sergio. In fact, any feelings outside of his sadism and greed were beyond his comprehension. Love was not part of his wanting her; she was just another acquisition. At first, the sex was tolerable, but now she was grateful that he rarely touched *her*.

Michael Rossi, Sergio's *consiglieri*, a financial wizard who handled all things financial for the family – including the laundering of money – stepped out of the room he used as an office. A slight look of concern crossed his face, which quickly dissolved into a smile. 'Lucia! You are back earlier than expected.'

'I was bored, Michael. Venice has lost its charm for me. Too many tourists.'

'And the Principessa?'

'The woman is a hypochondriac. Something that wasn't apparent when she invited me to stay,' Lucia groaned. 'Can you imagine every day having to listen to a person whine about "My back, my stomach, my knees." At first, I was sympathetic, but soon realised it was all in her fucking head.'

'Sometimes people can suffer the symptoms of an illness even if it is in the head,' said Michael. 'I'm sure your presence, no matter how short, was a comfort to her.' Knowing how selfish and self-indulgent Lucia had become, Michael doubted his own words.

'The palacio was cold and draughty. How they live in those damp places, I will never know.' She reached out to the handle on the study door, but his hand quickly covered hers.

'Lucia, I suggest you take some refreshment first. Don Sergio is holding an important business meeting.'

Lucia studied his face, which was, as usual, implacable and hard to read. With his chiselled features, blue eyes and dark blond hair, one could mistake him for German, despite his Italian heritage.

'He's never minded me walking in on his meetings before.'

'He left strict instructions he was not to be disturbed.'

She scoffed. 'I'm sure it doesn't apply to me.'

Michael could not tell her that it especially applied to her. Not prepared to restrain her further, he stood aside as she opened the door and walked into the room.

It took Lucia a moment to register what she was seeing. A thin, pale girl, all of fourteen or fifteen years of age with bouffant hair and exaggerated eye makeup, was on her knees in front of Sergio while he watched a daytime soap opera on a sixty-inch television.

'Sergio!' Lucia screamed in disgust. 'You filthy pig! She's a child!'

Sergio let out a sigh of impatience. Flicking his hand, he dismissed the teenager as he zipped up his fly.

Lucia slapped the girl's face as she scooted past her. 'Slut!'

Taking the girl's arm, Michael hurried her away.

Looking bored, Sergio turned off the television and surveyed Lucia. 'You're back early.'

Lucia's lips curled in disgust. 'In the name of Jesus. Kids? You know what they call people who do that with children? Do you?'

He appeared unperturbed as he looked her over. She didn't notice the slight tightening of his jaw as she shrieked, 'I want out. You hear me? It's over! I'm leaving. I no longer want your filthy, paedophile hands near me. You revolt me! You're a disgusting, impotent animal. I want out!'

'Have I ever denied you anything?' he asked Lucia in a cold voice. Without blinking an eye, Sergio reached into a drawer, took out a gun and shot her.

Lucia's mouth dropped open in stunned surprise as a blood stain spread across the front of her €5,000 couture dress.

Michael and Gino, Sergio's nephew, alarmed by the sound of gunfire, burst into the room, followed by a couple of armed men. They were stunned to see Lucia drop dead to the floor.

Seeing the look on their faces, Sergio shrugged. 'What? You want me to listen to that ageing, barren bitch nagging me for the rest of my fucking life? Get rid of her.'

At a diminutive five foot five, like his uncle, Gino was fit and whippet-thin. But if he could have added the chip on his shoulder to his height, he would have measured over six feet. His mouth, a little too fleshy for a man, was slack with shock.

'*Tio*, you shot Lucia…here?'

'No. I shot her in Rome and brought her here. What the fuck do you think I did? I said get rid of her.'

Wearing a garish, custom-made Versace outfit, Gino didn't relish the idea of hauling a bloody corpse around, but despite being related to Sergio, he knew better than to argue with the capo of the Gianelli Clan. He and the two guards were about to lift Lucia's body when Sergio shouted, 'Wait!' He removed all

Lucia's diamonds before kicking her dead body, muttering, 'Ungrateful bitch.'

***

Michael, well-practiced at hiding the feelings of contempt he felt for Sergio and the nephew Gino, displayed no emotion. Ever since his gambling-addicted grandfather lost the family fortune and became indebted to them, there was no chance of the Rossi family ever escaping the clutches of the Gianelli clan. The syndicates had as many idiot brutes as they needed, so they valued men with brains. They had paid for Michael's education as they did his father's, which meant they owned him.

He hesitated before breaking the news that could make the volatile man erupt in anger. A maid entered to say she had put food on the terrace as requested. Sergio, having locked away the diamonds in the safe hidden behind a priceless Italian masterpiece, grunted and walked outside to the spacious area where the food was laid out on a long, rustic table. He inhaled deeply the smell of garlic and lemons. Sergio loved only two things outside of money and power: food and daily soap operas. Michael often wondered if it was the family dynamic that fascinated him in the inane television stories of everyday family life: knowing he had little respect for family, having murdered his own father and brother to gain control, and now two wives with no conscience or fear of consequences.

No one acknowledged the maid as she passed Gino, who, after wiping blood from his hands with a silk handkerchief, pushed it into her hand, telling her to dump it.

'Don Sergio…' said Michael, following his boss onto the terrace, 'we have a potential problem with Fredo Sturla.'

Seated at the table in front of a platter of seafood fritto, Sergio grimaced. 'Sturla? That punk? What problem?'

'An informant tells me he has eyes on our business.'

Sergio shrugged. 'The drugs? No chance. It's distributed between the clans. He has his share. I have mine. It's tied up tight.'

'Not the drugs, the fakes.'

This caught Sergio's attention as he stuffed lemon-drenched calamari into his mouth with his fingers.

'The fakes?'

'Why?' questioned Gino. 'He has the waste.'

'The waste business is over,' said Michael. 'The syndicate have dumped millions of tons of toxic garbage into landfills around Naples in the last twenty years. It's killing people. Cancer rates are soaring. The World Health Organisation has its eyes on it. It's finished.'

'I thought we had resolved that years ago when we rid ourselves of Gianni Rinaldi.' He shrugged, 'So, it's over. He still has the cement business.'

Michael shook his head, refusing the leftover seafood pushed in his direction, and pressed his point as he poured himself water from a crystal decanter. 'Rumours are, his construction business is not doing too well.'

'Can't think why. The cement he sells wouldn't hold up a fucking tent,' Gino smirked as he reached across Michael to help himself to food.

This earned him a withering glance from Sergio, who picked at food caught in his €20,000 teeth that were a little too white in his lined brown face. 'Of course it's shit. The more his buildings collapse, the more he gets to build.'

'We should look into it, Don Sergio,' urged Michael. 'You don't want anyone challenging your position. The last thing we need is a problem when everything is running so smoothly.'

Sergio snarled at him, 'What problem? It took me years to build up factories and a supply line. You think he can compete with that overnight? '

'Maybe he doesn't intend to compete.' Michael's words hung in the air.

Gino shrugged, looking incredulous. 'Hostile takeover? He hasn't got the balls.'

'I have Africans all around the Med buying and selling my stuff. I built up that chain, and no one, not politician or Sturla, is going to break it.' Sergio sneered as he drank a glass of wine in one go and wiped the dribble on his chin, belching loudly. 'Gino is right. That *stronzo* wouldn't dare challenge me.'

Michael wasn't so sure. Fredo Sturla was a psychopath who had gathered an army around him. Unlike Sergio, who was old school and relied too much on brute force, he was astute and every move he made was calculated. Fredo risking war with Sergio was a stupid move, but then Michael had seen first hand how greed can eclipse intelligence. However, he wondered if there was more to it than Fredo wanting to take over the fake business; something bigger. Fredo, like himself, was a man who wanted to move forward to legitimise his financial operations. Inroads were being made into the banking business, but it was a slow job getting acceptance from the old dinosaurs who headed the clans. They worried that if they got a license to run a bank in Italy, the government could embargo it anytime they wanted and take their money. Michael knew there was a possibility of this happening, but believed it was unlikely. From experience, he knew they could buy and control politicians. He frowned, his mind racing. The beauty of the rag trade, which the Gianelli clan had built up only as a way to launder drug money, was that it had become so successful that it was producing millions legitimately. If Sergio gave up all his illegal activities, he would still be filthy rich from the profit he made, but his greed knew no bounds. The huge revenue taken on the streets from illegal fake goods was becoming more difficult to clean as more countries clamped down on money laundering. *So why,* he wondered, *would Fredo Sturla want to get involved in a business that would give him a massive headache?* He sighed, hoping it was nothing more than a rumour.

***

The Port of Naples, one of the largest in the Mediterranean, moving approximately twenty-five million tons of cargo a year, was alive with activity. Hundreds of giant, swinging cranes moved large metal containers from the massive COSCO ships recently arrived from China, onto the dockside where they were piled five stories high.

'Agreed,' Marco Falco said, handing a large wad of money to a customs official, whose stomach hung over his belt, his thighs so fat it amazed Marco that he could walk. The fresh sea breeze blowing in from the Mediterranean did nothing to combat the heat. The whole transaction had taken less than ten minutes, but already Marco's thick black hair lay plastered against his skull and large damp patches had formed under the arms of his impeccable white shirt. The man snatched the money and stuffed it inside his pocket.

'It's always a pleasure to do business with friends,' he smirked.

'I would rather cut off my right hand than call you a friend, you fat slob. Just do what you're paid for.'

In the back seat of a dark green SUV nearby, clan boss Fredo Sturla, his handsome face implacable, watched as Marco made his way back to the car. Fredo's head of security and hard man, who accompanied him everywhere as a bodyguard, sat at the wheel. At forty-five years of age, Luigi Ricci, previously a hitman for the Clementi family, had earned a killer reputation for carrying out any task assigned to him, without question.

Marco climbed into the air-conditioned SUV, wiped sweat from his forehead with a linen handkerchief and griped, 'Fucking Customs and Excise earn more black money than we do.'

'When will they release it?' asked Fredo.

'He said three days.'

'Good. I want the stuff on the streets pronto,' said Fredo.

Marco was a bit taken aback. 'So quick?'

'To get what we want, we must give the Chinese what they want, which is control of the fake goods. If we show any weakness, the whole deal is off.' Fredo turned his cold eyes on Marco. 'On your advice, the money I've invested securing a bank in China could buy all of Hong Kong. I don't want it to go wrong. The longer we take, the more of a problem we will have with Gianelli.'

'Don Fredo, I agree. But it's a matter of logistics. We will soon have the goods in the warehouse, but we don't have the delivery trucks set up or the workforce on the streets yet.'

Or a deal cemented with Sergio Gianelli, he thought. Fredo had agreed they would not make a move until he had first seduced Sergio with something more lucrative than producing the fakes.

'They will deliver the trucks soon. We already have people in place around the Med to take control before the Chinese take over.'

'Gianelli won't be happy,' Marco warned. 'What about the offer we discussed?'

'Forget the offer. Why should I give him anything when I can take it?' Fredo snarled. 'Sergio Gianelli is an old man who fucks goats. His day is over.'

Marco refrained from stating the obvious outcome. The conflicts between the different clans fighting for dominance, which had raged on and off for more than a hundred years, had been dormant for ten years: Fredo moving in on Gianelli in such a way was dangerous and could only lead to trouble.

'Don Fredo, I must caution you to wait until we have everything securely in place. We cannot risk word getting back to Gianelli about our intentions before we are in a position to act.'

Hearing this irritated Fredo and he snapped, 'So be quick about it. You can start by undercutting prices to the Africans here in Naples. Get them here and we get them everywhere.'

'We should start in other areas. Spain. South of France. The Gianelli clan will kill the Africans here if they buy from us.'

'And we will kill them if they don't,' Fredo replied, staring straight ahead, showing no sign of any emotion.

Chapter 7

The two-room apartment Joseph shared with Big Moses, Abdi, Bolo, Benjamin and Jacob, was damp, gloomy, cramped and sparsely furnished: a sagging sofa, well past its sell-by date, two chairs at a kitchen table, and a mattress on the floor for each of the six. Each bed was covered neatly with a sheet, clothes were folded, shoes were lined up with military precision. Music was playing from tinny speakers attached to a mobile phone.

'The water's cold again,' Jacob warned Bolo, who was about to step into the shower.

'So what's new, man? Nothing in here works,' shouted Benjamin.

From the Congo, Benjamin looked younger than his twenty-four years. He was shorter and rounder than the others, with perfect white teeth and a devil-may-care attitude.

Bolo grinned. 'I can do cold. It gives me an excuse to boogie in the shower.' He did a little wiggle to emphasise his point.

Jacob teased, 'You call that dancin' man? This is dancin'…' He turned up the music full blast and jumped about, singing and bopping. Laughing, Bolo joined in and Benjamin beat out the rhythm on the floor with his hands.

Joseph, busy cooking rice and vegetables on a two-ring hob, smiled at their antics. It didn't take long before the neighbours were thumping on the thin walls, threatening to call the cops.

To keep order in the apartment, they had a rota. Each man took turns to shop, do the laundry, clean or cook, but preferring his own cooking, it was often Joseph who dished up the food. They were also meticulous about personal hygiene and clothing. Bolo and Jacob were vain about their appearance and were often teased by the others. One thing they all knew for sure, customers responded better when they were well turned out.

Despite their good humour, they were all exhausted after two large cruise ships had docked earlier that day, releasing a thousand tourists who swarmed the sweltering city. It had been one long battle of bartering with people eager to get the fake goods they wanted, but anxious in case they paid too much and felt cheated. A set price wasn't possible because people assumed it was normal to beat the *'Looky Men'* down. Therefore, it was an ongoing game.

Big Moses and Abdi arrived home, lugging the merchandise on their backs and sweating in the heat, which was still intense despite the late hour. They dropped their bundles in a corner near the door, next to several others.

'I smell food,' Big Moses said, sniffing the air like a dog, a huge grin on his face.

'You ate a hamburger an hour ago,' Abdi said.

Big Moses protested, 'I'm a big man. I need food, but first I must shower. This humidity is killing me.' When the cold water in the shower hit him, he squealed. Within thirty minutes, both men had showered and changed. Soon, they were all eating the rice, vegetables and chicken, which Joseph had livened up with chilli and other spices. Big Moses' gleaming white trainers caught Jacob's eye.

'Hey, Big Moses, look at you, man. New trainers. Whoo hoo! You look like a capo. Big Moses the capo,' he teased.

Big Moses's face lit up with pleasure. 'Real Nike, too.'

'Yeah, like my real Polo shirt, which will fall to pieces after three washes,' Bolo said, tucking into his food. Abdi poked at the remains on his plate.

'I dream of a big steak…with an egg on top. No, make that two eggs and a mountain of fries.'

Big Moses looked amazed. 'When did you ever have that?' he asked.

'Never,' Abdi answered as he pushed the food around his plate. 'But I'm sick of rice and vegetables. I ate better in the army,' he grumbled.

Bolo scoffed, 'Are you serious, man? Beans and *posho* every day – except Sunday, when we had *posho* and beans.'

Hearing this, Joseph knew that like him, Bolo had been a soldier in the Ugandan Defence Force, because it was the standard menu, occasionally with a bit of meat added. But who you soldiered for was never discussed.

'The army was bad. No more army,' protested Big Moses, shaking his head.

Jacob nodded in agreement. 'I would rather eat rat shit than go back to that.'

'You have no family to support, so what's stopping you from eating your steak and fries, Abdi?' asked Benjamin, who supported a wife and kid back home.

'He'd have nothing to whine about. That's what's stopping him,' said Jacob, grinning.

Despite the teasing, they all knew that Abdi had been starved as a child, and hid money under his mattress. Little did it occur to him that by hoarding his earnings and denying himself the basics in life he was creating something to lose. But here, not one man would take something belonging to another. It was an unspoken code.

'I was eight when they took me,' said Abdi, surprising them all because he had never talked about what had happened to him. 'They murdered everyone in my family when they tried to protect me. Even my blind *Avo*.' He shook his head as if to dispel the memory of his dying grandfather. 'I didn't cry. It was as if all my feelings had died with them. I was numb, even when they beat me. Fuck the rebels.'

'Yeah, fuck rebels,' said Big Moses, rocking back and forth. 'They raided my school and killed my family too. My father was a doctor; he helped lots of people.'

***

Dr. Robert Akello was the only doctor in an area covering ten villages around the city of Gulu. As rebel forces drew closer to the area, he packed his wife and two young daughters into the car to make their escape south to Kampala. Driving to pick up his beloved son Moses at the Institute for Gifted Children, he smiled, remembering the day his boy had left to board there and how he had pressed his grandfather's Bible into his hand with the words, 'One day you will be a brilliant doctor. Never lose faith in Jesus, who will always protect you.' Unaware of the landmines laid by the LRA along the road to the school, he and his wife and daughters tragically died in the blast, never knowing that Moses and twenty other boys were already being transported to the rebel camp across the border into Sudan. Or that his gifted son, who had his head kicked repeatedly for refusing to kill, would never be the same again.

Moses wrapped his arms around himself. 'Why pick on kids?'

'Because they are easy to corrupt and maintain,' answered Benjamin.

Jacob scoffed. 'And dispensable.'

They all nodded, knowing it was the way it was.

'I escaped,' said Benjamin. 'And found my way back home. I thought they would be happy to see me, but my parents and everyone shunned me, thinking I was touched by the devil and was about to murder them all. I was on the streets for two years before someone took pity on me and gave me a job in a garage. At half the wage of everyone else. But it was something.'

'They used me…' Bolo's face contorted, remembering how they had sexually abused him. 'Kept telling me I was too pretty to fight.' Choking with emotion, he couldn't continue. Jacob punched him in the arm and teased, 'What? And you such an ugly fucker.' This broke the tension, and everyone laughed, including Bolo.

Abdi slammed his fork onto his plate. 'I didn't know what I was fighting for. I still don't.'

'Like us all, you were fighting to stay alive,' said Joseph in a quiet voice

Later, as they slept, Joseph lay awake on his mattress. The neon sign on the building opposite kept blinking on and off. Usually, exhausted from work, it didn't bother him, but not tonight.

Big Moses screamed and whimpered in his sleep. The men woke, but no one spoke. They all knew what his nightmares were about: they all suffered from them. The cries evoked in Joseph his own horrifying memories of his father being shot, his mother raped and killed, and little Mimi being chopped down in front of him. Of Tombe, marching off with a daft grin on his face but, like countless others, not returning; his body left to feed the predators in the bush.

Having given up on sleep, Joseph went to the bathroom. Looking in the cracked mirror, he touched the inch-long keloid scar on his cheek. He lifted a razor blade to his face. Without flinching, he cut into his flesh, changing the small straight scar into a letter 'K.'

Odango's words, spoken all those years ago, rang in his head. 'You are mine.' *I was never yours.*

Chapter 8

UGANDA 1995

Soon, it will be my turn. And soon it was. Squatting to eat a meagre breakfast after a long night of guard duty, Joseph was pulled roughly to his feet and marched through the camp to Odango's quarters.

Odango lived in a low building, guarded by four armed soldiers. There were no windows and no door across the entrance. It had a large bed, a comfortable chair and a table. Luxuries in the jungle. Seated at the table, Odango ate from a selection of foods.

No scraps for you, you fat hippo, thought Joseph, whose stomach cramped with hunger.

Dressed in jungle fatigues stained with sweat, Odango wiped away the perspiration which had gathered on his forehead and ran down his face. 'You? I remember you.' He grinned, showing his wolfish teeth. 'Yes. Perfect for the job.' He held out a piece of meat to Joseph, but hungry as he was, Joseph shook his head. The thought of accepting anything from Odango's hands repulsed him.

Joseph had been 'favoured' – chosen to accompany Odango and some troops on a mission to attack a government camp five miles south.

The Ugandan Government never gave up on its attempts to apprehend the rebel leader and his commanders. Kony had started the fight against corrupt politicians who were causing the people to suffer. But somewhere along the line, the campaign had become distorted. As always happens with despots, which Kony had become. Politicians were still corrupt, and it was now a battle between them and Kony for control over the people.

After a day's march the group of ten soldiers, including Odango, Joseph and two younger boys who were afraid of their own shadows, arrived at a clearing and set up camp. Mountains towered to the right, and dangerous rapids plunged to the left. The only way forward was to cross the open space ahead of them. Odango suspected the space was riddled with landmines laid by the Ugandan People's Defence Force (UPDF). One of the men took Joseph's gun; he soon realised why he had been 'favoured.' He was to be the sacrificial lamb, going ahead of Odango and his men to check where the government soldiers had buried the landmines. That he could be blown to smithereens didn't concern Odango, who had brought two more boys along to replace him if he died. To refuse meant death by the panga.

His throat dry, Joseph took his first step. Fear gripped him. Five more steps. Each one so uncertain. The sweat running down his face clouded his vision. *I might as well be blind*, he thought and froze to the spot. He glanced back at Odango and the others and saw one pointing a gun at him, ready to fire. A voice in his head said, *Kill the fear, Joseph.'*

As a seven-year-old, the story of a brave bushbaby had fascinated Joseph. Determined to see one of the small creatures, he wandered into the bush one night and became lost. Young as he was, when the pungent odour of a lion's warm urine assailed his nostrils, he recognised the danger, and was terrified, suspecting the beast was close by. He hoped it had eaten and was sleeping, but picked up a stick from the ground to defend himself, if not. The sound of a lion's roar made him tremble with fear. The big cat was awake and dangerous. Panicking, Joseph ran blindly. If his father, out looking for him, had not appeared and caught him, he would have headed straight towards the danger. 'You must learn to kill the fear, Joseph, before you can kill a lion,' Jacob said, taking away the stick.

Kill the fear. Kill the fear. He chanted to himself as he took a step forward, feet together and inserted a stick in the hard, dry ground behind him to mark the path as instructed.

He glanced back at Odango, who, with an impatient wave of his hand, urged him to keep going. Overcoming his fear and with grim determination, he made his way safely to the edge of the clearing. Wiping away the beads of perspiration from his face with his hand, he looked back. Despite having marked the way, he could see that the coward Odango had made the two boys walk across before him.

The clearing was edged by thick trees, through which Joseph could have escaped to the camp of the government soldiers to warn them of the attack and tell them the rebels had kidnapped him, but he had a promise to keep.

After all the others had gone before him, Odango finally found the nerve to cross.

His feet in their huge army boots, were twice the size of Joseph's which had paved the way, and with just one inch to left or right, there was a good chance he would be blown to pieces.

But this was not what Joseph wanted. There was no suffering in such a quick death.

Once across, Odango threw a rock into the field where it landed on a mine. The explosion was sudden and deafening. He grinned and punched the air: he had been right about the mines. Joseph hid his contempt and rage. The explosion had blown away all the markers he had planted, which meant he would have to take the walk of death again on their return. *But not if I kill him first.* Reluctantly, he put the thought out of his mind. *Not yet. Not yet.*

Chapter 9

NAPLES 2018

Bathed in the sweltering August heat, with no immediate hope of relief, the people of Naples wilted in the energy-sapping humidity that often deprived them of a night's sleep. The city bustled with locals pushing impatiently through throngs of sauntering tourists as they tried to go about their everyday business. Joseph, in his usual place outside the Café Borolo, handed a fake YSL bag to a middle-aged woman and took her money, ignoring her flirtatious smile. Joseph had only one woman on his mind.

Nearby, Big Moses haggled with a tourist. 'Fifteen euros. I'll give you fifteen,' said the woman, whose skin, burnt from too much sun, glowed in sharp contrast to her badly dyed blonde hair.

'I have to earn something, lady. It's all leather. I'll do it for twenty-five. Cheap as chips,' he said, with a winning smile.

The woman's partner grabbed her arm and pulled her away. 'Leave it. How many times have I told you they're a bunch of thieves.'

The smile died on Big Moses' face. 'I'm not a thief!' he protested.

Seeing his distress, Joseph called to him, 'Jesus knows that Moses. Take no notice, man.'

Outside the café, Carla was enjoying a cigarette when a young Italian shattered her peaceful moment, snatching her bag and making a run for it.

'*Ladro*! *Ladro*! Thief! Thief!' she shouted.

Hearing her cries, Maria came running to the door and watched as Joseph sprinted after the youth and grabbed the bag back. The teenager continued to run, making crude gestures and yelling abuse over his shoulder.

A little out of breath as he walked back, Joseph vowed to exercise more in the future.

Surprised that he had saved her bag, Carla reached out to take it from him. As she did so, the sleeve of her pale blue silk blouse rode up, revealing a dark bruise on her arm. She quickly adjusted it and said, 'Apparently it's the Italian thieves we have to worry about. Thank you.'

'We've got enough thieves without bringing more into the country,' Maria muttered, her eyes on the African boys.

With a kiss for her grandmother and a sideways glance at Joseph, Carla got into the Mercedes that had just arrived.

Maria's eyes filled with sadness as the vehicle drove off. She became aware that Joseph was watching her. 'What? You have nothing better to do than look at me?' She stormed back into her café, furious with herself for letting Joseph catch her with her guard down.

He wondered what had happened to make her so brittle and sad. Sighing to himself, he knew everyone had a story – some worse than others. His fingers went to the scar on his cheek. *Kizza.*

UGANDA 1995

The scar made on Kizza's cheek by Odango's panga felt angry and sore. She was shoeless when they took her, so had suffered from each thorn that pierced the soles of her feet on the long trek to the camp. The rope that attached her to the others in a human chain had chafed her waist, making the skin raw and angry. A turmoil of conflicted feelings raged inside her. Despite knowing Joseph had saved her life and watched out for her on the long march to the camp, she was not yet ready to accept his killing of her mother. The brutal scene haunted her day and night. Despite this, she was alarmed at being separated from him. No longer trusting anyone, she kept her eyes to the ground, not wanting to make eye contact, and turned a her face away when anyone tried to speak to her. She found it tedious to listen and recite the same mantras every morning, led by a man posing as a priest who bellowed, 'We believe in the Messiah, a Holy Spirit sent by God to cleanse his Acholi people from their arrogance for not supporting his rebel army.' The very mention of the Messiah, who ruled from a camp on the border of Sudan, was enough to terrify her. Odango was a monster; to her mind, the man who ruled him had to be worse.

'Recite after me: we will fight for the Messiah and will be rewarded. I love Jesus. Jesus loves me.'

Paying lip service, Kizza inwardly prayed to God, begging him to end her nightmare.

Tears running down her cheeks, a young girl squatting on the floor next to her, nails bitten to the quick, stopped reciting. Without warning, the 'priest' sliced through her neck with his panga, spattering Kizza with blood. She gasped in horror.

The man displayed no emotion at his cruel action, simply stood over the dead girl, preaching.

'The Bible says that if your hand, eye, or mouth is at fault, we should cut it off. So, I ask you, Who is to blame?'

Kizza, isolated, alone, vulnerable to the dangers surrounding her, shuddered with fear. *Joseph. Where are you?*

Chapter 10

NAPLES 2018

Joseph waited with Big Moses outside the Gianelli warehouse on the edge of the city, and watched as two Camorrista brothers, Frankie and Toni Esposito, beat up a youngster. He had known many men like these in his life. Unable to think for themselves, but with a penchant for violence. The boy slightly built, in his early teens, cowered in the dust as they attacked him.

'You steal from us?' Toni demanded as he landed a vicious kick to the boy's ribs.

'It was five euros. Just five,' the boy cried, receiving another kick to the head.

'Five or five fucking hundred, it's the same! No one steals from us!'

Blow after blow rained down on the boy. The other kids, their eyes averted, collected their supply of drugs to distribute around the city, and sped off on their motor scooters, leaving clouds of dust and the stink of petrol behind them.

A gleaming yellow Maserati approached, catching Joseph's attention. In what appeared to be a deliberate action, it pulled in close to the queue of African men, making them scatter. Joseph recognised Gino Gianelli with his slicked-back black hair, as he stepped out of the car and swaggered into the warehouse. He was wearing tight, skinny jeans, which made his feet appear too large, a garish jacket and mirrored sunglasses to hide his eyes.

A clown, but a dangerous one.

'Keep your head down,' Joseph advised Big Moses. 'No one needs trouble from anyone named Gianelli.'

Big Moses shook his head. 'I want no trouble. No trouble.'

Once inside, the boys picked up their supplies from Fat Guido, who didn't cheat them this time. Not with Gino around, which meant Guido was probably skimming off the top. They had bought six Dior copies and six YSLs, the brands most women were after. As they were leaving, Joseph dropped a bag.

'Hey! Monkey face, you dropped something,' called out Gino.

Joseph stopped in his tracks and turned to look back at Gino.

'He's not a monkey,' protested Big Moses and stooped to pick up the bag.

It surprised Gino that someone had spoken up. He walked towards Big Moses, a menacing look in his eyes. 'He is what I say he is, you Black ape.'

Joseph stepped between them. Gino glared at him, but something in Joseph's coal-black eyes unnerved him a little. He took a step back, reaching inside his jacket for his gun.

'You're right,' Joseph shrugged. 'But I can't help having a baboon for a mother.'

Hearing this, Gino relaxed and grinned, calling out to the watching Camorrista, 'Did you hear that? A baboon for a mother!'

Joseph smiled, but the smile didn't reach his eyes.

As they walked away from the warehouse, there was a loud Whoosh! behind them as a motor scooter went up in flames. Big

Moses looked back, fear in his eyes. 'They burnt his bike. He's just a kid.'

As were we, thought Joseph.

UGANDA 1995

Sickened by the slaughter and chaos, Joseph as usual fired his gun wide, not wanting to kill anyone. People died anyway, at the hands of the rebels. Villagers at gunpoint despaired watching them round up their young to be taken away. Unable to help them, Joseph did what he could to make sure the children had enough water on the march back. When Bako, who was leading the raid, asked him what he was doing, he answered that he was keeping them alive. Bako responded by striking him across the head.

*****

Back in camp after the long trek and a meal of vegetables and hippopotamus meat, which was as tough as leather, Joseph, head aching from the blow, made his way to the open area in the camp where the visiting leader of the rebels, surrounded by armed bodyguards, spoke to a huge gathering. He ranted with fervour about the wickedness of the Ugandan Government, which forced him and his soldiers to become rebels.

It was the first time Joseph had seen the man who called himself 'The Messiah.' The man who likened himself to Jesus, who enslaved children and encouraged all to commit atrocities in God's name. In a powerful voice, he raged about the President who would kill them all, and the treacherous priests working hand in hand with the government, who refused to accept that he was a gift from God, sent to lead his people.

'They are damned Pharisees! Betrayers! Traitors!' He yelled, raising his voice and eyes to the heavens. 'They betrayed Jesus, and now they betray me!'

Forgetting the pain, anguish and suffering he had inflicted on them, and desperate to believe their lives would get better, the rebel soldiers smiled in rapture when he promised that the Lord Jesus would make them rich fighting in his army. Not one word touched Joseph.

Chapter 11

NAPLES 2018

With no cruise ships in port and few tourists to be seen, the city embraced a peaceful Sunday morning atmosphere. Locals ambled to and from their local church, often stopping on the way home to indulge in a sizzling mozzarella, tomato and basil pizza, with a glass of wine.

Joseph made his way to Jamal's to send his weekly money order to Kampala. Money to pay for his wife and son's passage to Tunisia, from where they could make the journey to Italy. Approaching the shop, he frowned when he saw boards covering the shop windows and the words 'Filthy Muslim' sprayed on the door.

Saba sat behind the counter, holding baby Sami. There were no warm smiles or spicy smells of cooking today. Jamal, serving Abdi, looked despondent.

'What happened, Jamal?' asked Big Moses as he entered behind Joseph.

'They attacked my shop, Moses.' He shrugged, shaking his head in disbelief. 'Fifteen years I've lived here. I speak Italian and pay my taxes. My wife and child were born here, and now I'm a filthy Muslim.'

The men in the shop sympathised; they lived with racism daily. Not because of their religion, but because of the colour of their skin.

'We do nothing wrong. Why do people hate so much? We don't hate, and this happens,' said Saba, rocking her child, more to comfort herself.

'Who did it?'

Jamal shook his head. 'Just kids. Teenagers on bikes.'

Kids who had grown up in the slums of Naples knew no other life than the one in which they survived. They felt threatened by anyone who was different and acted to protect their identity, because most times, it was all they had. It gave them a false sense of power.

'Someone has got them riled up on the internet saying Muslims took Italian slaves,' said Jamal. 'It was hundreds of years ago, and the Italians had Muslim slaves. It worked both ways, it was the way it was. What does it have to do with me, Joseph?'

'Nothing. If they bother you again, let me know.'

'Jesus will take care of you, Jamal,' Big Moses offered.

'I'll take help from anyone, Moses,' Jamal answered with a weak smile.

After concluding his weekly business, Joseph left the shop, followed by Abdi.

'Why are you sticking up for a Muslim, Joseph?'

'Jamal is a good man. He and his wife are good people. It might have escaped your notice, but here we are all Jamal.'

'We're not Muslims,' he protested.

'No Abdi. We're Christians, like the Messiah. And the Camorra.'

***

The black Mercedes pulled up at the kerb outside the Café Borola and Carla climbed out, carrying flowers. She hesitated until Mario drove off to park, before walking to Joseph at his usual workspace.

'I'm sorry about yesterday. Please forgive me. I didn't mean to be rude. Thank you again for what you did. It wasn't the bag that was valued, it was a treasured photo of my dead parents, which I always carry with me.'

She's young to have dead parents. But then, so was I.

Joseph nodded his head, smiled a small smile.

'Let me buy you a coffee,' she offered. 'It must be hard standing out here all day.' Joseph, taken by surprise, shook his head.

'No, thank you. I need to work.'

Carla took him by the arm and, with a quick glance round, ushered him towards the café.

'I insist. Please. You can watch your stuff from the window.'

Joseph frowned as she nudged him through the door. He would rather do battle in the Congo, as he had many times, than be in Maria's café.

Maria raised her eyebrows, and her mouth dropped open, thinking that her granddaughter had gone mad bringing Joseph into her establishment. Carla ignored her disapproving looks, handed her the flowers, and invited Joseph to sit down.

He hesitated then took a seat in the window, from where he could see his bags. Carla sat opposite him. It was the last place Joseph wanted to be, but the aroma of hot, melted cheese set his taste buds tingling, reminding him of better times when there was a woman in the kitchen and a warm welcome home. He was uncomfortable sitting with an obviously rich, beautiful young woman, wearing a large heart-shaped diamond and a wedding band on her finger

'Two coffees please, Nonna,' she ordered, emphasising the 'two' with a smile. Huffing, Maria displayed her disapproval by banging around as the machine hissed and spluttered. Coffee cups were clattered onto saucers. Ignoring Maria's displeasure, Carla turned to Joseph. 'So, what's your name?'

He had picked up a fair amount of the language while working the streets, but had never held a proper conversation in Italian.

'Joseph,' he answered, still wanting to be anywhere but there.

Carla held out her hand for him to shake. He hesitated before taking it. *I've never shaken hands with anyone before.* He quickly let go.

'Nice to meet you, Joseph. I'm Carla. Maria is my Nonna, my grandmother. I used to live here in this café,' she said with a smile.

Maria and the café had been home to Carla until she left to study architecture at a university in Rome. She returned halfway through her studies, married at just twenty. Maria hadn't trusted or liked Carla's choice of husband. Accountants, according to Maria, were on a level with lawyers – a bunch of sharks. He was ten years older than Carla, too handsome, too well dressed, and too sure of himself. Just too much of everything, in her eyes. She also detected that the charm he exuded was skin deep. But Carla was in love and could see none of those things.

Maria put the two coffees on the table before them and scowled at Joseph. Carla winked at him. 'Nonna, I was just telling Joseph that you make the best coffee in Naples.'

'Nothing wrong with the truth,' Maria retorted.

'And please, can we have some of your famous cannoli? Joseph, you really must try it. Nonna makes them herself, and they are utterly delicious.'

Maria returned behind the counter, muttering. 'Huh…cannoli now, is it?'

'Do you have family here, Joseph? Sugar?' Carla pushed the sugar dispenser towards him.

Not a man to open up about himself, and disarmed by her questions and her friendliness, Joseph, answered awkwardly: 'Err…no. No, not here.' The coffee smelled inviting, and it looked like there was no escape, so he helped himself to sugar. He liked his coffee black and sweet, so he piled in three teaspoons and took a sip. *Ahh, arabica.*

'In Africa? Is that where you come from?'

He was reluctant to discuss anything about himself, but it had been years since anyone had smiled warmly at him. 'Yes. From Uganda. I have a wife and a boy there.'

'I've heard Uganda is a beautiful country.'

'It is. Apart from the evil men warring over it.'

Carla scoffed. 'Same here.' She gave him a wry smile. 'But getting rid of them would take a miracle.'

'I'm not a believer in miracles.'

'I live in hope. It must be hard for you being separated from them. Your wife and child.'

'It is. I haven't seen them for three years.' *Why am I telling her this?*

'You've been here three years?'

'In Naples? No. Just a year. I worked in Tunis for one year.' *To earn my passage here. A year because I could not take a legitimate route, as I had absconded from the army, which only allowed you to resign when they carried you off in a coffin or when you were too old to hold a gun.*

'I arrived in Italy, Lampedusa, and spent a further year in an internment camp for immigrants.'

'Sounds unpleasant.'

***

Lampedusa, a small island lacking in the human resources needed to deal with the thousands of immigrants who flooded onto its shores, was finding it difficult to process everyone. Waiting to be granted refugee status and knowing it could take months, even a year, Joseph wanted nothing more than to get out of the overcrowded holding centre, surrounded by barbed wire and patrolled by soldiers. When the chance arose, both he and Big Moses volunteered, along with others, to help retrieve bodies from the sea after a ship transporting refugees from Eritrea had sunk off the coast, taking the lives of all those on board. They worked day and night. The sea never stopped giving, and the bodies piled up. Over one thousand men, women and children seeking refuge in Europe, perished in the first three months that Joseph was there.

He was used to death, but Joseph felt his heart lurch at the sight of fifty small white coffins containing the tiny bodies of children, which lined the floor of an airport hangar. He could imagine the children laughing and singing during the voyage before they were so cruelly silenced. The image of the coffins became etched in his mind's eye as he struggled to come to terms with the hardship and cruelty fate inflicted on so many people.

***

'It was what it was,' he said to Carla.

Maria pretended not to listen as she put a cannoli down in front of him.

'I have a son too. How old is your boy?' Carla asked, smiling.

'He has six years.'

'The same as Giancarlo. I could never be apart from him.' A shadow passed over her eyes as she spoke, which made Joseph wonder what lay below the statement. She shook her head. 'I can't imagine the heartache, being separated from your wife and child for so long.'

'It wasn't my intention, but soon I will bring them here.'

Eavesdropping behind the counter, Maria rolled her eyes, muttering, 'Huff! More of them coming.'

'Good, a family should be together,' said Carla, tugging at her sleeves; ensuring they were in place. Suddenly alert, she jumped to her feet when the black Mercedes pulled up outside of the café. She moved out of view of the window.

'What? Now he doesn't give you time to drink a coffee?'

'I must get back, Nonna. Giancarlo has a dental appointment. I just came to thank Joseph, and bring you flowers, of course.' With a muttered apology to Joseph and a quick kiss on Maria's cheek, she hurried from the café.

Joseph, not wanting to stay where he was not welcome, stood up to leave.

Seeing him about to go, Maria crossed her arms and glared at him.

'Finish your coffee and eat your cannoli. You think I have nothing better to do than make food for people to waste?'

Joseph sat back in his seat.

'And I am telling you now, just because my granddaughter is grateful to you for saving her bag, it does not mean that you can take advantage and move a little further onto my pavement. *Capisce?*'

'Si. Capisco Señora.'

'Good. So long as we understand each other.'

Joseph didn't think that he would ever understand the woman standing over him as he pushed the cannoli into his mouth, admitting to himself that it was indeed delicious.

An elderly couple entered the café to a warm smile from Maria. '*Buongiorno* Fredi and Gina, what can I do for you today?' she asked before muttering to Joseph, 'Don't know why I bother asking. Always the same thing. Ravioli with butter and sage sauce. Bad for their cholesterol, but that isn't for me to worry about. I have enough problems of my own with my damned arthritis.'

As the couple took a seat at a nearby table and Maria busied herself behind the counter, Joseph slipped out the door. Once outside, he stood by his bags, wondering what was going on with Carla and who was hurting her. *Who is she afraid of?* His mind went to Kizza, who was always afraid.

***

UGANDA 1995.

After a month, Kizza was housed in a hut with Odango's four current wives. Their ages varied from fifteen to eighteen. Each had borne children to him and appeared to have accepted that living in the bush and servicing Odango was now their life. Believing they possessed some sort of status, they guarded their positions like lionesses protecting their cubs, and had become cruel and indolent.

Kizza was chosen to perform 'Ting, Ting', maid service for the women, joined by Okeny, aged eleven. Their task was to care for the children and do the laundry, but Kizza soon realised that they were nothing more than slaves. If she or Okeny, with her stick-thin arms and legs, failed to meet the many demands made of them, they felt the sharp sting of a slap. There was no compassion in the young wives. Regular abuse and rape when they were little more than children had made them heartless.

Kizza felt a small sense of freedom when she and Okeny carried the dirty clothes to the nearby riverbank to be washed. It was a welcome escape from the overcrowded, stinking hut and the hands always ready to lash out. Apart from the guards and the crocodiles, the swiftly moving water was murky, deep and dangerous, as proven by the unfortunate few attempting to flee by swimming across it.

She loved the cool feel of water swirling about her legs as she pounded the clothes against the rocks. Taking advantage to clean herself, knowing from her mother that cleanliness was important to stave off disease, she urged Okeny to do the same.

The musty, earthy odour of the river reminded her of home and the river where she and the other village children would swim to cool off in the heat. Joseph was the strongest swimmer. She often cheered him on to win races when challenged by other boys who were much bigger. At one time, she wondered what it would feel like to kiss him. She didn't know where Joseph was, and she didn't dare ask.

Okeny, a rare name given only to a girl born into a family of male siblings, feared the water and would only enter ankle-deep. She always sang as she worked when washing the clothes – it was strange because she had not spoken one word to Kizza or anyone else since her indoctrination. Kizza could not find it in her heart to join in, and at first thought that anyone who could sing but not speak must be touched in the head. But over time, as they worked together, she came to understand that singing was Okeny's way of escaping the surrounding madness. After a while, her sweet voice became a comfort to Kizza, who, like Okeny, had become introverted and was no longer the smiling, outgoing girl she had once been. Distrusting others with her words, she spoke only when spoken to, and to avoid punishment, she answered only with what they wanted to hear. Sometimes, with the washing piled up beside them, the two girls would sit on the riverbank in silence, taking comfort from holding hands. In time, and being a year older, Kizza would watch out for Okeny like one would a little sister. A feeling of responsibility gave her a sense of purpose and a way to ignore her own reality. She would often protect her from the viciousness of the wives by claiming to be the one who had made them angry. Each stinging slap she saved Okeny from felt like a small win.

A feeling of dread enveloped Kizza when she woke early one morning to discover Okeny wasn't in her usual sleeping place. Concerned that Okeny would be punished if the wives woke to discover she was missing, she slipped out of the hut and searched for her near the river area, but was disappointed.

Returning to the hut, and receiving a sharp blow from the youngest wife for being missing when her baby had soiled himself, she saw Okeny stagger from Odango's nearby hut with swollen eyes and a split lip. But it was the blood running down her legs that horrified Kizza, who realised Odango had taken Okeny during the night. She reached out to help the distraught girl as she staggered past. But the claws of the wife dug into her shoulder, preventing her from following, and she was pulled into the hut and told there was work to be done. Later that day, Kizza learned that despite being afraid of water and crocodiles, Okeny had chosen death to escape from the clutches of Odango. The wives were unconcerned about the loss of a female who might have threatened their position.

Please God, help me. Don't let me lose my soul like them. No sooner had the prayer left her lips when Kizza, herding the children together to take them to the river to bathe, saw Odango on his knees in front of his hut, praising Jesus, and murderous thoughts invaded her mind.

A few days later, going about her task of washing the clothes, Kizza became aware of Odango watching her. The hair on the back of her neck rose up. Standing in the water, the urine trickling down her legs went unnoticed. Praying would not help. She knew now that no one was listening, and she could not escape the monster.

Chapter 12

NAPLES 2018

The black Mercedes car arrived at the entrance of a modern tower block in Chiai, an affluent resort area south of the old city. Each floor of the fifteen-story edifice had four apartments – apart from the penthouse, which comprised two hundred square metres of space and a large terrace in contrast to the small balconies of the apartments below. Surrounded by manicured gardens, the building stood at the end of a tree-lined cul-de-sac, set apart from other buildings in the area.

Upon the Mercedes' arrival, one of the two armed men standing guard at the entrance rushed forward to open the car door. Carla got out of the Mercedes, took Gianni by the hand and entered the marble foyer of the building. There were two elevators, one that served every floor and one that went directly to the rooftop.

'Mamma, let me do it,' pleaded Giancarlo.

She handed him the key needed to access the penthouse. Her anxiety kicked in as the elevator rose, taking her closer to home. When the doors opened into the apartment, Fredo Sturla was there to welcome them. He swept Giancarlo up in his arms.

'Hey Gianni! So, were you a brave warrior at the dentist's today?'

'Si, Pappa.'

'That's my boy.'

Carla gave him a nervous smile as he kissed her on the cheek, asking, 'And where did you go this morning?'

You know damn well where I've been. 'Didn't Mario tell you?' She asked innocently. 'I visited Nonna.'

'It's not your day to visit.' He tickled Giancarlo, making him laugh.

'I know, but she wasn't herself the last time I went. I wanted to take some flowers and check on her.' As she lied, she smiled, hiding her anxiety.

He eyed her suspiciously. Heart pounding, she turned her attention to Giancarlo. 'Go change your clothes, and then we can eat.'

'I want to eat with Pappa.'

'Pappa is busy, do as your mother says, and tomorrow we can play some football on the terrace,' Fredo said, smiling.

Happy with this, Giancarlo wriggled out of his father's grasp and ran to his bedroom. Once he was out of sight, a snarl replaced the smile and Fredo's fingers dug into her shoulder, but not too much, as he didn't like to leave marks that people could see.

'How many times must I tell you? I like to know where you are. I worry about your safety.'

' I took Gianni to the dentist.'

'Before that.'

His face was so close, she could see a small red vein in his eye and smell the whisky on his breath. He always drank when he was angry about something. But not enough to make him drunk; he liked to be in control. *Placate, placate, placate.*

'Fredo, you were busy when I left, and I didn't want to disturb you with something so trivial. Besides, if you are worried about my safety, Mario is always with me.' *To spy on me.*

He seemed satisfied by this answer and released her.

'Your safety is all I worry about, Carla.'

Goddamn liar!

'I won't be eating with you today.' He patted her cheek and walked into the area separate from their living space, where she could see Marco Falco, Luigi Ricci and Donato Gallo waiting for him. *All the King's men …*

The bedroom, which should be a place of tranquillity, was a place of nightmares for Carla. She sat on the bed, kicked off her shoes, and sighed heavily, wondering how she had come to this.

***

She was realising her dream of becoming an architect when she entered Rome's university. It had taken her a long time to get over the loss of her parents, but life was gradually beginning to feel good again. When not in class, she would scour Rome in search of the abundance of ancient and modern architecture. Every day brought a feast to her eyes.

She carried a small sketchbook everywhere with her and would sit and draw various buildings as she ate a sandwich bought at the university café. Occasionally, she would sit outside a local eatery she favoured, and drink a coffee. It was here that Fredo first saw her, glossy hair hanging down her back, deep blue eyes, inherited from her mother, who hailed from Lake Garda in Switzerland, which sparkled as she ordered a drink. The server, impressed by her fresh beauty and her smile, smiled back.

'For you, Signorina, pronto.'

Adjusting her chair so it didn't wobble on the uneven cobbles, she knocked her sketchbook to the ground. As she reached for it, another hand covered hers.

'Allow me.'

She looked into Fredo Sturla's brown eyes and fell in love.

It was a whirlwind affair. Fredo, an accountant, was intelligent, handsome, charismatic, and came from her hometown of Naples. They met every day, drinking each other in, walking in parks, visiting galleries, eating in pavement cafés. On Carla's birthday, he surprised her by taking her to an expensive-looking shop where the assistant, obviously expecting them, held a tailored white dress over her arm. At his insistence, she agreed to try it on. In sharp contrast to her preferred relaxed look of jeans and crisp white shirts, the dress made her look very sophisticated, something she didn't feel. Fredo voiced his approval, telling her she looked beautiful. With a gasp, seeing the price tag of €1,200, she shook her head.

'Fredo, this is far too expensive. I can't accept it.' Living with Maria had made Carla independent and frugal with her money.

'Please, Carla, it's your birthday. Allow me the pleasure of doing this,' he begged. 'It's my gift to you. I want to make you happy.'

A bunch of flowers or holding hands as they walked would have made her happy. But it appeared important to him, so, not wanting to hurt his feelings, she eventually accepted it with good grace and agreed to wear it that evening.

A small intake of breath betrayed her uncertainty as she paused before entering the rooftop restaurant in the luxurious Cavalieri Hotel. Showing them to their table, the maître fussed over them, addressing Fredo by name. When presented with a separate menu from which to choose the bread, and another for salt, Carla supressed her amusement as she imagined Maria's reaction. The delicious meal ended with handmade chocolates, each one a luscious creation that melted in the mouth and made Carla groan with pleasure. Fredo walked her out onto the restaurant terrace, past the approving stares of the other male diners. Only in Rome could a wife nod approval of her husband's admiration for a beautiful young woman.

To her delight, the city lights glittered below them in the near distance, and the fragrant smell of night-blooming jasmine pervaded the air. Fredo folded her in his arms and told her he loved her.

It was music to her ears; her heart was racing when she answered that she loved him too. He kissed her, as he had done many times since they had met. *Was it only a couple of months?* she wondered, feeling like she had known him forever. He looked deep into her eyes, making her heart pound.

'Carla, I have to return to Naples. My father is ill.'

She was immediately concerned. 'Oh, I'm so sorry, Fredo. Is it serious?'

'Yes. But I don't want to leave you.'

'Fredo, you must. It's your father.'

'Come with me,' he urged. 'I want you to be my wife, Carla. I want to marry you.'

The suggestion flattered, stunned, bewildered her. 'I can't,' she protested. 'I'm studying at the university, remember?' Marriage was not something she had contemplated. Being an architect was a lifelong dream, that had begun when she first learned to draw. Other kids would sketch funny figures, but she had drawn houses and buildings, fascinated by their shapes and sizes.

'You can continue your studies in Naples. You would have no problem adjusting.' He pulled her close as his lips met hers again. 'Please say yes.'

But even as she wanted to melt from the desire the kiss had kindled, she hesitated, shaking her head.

'Fredo, after tonight…I don't think I would fit into your world.' Glancing back into the restaurant at the unsmiling but elegantly dressed women seated there with their affluent husbands, she wasn't sure she wanted to. 'I'm just a student. In Naples, I live with my Nonna above a café.'

'You will shine in my world,' he insisted, pulling her closer. 'Say yes, Carla,' he begged. 'Make me the happiest man on Earth. I have plans for my life and want you by my side.'

'I'm a bit…I…'

Releasing her, he looked sad. 'If not, it's goodbye. I will not be returning to Rome.'

Stunned, her heart lurched. Her emotions were in turmoil. 'But Fredo, we haven't even slept together.'

'Because I love and respect you. God made us for each other. I knew it from the first moment I saw you.' He pulled her to him, his eyes boring into her, making her knees weak. 'If you don't say yes, then it's goodbye. If you are not sure now, you never will be.' His intensity sent a thrill down her spine.

He's right, I can continue my studies in Naples. What is Rome compared to a life with someone I love?

'Please, Carla. Be mine!'

The thought of life without him was unbearable. Inhaling deeply, she said, 'Yes, Fredo. I will.'

Laughing, he picked her up and swung her around, calling to a server to bring champagne. To her surprise, he produced a ring set with a heart-shaped diamond and slipped it on her finger, announcing he had booked a suite for them to spend the night at the hotel. A thought niggled in her mind…*Was he so sure I would say yes?*

She wanted Maria at the wedding, but Fredo insisted that there was no time, as his father was fading fast. The marriage took place the next day in a chapel in the Vatican. His family, she learned, were big donors to the church, which was the reason they performed such a rushed union.

Travelling back to Naples by private jet, she realised she had married a man she knew little about. Anxious about how Maria would react to her leaving university and becoming someone's wife, she convinced herself that her grandmother would love Fredo as much as she did and would only want her to be happy. Maria, however, had taken an instant dislike to Fredo Sturla. It was the cold, controlling nature she saw deep in him. Things she herself had been blind to, when he had totally manipulated her.

***

Carla heaved another deep sigh as she glanced around at the clean lines of the bedroom furniture. The luxurious apartment, furnished in ultramodern style, wasn't her idea of a home, but Fredo, always in control, had never once consulted her about what she preferred. Ironically, among other works of modern art, a Mark Rothko canvas of varying yellows that glowed with an inner, mesmerising power, caught the eye as soon as one walked into the central living area. It was chosen not because it appealed to Fredo on any artistic level, but because he was told it was a sound investment for the future. Fredo, who would try to soothe her after every blow he delivered, liked to look forward.

Bored to death with doing nothing, she long ago planted a seed of fear in him by relating the history of emperors and kings who employed food tasters, fearing their enemies might poison them. He soon agreed to her cooking his food, which made her wonder why, as she was the one most likely to poison him…

Leaving the kitchen after preparing Giancarlo's meal, she overheard Marco informing Fredo that everything was now stored in the new warehouse. She stopped to listen, wondering what Fredo was up to now, knowing it was nothing good.

'And the Africans?' Fredo asked Marco.

'Once we have priced the goods, we will give them the choice. They work for Gianelli or for us.'

'I told you it's not a choice. We need to be established before I fly to Shanghai. Fuck Gianelli.'

A shiver of fear ran down Carla's spine. She had been around Fredo for seven years, long enough to learn about the clans. If he disrespected the unstable Sergio Gianelli, there could only be one outcome.

***

Sergio Gianelli seethed with anger as he faced Michael and Gino. 'China? He's bought crap from China?'

'It's confirmed, Don Sergio. They offloaded the containers yesterday.'

'That son of a *puttana*! What the hell is he playing at?'

Michael hesitated before suggesting, 'Maybe we should talk to Fredo, find out what he's about. Work out some terms.'

'Terms? He's pushing into my organisation and you talk about fucking terms?'

Gino shrugged. 'It's crazy.'

Michael, who thought Gino was a yapping dog with no brain, ignored him. 'Why not let him have the street trade, buying his goods from us?'

'There are thirty thousand Africans working the streets in Europe, most of them selling my stuff,' ranted Sergio. 'You know how long it took to build that up. The bribes I had to pay. Why should I give anything to that *stronzo*?'

'Don Sergio, you would earn twice as much from manufacturing if we expanded. Plus, we wouldn't have the transport or distribution costs. Let him sell our goods. Think about it – Fredo Sturla and his clan working for Sergio Gianelli.'

Sergio had a dark, brooding look as he contemplated what Michael had said. He ran his hand through his sparse, dyed black hair before turning his eyes on him, shaking his head.

'We give him nothing! With control of the distribution, he would have me over a barrel.' He poked his finger at Michael. 'You're the money man, you should know that. If you don't, you're no fucking use to me.'

Michael swallowed hard, knowing he was on slippery ground.

'Si, Don Sergio, you are right, of course.'

Sergio snorted like a pig. 'Fucking Chinks are like rats. They steal every design, every idea and then try to sell them back to us. Where is he keeping the Chinese shit?'

'A warehouse south of the city. It's on his territory.'

Gino sneered. 'Fuck territories. Sturla has no respect for you. He's trying to steal your business, Tio.'

Michael knew where this was heading and didn't like it one bit. He had just graduated from law school when the last clan war raged, and his father and many others had died.

'If you hit, they will hit back. Business will stop. War will cost you money. Lives. Set up a meeting. Let's talk to him. Find out what he's up to. There must be something more than we are seeing here.'

Sergio leaned back in his chair and surveyed the two men, then shook his head.

'As Gino said, it's all a matter of respect. One good hit should be enough to put him in his place. Gino, you see to it.'

Gino grinned at Michael.

Michael held back a sneer of contempt for Gino, who was strutting around like a peacock in his garish clothes. *The stupid moron will get us all killed.*

Chapter 13

With a sigh of relief, Maria kicked off her shoes. It had been a busy day and her feet ached. Soon undressed, she put her clothes straight into the washing machine to wash away the smell of cooking and stepped into the shower. Using expensive bath products, the only luxury she treated herself to, she scrubbed the day's perspiration from her body and let the warm water ease her aching muscles.

Her long hair shampooed, conditioned and wrapped in a towel, she slipped into a silk housecoat. It had been an anniversary present from Enrico, which she had lusted for after seeing Sophia Loren wearing something similar in a movie. She smiled, remembering how he would often say that she was his Sophia Loren and that he would die for her. She loved him for it.

At the window, closing her curtains, she saw Joseph still working on the pavement, enticing the few tourists still wandering around after eating in one of the many restaurants in Garibaldi Square. There was no sign of the other Africans who had disappeared for the night.

God knows when he ever eats, thought Maria. *I don't know why he bothers to go home, wherever that is. Why do they come here? It's not an easy*

But even as these thoughts ran through her mind, she knew this was often impossible. Once criminals had become an integral part of running a country, they were hard to defeat.

The heat from the mug of hot chocolate eased the pain in her arthritic fingers as she wrapped her hands around it. Savouring the smooth, velvety taste and inhaling its sweet aroma was a pleasure that she enjoyed every night before retiring. After washing the cup and putting it away in the same place it had occupied for years, she climbed into bed, wondering if it was her body or the bed that was creaking. Reading was a pastime Maria enjoyed, after the death of her husband. A good story took her to places she would never visit and into the lives of people she would never meet. She put on her reading glasses, reached for the book lying on the bedside table, and read the blurb printed on the back cover. It was about an American woman called Nellie Bly, who had travelled the world in eighty days. Puzzled as to why anyone would want to do such a crazy thing, she put it down. Her eyes were heavy, and she was soon asleep.

Maria cooked from scratch, never using frozen food as had become the habit in a lot of the city's cafés, much to her disgust. This meant she had to visit the food market for fresh produce, a trip she made at least three times a week. To the sound of morning church bells ringing out the hour of seven o'clock, she cut through the streets, making her way to the local Porta Nolana market, named after two enormous circular towers that flanked the stone archway built by the Aragonese in the 15th century. Pignasecca was the most central, more famous of the two markets in Naples, and a favoured tourist attraction, but Maria always shopped locally. It was important to her to keep the traditions of her neighbourhood alive, even if the Porta Nolana area was dying of neglect, the district seedy and menacing. Pickpockets were rampant, and she cursed the kids who sprayed graffiti on every wall and door, but having been born in the neighbourhood, it was what Maria knew, and here she felt at home.

The market, close to the sea, was a hive of activity. Fishermen in long rubber aprons and boots gutted and cleaned their catch, calling out and joking with each other and their customers as they laid fresh fish and seafood on makeshift tables. It was a daily ritual for restaurant owners to haggle, prod and smell the goods before caving in to pay the price.

Many of the weather-beaten men had been chasing Maria's tail since they were teens. Most of them knew and admired her. But none so much as Enzo Baldacchi. As she approached his stand, he greeted her with a big smile.

'Ciao bella, my favourite woman. Here she is. Come to make my day!'

'How happy I am for you, Enzo, that it takes so little to make your day. How are your wife and six children?'

'As to be expected, Maria.' He dropped his voice, trying to sound seductive. 'But what a life we could have had if you had chosen me!'

'Yes, I often regret not spending my life with you, stinking of fish.'

The men close by, laughed. They were used to the good-humoured banter between the two.

She ordered *vongole veraci* and watched Enzo to make sure that each clam was perfect and she wasn't being cheated. Not that any of the fishermen or vendors would dare take advantage of Signora Maria Rinaldi.

After also buying fresh bread, a lump of her favourite cheese, a bunch of parsley and sprigs of fresh basil, she stopped in at Arturo's Café nearby to take a morning cappuccino. Like most Italians, Maria only drank milky coffee in the morning and never after a meal, for fear of it upsetting her digestion. The café was bustling with life despite the early hour. She took a seat outside, where she preferred to sit, avoiding the gossiping local women huddled inside. Sipping her coffee, she watched people shop, argue and joke with each other. If asked, she could name most of them.

Her eyes narrowed as she saw Joseph emerging from a doorway nearby. Because of landlord neglect, the building, like those surrounding it, was a slum. It didn't surprise her that he lived there. A lot of Africans did and paid outrageous rents to do so. She didn't want them in Naples but didn't agree with them being taken advantage of in such a way. Joseph walked past without seeing her. He was carrying his bundle on his back. It was 8.00 am, and he was already back at work. She frowned, wondering what drove him. *Whatever it is, with a work ethic like his, any employer would be happy to have him*, she thought.

At midday, before her regular customers arrived to taste her freshly made spaghetti alla vongole, made with the local clams, garlic, white wine and parsley, Maria took Joseph a coffee in a styrene cup, together with a sandwich of Parma ham.

Bewildered, he was reluctant to take it. 'I can't pay for it.'

'You work all the hours God sends. Of course you can pay for it. But who's asking you for money? Take it. You can't live on air and water.'

Joseph hesitated.

'You think I want you dying on my doorstep, bringing me bad luck?'

He took the coffee and sandwich and thanked her.

As she was about to walk back into her café, Maria hesitated, seeing a black SUV approaching. The Gianelli clan was on her doorstep, which would mean trouble for someone. They parked outside the café. Frankie and Toni jumped out, guns showing.

The coffee and sandwich fell to the ground as they grabbed hold of Joseph and manhandled him into the vehicle. Joseph put up no resistance.

Big Moses, watching anxiously nearby, hurried to wrap Joseph's bags into a bundle to keep them safe, muttering a prayer to Jesus to keep Joseph safe.

As they drove off, Carla arrived and saw Maria standing in the street. Climbing out of the Mercedes, she went over to her. 'What is it, Nonna? What's wrong?' she asked, concern clouding her eyes.

'Gianelli's men. They've taken him. I knew it. He's trouble, that one. I can see it in his eyes.'

'Taken who?'

'Joseph, or whatever his name is.'

'Joseph? Why? What's he done?'

'You're asking me?' answered Maria, with raised eyebrows and a shrug of her shoulders.

Carla, always aware when visiting her grandmother that she was in Gianelli territory, wondered if Joseph had upset them, knowing it could go badly for him if he had.

Chapter 14

The SUV drove through the campagna, the country, east of the city. The road led through a dense area of trees desperately in need of rain, eventually opening onto a twenty-metre clearing, revealing an eight-foot wall encircling the compound. Two armed Camorrista opened the large iron gates. Driving in, the car made its way past the lush, flowering oleander bushes bordering the gardens that surrounded the house. Climbing out of the SUV as ordered, Joseph hunched his shoulders to make himself appear smaller, something he had always found to his advantage around men with guns.

As they patted him down, he noticed that there were many men patrolling the grounds. *Rich men and their fears.*

To further ensure he carried no weapons, he was pushed through a metal detector, which looked incongruous in the luxury interior.

Joseph knew the sort of person he was about to meet. He had been in many such houses in his own country, belonging to men who thought they ruled the world. But in his experience, no matter how secure they tried to make themselves, they were only displaying their insecurity and vulnerability.

Frankie and Toni walked Joseph through the house to the main living area, where Sergio was sitting in an arm chair, fondling a young girl while watching a soap opera. The girl looked terrified. It was a look Joseph had seen many years ago.

***

UGANDA 1995

Joseph's heart thudded in his chest, watching Kizza tremble with fear and humiliation as Odango mauled her in front of him. He felt an overwhelming urge to put his arms around her, hold her tight, and tell her none of it was her fault. But he didn't dare.

Despite it being dangerous to question anything in the camp, it was a risk he took to discover Odango had taken Kizza as a wife. Joseph's driving force was to save her and escape, but as long as Odango kept her in his quarters for his own use, there was little chance of doing so, but he would never give up trying. Positioning himself close enough to Odango in order to reach Kizza was not an easy task.

Learning Odango would only drink water from a mountain stream, Joseph bribed the young soldier whose job it was to collect it, and took over the task.

Delivering the water for the first time, he now stood in front of Odango, careful not to show any emotion at his crude actions against Kizza, knowing the sadistic monster would use it to hurt her even more.

'Now that she has been blessed by me, I think she will do well in the brothels,' Odango announced.

The brothels were stinking holes where syphilis was rife. The women working in them didn't survive very long. Joseph dropped his eyes so that Odango would not see the rage burning deep inside him.

Odango scratched at an infected insect bite on his leg, filled with pus, and troubling him. If not attended to, it would soon stink. Infections in the bush were hard to cure, and people often lost limbs because of them. Some even died.

Joseph knew Odango had lost many soldiers to ailments that a camp doctor could have cured. The last doctor, kidnapped from a hospital in Gulu, died of typhus, and they had been unsuccessful in abducting another. Seizing the chance to help Kizza, he pointed out that she could heal his leg. 'The girl can help you; she knows the herbs. She can help others too.'

Odango frowned, his eyes sliding sideways to Kizza. 'You know the plants, girl?'

Kizza nodded. He studied her for a moment, his eyes narrowing in suspicion.

'I remember you. Your mother was the witch.' He glowered at her. 'You're a witch!'

Terrified, fearing the same fate as her mother, Kizza shook her head.

'Not a witch,' said Joseph. 'The village healer. She cured many people.'

'She cursed me,' Odango snarled.

And made you afraid.

'Her daughter also has the gift of healing. The elders in the village said so. She can save your leg.' *Be careful. If he thinks I am desperate to save her, he will do his worst.*

At the thought of losing his leg, Odango scowled and scratched at the wound again, causing a trickle of blood to run down his calf. He studied Joseph for a moment before looking at Kizza, who, not daring to look at him, had her eyes fixed on the floor. He stroked her under the chin, grinning.

'She loves me, just like all my wives, and the Lord.'

The lord Satan.

The grin dissolved into a sharp look as he turned his eyes toward Joseph. 'If she fails, she will join her witch of a mother, and so will you.'

Joseph shuddered, hoping he had done the right thing. But if it worked, it would keep Kizza out of the clutches of men in the brothels and the monster seated before him.

***

Sergio dismissed the girl with a slap on her backside. The teenager, lured by the promise of work in a wealthy man's house, fled, thankful to escape his clutches. Gino strutted in, and, seeing Joseph, asked: 'What the hell is a *mulignan* doing here?'

'If you had bothered being here instead of off humping some bitch, you would know,' Sergio snarled at him.

Ignoring Gino's racial insult, Joseph scanned the room and saw a Roman broadsword mounted on a wall next to a framed photo of Gino climbing a mountain. Sergio caught this.

'The Romans ruled the world with the broadsword. Now the Romans are fit for nothing,' he sneered. 'But my nephew Gino, he climbs mountains. Isn't that right, Gino?'

'That's right, *Tio*.'

'And you, Blackie, can you climb mountains?'

Images of himself as a young soldier invaded Joseph's mind: scaling a steep cliff-face in the mountainous region of the borders of Sudan, barefoot with an AK-47 automatic on his back and a panga in his belt. Sergio sneered again when he didn't answer. 'I didn't think so. You're all good for nothing.' Turning off the television, Sergio noticed the keloid scar on Joseph's cheek. 'What's the mark on your face? Some kind of tribal crap?'

Like the tattoos on your thugs? 'No.'

'Never known a *mulignan* working the bags at your age. What are you, fifty?'

'Thirty-five. A man must survive.'

'And that's why you're here. You Africans work for me, and that's the way it stays. If any of you buy goods from Fredo Sturla, I will cut off your balls and post them back to Africa with the rest of your body parts. That goes for all you Black bastards. You tell them that.' Joseph had heard of the Sturla family, but had never come across them. He knew the clans had boundaries, and each one kept to its own territory, so he didn't understand what Sergio was on about.

'We buy from you. I don't know this Sturla.'

'Make sure you keep it that way if you enjoy breathing.' He motioned to Gino, 'Get him out of here before he stinks the place out.' His hooded eyes narrowed as he watched Joseph leave.

Gino, Frankie and Toni walked Joseph out of the house and down the drive toward the gates, passing caged dogs and a well guarded low-lying building set into the walls surrounding the grounds. As Joseph walked out of the compound, Gino mocked him with ape sounds and gestures, to the amusement of Frankie, Toni, and the other henchmen.

'Enjoy the walk back,' Gino called out, grinning. Unaware that the fifteen-kilometre hike back to the city for a man like Joseph, who had walked hundreds of miles as a soldier, was nothing other than an inconvenience.

'When I'm capo, I'll rid the streets of the Black bastards. I'll get Italians to do it,' Gino boasted, as Joseph walked away.

'They wouldn't work for the money, Gino. Even the pushers and the lookout kids earn more. It's peanuts,' Frankie said.

'Yeah, that's true. Pay peanuts, you get monkeys,' sniggered Gino.

Within earshot of this, Joseph stopped at the edge of the clearing to look back at the compound. A bullet hit the ground in front of him, and the order to keep moving was yelled. Not flinching, he turned and walked away.

Chapter 15

Relishing his first meal of the day, pasta in a spicy tomato sauce, Joseph related to the others what had happened and issued the warning.

'One day, I'll be rich, and no one will tell me what to do,' stated Abdi, pushing a forkful of food into his mouth.

'Dream on, man,' Jacob said with a big grin.

'You want to live in a prison with an army to guard you?' asked Joseph.

Abdi scoffed, 'Why not? We have nothing. Working ten, twelve hours a day for what? So stinking Gianelli can earn more money?'

Big Moses looked uncomfortable. 'That's true, Joseph. What do we have?'

'We have freedom.'

'Freedom? Living in this piss-hole and eating rice? I want a proper job,' Abdi said, raising his voice.

Benjamin patted his arm. 'Calm down, Abdi. It is what it is.'

Jacob nodded in agreement. 'You have no papers. None of us have.'

'So how come Jamal can get papers and we can't?'

'He's been here since he was a child. Why shouldn't he have papers?'

'He's a Muslim.'

'So what? Why can't you just shut the fuck up, Abdi? Always running your mouth, moaning and complaining. What don't you understand? It is what it is, and if you don't like it, you can fuck off back to Africa,' Bolo said, getting up to take his plate to the kitchen.

'Joseph, when does your wife come?' asked Moses, uncomfortable with the way the conversation was going.

Abdi whined, 'I'm just saying if we had papers, we wouldn't have to work the streets.'

'Will I meet your boy, Joseph?' Moses asked, still trying to diffuse the tension.

'Yes Moses. You will meet my boy.'

'You will if they don't drown,' scoffed Abdi.

'For fuck's sake, Abdi, shut your mouth!' said Bolo.

The sound of an explosion rocked the building, making them all scramble to their feet. Moving onto the small balcony that led off the main room, they could see fire and smoke in the distance.

'Is it a bomb, Joseph?' asked Big Moses, wringing his hands.

'I don't know, Moses. Maybe just a gas explosion,' he answered, trying to calm him. But Joseph knew the sound of war. The sound of death.

Chapter 16

Marco had delivered the bad news, and now watched Fredo glower like a caged tiger as he paced around the room, seething with anger.

'He bombed my warehouse. Is he insane?' Fredo, brutality lurking close to the surface, never raised his voice and calculated every move. It was this ruthlessness, together with his assassination of the Clementi family members who had stood in his way, that had raised him from monetary advisor to Don of the clan. Despite his good looks and practiced charm, which, when he was young, had successfully hidden his true nature, these days he exuded menace.

'Don Fredo, we tried to muscle in on his business.' Marco had repeatedly warned Fredo of the outcome of his plan. 'Gianelli has ears everywhere. It was to be expected.'

'With a bomb? Is that what you expected?'

Marco, knowing that Fredo would have done the same thing, hesitated before continuing: 'Michael Rossi called me to set up a meeting. Now that the warehouse has gone, they are prepared to forget what you did.'

Fredo's eyes bulged with contained fury. 'What *I* did? He's prepared to forget what *I* did? He blew up my warehouse and killed three of my men. Not to mention that he could have ruined my deal with the Chinese.'

'I've taken care of the families of the dead men,' said Marco. 'They will move out of the building within the week, into more suitable accommodation.'

He knew it would be no problem to find others to replace the men who had died in the bombing. It was like a badge of honour for a Camorrista to live in the Sturla building. But this was not something Fredo was interested in hearing. Marco could almost hear the machinations of his mind, twisting and turning as he thought about how he could avenge himself against Sergio Gianelli, instead of trying to bring the situation under control.

'We still have a container of goods on the dock and more coming in. The Chinese offered us a place to store the stuff near the port before we bought the warehouse. It's an option that's still open. They need never find out about this attack,' Marco offered.

'Sergio has friends among the clans who may condone his action. They could react by taking his side if you retaliate,' Luigi warned.

'He has more enemies than friends,' Fredo snorted. 'They will soon see the benefits I put before them.'

Not thinking to offer a drink to the two men, he poured himself a large Scotch and drank it in one go before refilling his glass. 'It's the only road if we're to move into legitimate business. Give the Chinese what they want – control of the fake market in Europe, and they give us what we want.'

Initially proposing the idea of owning a bank in China, enabling them to launder money worldwide, Marco could see Fredo's vindictive, greedy nature becoming a stumbling block. He suggested, 'Gianelli might go for the idea if you make him the proposal we discussed.' *And agreed to…*

'No. That old goat would want a bigger share than I'm offering, or try to deal direct with the Chinese himself. He can't be trusted.'

'Don Fredo, if you hit back, it will be war. Think about what you have within your grasp. Legitimate offshore banking in China. No bribes, no cops, no politicians. In a few years, you could wash money for every clan boss. We're talking billions.'

Fredo smiled without humour. 'Legitimate is good, but realistically, you and I both know it won't happen if Gianelli stands in the way.'

Marco was about to protest, but Fredo said, 'First, I will destroy that decrepit old bastard and his idiot nephew. Let's drink to that.' Marco jumped up, poured whisky into two glasses, and handed one to Luigi. Fredo held up his glass. 'To the death of our enemies.'

Marco, thinking that Fredo Sturla would have to annihilate the whole of Italy to rid himself of his enemies, drank the twelve-year-old Macallan whisky, the price of a single bottle of which could feed a family for a month, and thought with dread of the bloodshed to come.

Always alert, Luigi, savouring the warm, woody taste in his mouth, didn't miss the sound of a door closing. He guessed it was Carla who had been listening, but it was not part of his job description to rat on someone unless it meant Fredo's life was in danger. Fredo was his boss, but Luigi had no respect for a man who beat women. Being a killer, he felt it was always in his favour to know a man's weakness, but he never questioned his own. Draining the last drops of Scotch from his glass, he listened to the order given by Fredo and nodded his head. That night, another bomb exploded.

Chapter 17

Gennaro Bianchi and his crew offloaded their catch and swabbed down the decks of the boat. The acrid stink of fuel overrode the smell of fish as the returning trawlers chugged into port, polluting the air. Covering his mouth, Joseph wondered how the fishermen lived with the foul odour. Men piled boxes of the day's catch on the dockside, ready to be loaded onto trucks and delivered to city restaurants as far away as Rome.

Bianchi stank of both fish and garlic. His face bore the look of a man who had worked hard for too many years. A man who wouldn't be easy to bargain with. He was evasive when Joseph approached him, denying that he knew anything about carrying illegals and threatening to call the police if Joseph didn't clear off. But Joseph was persistent, knowing he had the right boat and the right man.

Not wanting his wife and child to travel from Tunis with traffickers who didn't care if they lived or died, as was his experience, Joseph looked for other options. He sought a Congolese man called Benno, working the streets around the cruise ship terminal, Molo Beverello, in Porta Di Naples, rumoured to have arrived seven miles from the city, bypassing the Island of Lampedusa.

At first, Benno had refused to talk to Joseph. He was not well disposed towards Ugandans, as they had fought a terrible war against each other, but a reasonable bribe made him more amenable. He told Joseph that a small boat with an outboard engine picked up a small group of them from a designated place on the shore a mile from the city of Tunis. It delivered them to the *Michael Angelo,* anchored three miles off the coast. Joseph assumed that by staying in international waters, the fishing boat was less likely to be targeted as a trafficking vessel. Not that the Tunisian coast guards gave a damn about the trafficking of illegals from their shores. If they weren't staying in their country, it suited them fine. But corruption was rife, and bribes were often received for informing the Italian coastguards of any such activity.

'We came halfway, then stopped. The four-man crew fished for two days with us on board.'

'Why waste time fishing? Didn't it leave them open to being caught?' asked Joseph, frowning.

'It's what I thought, man. Like, what the fuck? Get us to land. Turned out the old guy knew what he was doing. A border patrol stopped us off the coast of Italy. Gennaro, the captain, had buried the six of us under the catch.' He grimaced at the memory, then grinned. 'The sea patrol guy took a quick look into the hold and all he could see was fish. Man, covered in slime, we stank.' He shrugged, 'But I've known worse.'

Seeing two fingers missing from Benno's right hand, Joseph was sure he had, if he had been fighting in the Congo. The bloodiest of conflicts, in which more than five million people died.

'A mile out, he dumped us by motor dinghy onto a beach. It was a half day's walk to Naples. Cost a lot. If the six of us had clubbed together, we could have bought our own fucking boat.'

And would have sunk halfway here, thought Joseph

'One is just a boy,' Joseph reasoned with Gennaro Bianchi. 'I can pay you three thousand. Include a life vest for them both, and we have a deal.'

Luckily for Joseph, Gennaro, who would have been a rich man if it weren't for his gambling addiction and a run of bad luck, needed the money. He did not move refugees regularly, for fear of being caught, not that he would go to prison, but because the bribes to keep him out would be extortionate.

Shrugging his shoulders, he held out his hand. Joseph counted out the euros and handed the money to him. He wasn't worried that Gennaro Bianchi would take the money and run. He knew where to find him and his boat.

'Don't take chances with my family,' Joseph warned.

'Your family?' the Captain sneered in reply. 'I take no chances with my boat. It was my father's and his father's before him. You have the location where we will drop them. Be there.'

'I'll be there. Make sure you are.'

On his way back, Joseph stopped at a small group of weathered fishermen who were gutting and cleaning fish, which they were cooking on a brazier. He needed all the money he could get to provide for his coming family, but the aroma of the garlic and lemon on the fish was too tantalising. He bought a small portion, which was put into a polystyrene container and handed to him with a plastic fork. It melted in his mouth, and he savoured the taste. Delicious. A grizzled-looking man squirted some fuel onto the coals, which burst into flames with a whoosh, making Joseph step away, the fumes making him gag.

***

UGANDA 1995

The toxic reek coming from a burning hut, scorched Joseph's nostrils and screaming filled his ears. The raw face of suffering turned Joseph's horror into a raging anger. He knew that avoiding shooting people was not enough. To the astonishment of the terrified people, he shot the four hardened rebel soldiers, who, intent on abducting the children, were revelling in murder and destruction. He distributed the guns from the dead rebels to the bewildered villagers, instructing them to use them if more soldiers came back. He ran a finger across his lips as a signal to tell no one. Overwhelmed by their survival, they were speechless as he disappeared into the bush before they could thank him.

Back at camp, with a self-inflicted cut on his arm and a gash on his head, he was ordered to report to Odango. He reported that government soldiers had been lying in wait for them in the village. He had been left as a lookout outside the village but was discovered by a soldier taking a leak. He fought and killed him before he escaped. Knowing that a hint of nerves could be his undoing, Joseph remained steadfast and locked eyes with him as he related the story he had invented. Odango studied him, frowning.

'You must be blessed by the Lord. Maybe next time they should use someone else to watch out, and you can carry your luck with them.' Shifting in his chair, he weighed Joseph up. 'You survived the mine fields…and my leg …the girl Kizza did a good job.'

Kizza lives.

Surprising him, Odango announced he was to be his lucky charm as one of his bodyguards.

Close, at last.

Although it was against the rules to leave their assigned area, his injury granted him permission to move through the camp and locate Kizza, whom he had learned was working as the camp healer. Her face, lean from lack of nourishment, lit up in a smile when she saw him.

Has she forgiven me? he wondered. A frown quickly replaced the smile, and his heart sank. Kizza dressed his wounds, which were superficial, with a poultice made from herbs and showed no further emotion at seeing him. If anything, she seemed both nervous and anxious.

'Is someone hurting you?' he asked, taking hold of her wrist.

She pulled her hand away, not wanting to answer.

His heart was heavy, knowing the truth of it. *They have stolen everything from her...everything but me.*

'I am going to escape. You too, Kizza. We will get out of here.'

A small flicker of hope came into her eyes. 'When? 'she whispered.

'When I know it's safe. There is something I must do first.'

'Will you kill him?'

'Yes, I will kill him.'

Chapter 18

NAPLES 2018

Despite Carla telling him she would be at least two hours having her hair done, and to go and drink a coffee, Mario parked in front of the beauty salon, adamant that he would wait as instructed by Don Fredo.

The salon owner, Irina, an old school friend, welcomed her warmly with a hug.

As young students they had been inseparable. They had talked and dreamed of what the future held for them: Irina wanting to open a beauty salon and Carla wanting to be an architect. Back from Rome, she was the first person Carla had called with the news of her marriage. Irina, stunned, couldn't believe her friend had abandoned her dream, and after her one and only visit to see her, that she was living in such splendour.

Fredo and Carla had moved into his father's house in the old, affluent part of the city, a home far richer than anything Carla had ever dreamed of. Discouraged by Fredo from 'acting like a servant,' as he put it, cooking or performing household tasks, the house didn't feel like a home that had been nurtured with love into being. Grand as it was, it lacked the warmth of Maria's small apartment, where every item was a part of its story. Its only saving grace for Carla were the surrounding gardens, tended daily by two grizzled gardeners. Determined to further her studies, she broached the subject of enrolling at university, but Fredo persuaded her to wait, claiming he needed the comfort of her presence at such a difficult time.

Fredo, whose mother had left his father years ago and then died in Paris, was the only person at his father's bedside when he closed his eyes for the last time. His death was surprising to Carla, as the doctor had sounded positive about his recovery from the minor stroke. It was at the lavish funeral that followed when Carla discovered that her husband's father was an important man in the powerful Clementi clan. It alarmed her to learn that Fredo would take his place as their monetary advisor.

Within months, she was in a state of denial, refusing to believe the rumours that Fredo, an accountant, was responsible for the alarming rate of deaths in the Clementi family. She became irate with Maria, whose face and the raised eyebrow said it all whenever she mentioned his name.

Once Carla was pregnant, Fredo became more obsessive and controlling. Attending university was no longer discussed, and he disapproved of her meeting old friends. All but Irina disappeared from her life. He kept tabs on her every movement, insisting a bodyguard accompany her everywhere, even to Maria's café. Always insisting it was because he loved her and wanted her to be safe, especially as she was carrying his heir.

Out strolling with Fredo on a sunny Sunday morning, she smiled and greeted an elderly neighbour out walking his dog. Fredo, who had been attentive, talking about what they would do when the baby arrived, grabbed her by the arm and marched her back to the house. There, in a furious mood, he slapped and punched her time and time again, yelling that *his* wife did not talk to other men. Knocked to the floor, she curled up in the foetal position to protect her baby as the blows rained down. The rage in him terrified Carla, who realised she had been blind and had married a monster.

After Giancarlo was born, she became nothing more than a prisoner in the towering block of apartments they called home since Fredo had become capo. The high-rise building was a fortress with rigid security measures in place. Apart from the two armed men who stood guard at the entrance, there were two more on the roof above their private terrace, where, in the summer, Fredo liked to eat. His army of thugs and their families occupied the rest of the building, none of whom she or Giancarlo were allowed to mix with. The small local salon, where she had her hair washed and conditioned, was the only way she had to keep in contact with Irina, her one remaining friend and confidante.

Walking to the back of the salon, Irina opened a door that led onto a narrow street, and Carla slipped out. At a brisk pace, making her way through the narrow, chaotic streets straddled by laundry hanging limply overhead, Carla avoided the broken flagstones and ignored the smell of garbage.

***

Maria was delighted to see Carla, hugged her close, wondering why she was earlier than expected and without her son. 'Has something happened to Giancarlo?' she asked with a worried look.

'No Nonna. He's fine. I needed to talk with you before I brought him. I didn't want him to hear.'

'Where's the goon?'

'He's parked outside Irina's, thinking I'm having my hair done. His mind is on other things. His wife has just given birth to a baby girl. It's all he can talk about.'

'He talks to you?'

'Yes. The only one who dares. Of course Fredo doesn't know.'

Maria hugged her closer. 'You shouldn't take these chances coming here. I dread to think what will happen if he finds out.'

Carla shuddered at the thought, but escaping her chains, even in a small way, gave her a sense of freedom that was badly missing in her life, and she was driven by the desperate need for it. 'Irina and the women there, are very good. They'll cover for me.'

'So, talk,' Maria urged. 'Is it true that Fredo retaliated against Gianelli?'

Carla nodded. 'He bombed his warehouse. Tit for tat – it's war,' she said, twisting the ends of her Hermes silk scarf nervously in her hands. 'The streets will be dangerous.'

'It's you and Giancarlo who are in danger. The man is a lunatic. I pray God answers my prayers and strikes him down, but it seems the Devil takes care of his own.' Maria's eyes burned with indignation.

'Nonna, that's why I'm here.' She took Maria's hand in hers. 'I want to take you and Giancarlo out of this damn city. Away from it all.'

'No chance of that. He doesn't let you breathe without his apes watching you,' Maria scoffed. 'You can't even take your child to the beach on your own.'

Taking a deep breath, and afraid of what she was about to say, Carla looked around, checking that no one was within hearing distance.

'But what if I take Gianni to the salon to have his hair cut and leave through the back door, where I could arrange for a car to be waiting for us? I still have the money from the sale of my parents' house, which Fredo knows nothing about. Thank God you put it in trust until I was twenty-five. I could get tickets to London or Paris. Any place he wouldn't find us.'

Horrified, Maria shook her head. 'No! *Mia caro*! Too dangerous. You know what happens to clan wives when they run? They all come after you in case you talk.'

'I wouldn't.'

'They don't believe in taking chances. And if you were to succeed, what kind of life would it be for you and Giancarlo, always hiding and afraid?'

'Better than this. I don't want my son growing up to be a killer like his father.'

'But Carla, the airport is the first place he would look. He probably has paid informers there, and it would take no time to find you.'

'True. Maybe I could take Grandpa's old car and drive to Switzerland or Germany.'

'Child, they have the police in their pockets. You would never reach the border, and I doubt the car would. It's so old.' Maria could see the desperation in Carla's eyes and her heart lurched.

'I can't take it much longer, Nonna. One day, he *will* kill me. And what will happen to my Gianni?' Carla dropped her head into her hands and sobbed.

Maria was torn seeing her beloved granddaughter in such pain. 'Mother of God, don't say such a thing. I can't bear to see you like this, child.' Taking a deep breath and pushing stray hair from her face, she reluctantly said, 'Maybe …maybe I could convince Enzo Baldacci to take you both on his trawler and drop you in North Africa. You can take a plane anywhere from there, even to South America.' *God forbid,* she thought.

'You would?' Hope sprung in Carla's eyes as she raised them to look at Maria. It hurt Maria's heart to see it.

'It's the last thing I want to do,' she said, shaking her head. 'But if you cannot bear it a minute longer, I will, although it would break my heart to see you go.'

'You could come with us…?'

'No, *tesoro*, no one drives me away, especially those pigs,' Maria stated, shaking her head. 'They have more money than the damned government, but they still fight for even more. Politicians are just the same; legalised gangsters only interested in filling their pockets. This is a beautiful city: a lot of old families, old wealth in big houses, and lots of good people, but there are no real opportunities for the young here, only crime.' Maria sighed. 'If Enrico and I had left this city when we were young, maybe your mamma and my beloved son would still be alive. But it's where I was born, and God forgive me, I was determined not to be driven out.'

Knowing her grandmother was Neapolitan to her core and would feel amputated at her roots if she had to leave, Carla sighed again. 'It wasn't your fault that Mamma and Papa died. They did it. I wanted to think it was an accident …to believe that people were not that wicked.'

'You were just a child.'

'Yes, and naïve,' Carla snorted in derision. 'I've learnt a few lessons since then. They will kill anyone who stands in their way.' She took Maria's hands, her eyes full of compassion. 'Having Giancarlo, I can't imagine how much pain it caused you to lose my father.'

'Tears are the price of love. I've learned that in my many years.'

'Dare I hope I can get Giancarlo away from here?'

'I pray to God,' said Maria. 'Not that he ever listens to me. Better you go back to the salon now before you're missed.'

Maria hugged her again and held on to her. She loved her granddaughter with her whole being and would sacrifice her life for her and Giancarlo to reach safety. As she was leaving, Carla noticed that Joseph was not in his usual place.

'Joseph?'

'Haven't seen him since they took him yesterday.'

'Maybe he's working somewhere else, Nonna,' Carla said, frowning.

'He's worked here for over a year. Where else would he be?' asked Maria. 'If it's not him on my doorstep, it will be another. Better the devil you know,' Maria said before welcoming a customer arriving at the café, with a smile. 'Buongiorno, Margarita. I hope you are hungry today. I've made your favourite.'

'I am always hungry for your food, Maria, whatever it is. But It's true I love your veal parmigiana the most,' she answered, the eighty-year-old lines on her face crinkling into a smile. 'Carla, you are still looking beautiful,' she said, sitting at the same table she had sat at for the ten years since her husband had died. 'God rot his soul,' she said. 'I hope someone kills him soon.' She made a show of contempt by pretending to spit on the floor.

'Who, Margarita?' asked Carla, wondering who had upset the old lady.

'Your pig of a husband. All this bombing and killing going on. Is it true he beats you?'

Carla was stunned. *Sheesh! Does everyone know?*

Maria looked at Carla, nonplussed. She always made light conversation with Margarita, who lived alone and left the house only to come to the café, but she had never discussed Carla with her. She shrugged, knowing it was a fact that the old ladies of the city, including herself, all had family members who knew someone who worked for someone. There were few secrets in Naples, even one as personal as this, that they didn't know about.

'My husband was no better. I wish I had shot him years before he died, the philandering, sadistic pig. I can get you a gun if you need one.'

Carla almost laughed at the absurdity of this eighty-year-old woman, dressed in a dated Chanel suit with fake Hermes scarf draped around her neck, offering to get her a gun, but she knew if she said yes, Margarita would arrange it. Such is the covert power of elderly women in the city. 'Don't tempt me, Margarita. Nonna, I must go,' she said to Maria and quickly left.

No one glanced at her as she hurried back through the streets to the salon. Irina smiled, seeing her. Her long, lustrous hair, which Fredo had forbidden her to cut, was rapidly washed and dried. In the car and sinking into her seat, it puzzled her when Mario hesitated before driving off. 'Mario?' He twisted around to look at her. 'I know you left the salon. Her heart missed a beat.

Chapter 19

Walking back from the port area, Joseph stopped to look in a shop window filled with African antiques and shook his head in disbelief at what he was seeing. Among the carved masks and beaded tribal neckwear, a panga was being sold as some sort of decorative item. The memory of his sister, Mimi, being chopped down, filled him with pain and misery.

Twinkle, twinkle, little star.

A nearby commotion caught his attention and chased the painful image from his mind, replacing it immediately with another scene of violence. An African man, one of many who worked the area where cruise passengers had to pass through to reach the heart of the city, was being beaten and kicked by two Camorra gangsters.

'When we say you buy from Sturla, you buy from Sturla. Understand?' A muscular older guy whom Joseph judged to be in his mid-forties, with the outline of a gun visible beneath his expensive tailored suit jacket, yelled at the man, now prostrate on the ground.

The African, blood streaming down his face, nodded his head while his attacker watched without concern. With a last kick, the thugs took all the man's goods and threw them into the boot of the SUV. The aggressor appeared bored as he slipped off his sunglasses to polish them.

'Who the fuck you looking at?' growled Luigi, seeing Joseph watching him.

Joseph walked away. *Not my war.*

He found Big Moses and the others hiding in a narrow side street with their stuff, near Garibaldi Square. Eager to not get involved, they had moved away when the violence erupted. They were all disturbed and talked of buying from Sturla to avoid confrontation with them. Joseph reminded them of what Gianelli would do if they did.

When things had calmed down, he approached the café with his bundle of goods, which Moses had been minding, and got back to work, spreading his stuff on the pavement; always mindful not to intrude on Maria's café space. Carla arrived in the Mercedes. Joseph noticed that the driver was different, more alert. As he jumped out to open the door of the car, his coat flapped open, revealing a weapon in a shoulder holster. A child holding an iPad followed Carla, who gave Joseph a small smile. Taking her son's hand, she moved towards him and picked up one of his bags, as if examining it. The bodyguard, standing by the Mercedes, watched suspiciously.

'This is my son, Giancarlo,' she said.

Joseph answered with a smile.

'I was concerned for you. Did the Gianelli thugs hurt you?'

'No. It was a warning.'

'A warning…?' She was about to ask what the warning was about when she saw the bodyguard walking towards them. She put the bag down and shook her head. 'No, thank you,' she said in a loud voice, handing back the bag, pretending she had been a potential customer.

The bodyguard ushered them quickly away from Joseph and into the café. Unlike the usual driver, who waited in the car, he entered the café with them. *She must be married to a powerful man to merit so much protection.*

***

Maria, happy to see Giancarlo, smothered him with kisses and hugs, '*Mio caro figlio. Mio prezioso regalo.*'

'Nonna Maria, you're squashing me!' Giancarlo protested, laughing.

She let the boy go, looking proudly at him. 'My beautiful boy. It's so good to see you. And what have you got there?'

Giancarlo, who had inherited his mother's blue eyes, held out the iPad to her.

'It's for you. A present from Mamma.'

'For me? A present? What a surprise!'

Maria took it, frowning, and turned it over in her hands, looking puzzled. 'What's it for?'

He rolled his eyes. 'It's a tablet. On it, you can find anything you want to know in the whole universe.'

'In the whole universe, you say? It must be very clever.' Her amused look said she didn't believe a word of it.

Carla laughed. 'Nonna, it's the 21st century. You have to catch up. On this, you can speak to Gianni every day. Just like on the phone, but you can see him, and he can see you. I'll show you how. It also translates languages, so when foreigners come into your café, you can understand what they say.'

'Harrumph. If people don't speak Italian, I'm not interested in what they have to say.'

'You can also get the daily news and see what's happening in the world.'

'I already know what's happening in the world. Nothing good.'

She looked at the tablet suspiciously. 'Whatever will they come up with next? I can speak to Giancarlo every day and can also see him. Is that what you said?'

'Yes. I'll show you.'

As Carla took it from her, Maria's eyes went to the bodyguard standing in the café doorway. 'Mateo Bagli, what?' she snapped. 'You think I'm going to steal my granddaughter's son, so you have to watch his every movement? Get out of here, or I'll tell everyone you've been cheating on your wife. Get out!'

'Nonna, be calm. It's okay,' said Carla, who didn't want any problems reported back to Fredo.

The bodyguard, looking guilty, moved outside.

'No. It's not okay. I don't have to accept that scum in my café.'

'How do you know he's cheating on his wife?'

Maria shrugged. 'Tell me an Italian that doesn't, apart from your grandfather and your father, of course.'

'Of course,' Carla said, suppressing her amusement. Knowing her grandmother, she didn't doubt the two men in her life were faithful, if only out of fear of her.

'Come Giancarlo, let Nonna get you biscotti.'

'Did you make them Nonna Maria?'

'No,' Maria admitted, 'But, they are still good.'

'Espresso for me, please Nonna,' said Carla, taking her usual seat in the window.

Maria moved behind her counter and set the coffee machine in motion. It hissed and spat out steam.

'Can I have an espresso too, like Mamma?'

'Espresso? I should think not. You'll be asking for beer next. It's juice or water for you, my boy,' she answered with fake outrage, making him chuckle.

Carla spent some time showing Maria how to use the iPad. It impressed her when she saw how it translated languages into Italian, but had no intention of ever using it for that. What she did like was FaceTime with Gianni, who was sitting in front of her but appeared on the screen as well.

'It does this, even if he's somewhere else?' she asked.

'Yes. Even if he was in America.'

'God forbid he should go to such a place, more gangsters there than we have here. Why does it keep disappearing?' she asked, looking puzzled.

'It's the battery saver. Just press on this button, and it comes back.'

'You can play games on it as well. Mamma lets me sometimes,' said Giancarlo, who had been patiently watching Maria learn what he already knew.

Maria passed it to him. 'I'm sure she will let you now.' He took it with a big smile as he sat at a nearby table, becoming immediately engrossed in what he was doing.

Carla encouraged Maria to sit at the window table, so Giancarlo could not hear what they were saying. 'We need to talk.'

'Yes. Tell me what's happening,' Maria urged, as she took a seat.

'It's quiet at the moment, but I'm sure there is more to come.' Carla hesitated before breaking the news that Fredo had forbidden her to bring Giancarlo to visit her again.

'Until the war is over. He doesn't want him to become a target.' She scoffed, 'Just another reason to keep us prisoners. I'm sorry, Nonna.'

Carla had pleaded with him, but Fredo had been adamant. Acutely aware that Maria, whom he had met only twice – when they first married and again at Giancarlo's christening – could see behind his mask, he would like to keep her out of Carla's life. As befitted his narcissistic nature, he didn't like outside influences on those he controlled, so he limited her visits to Maria to twice a week.

Maria, clearly disappointed, sighed. 'So be it. With all the craziness about to happen, I would rather be safe. That both of you are safe.'

Even as she spoke, she knew her granddaughter would never be safe as long as Fredo lived. But so far her prayers, said once a week in the local church of Santa Maria, asking God to strike him down in the worst possible way, had gone unanswered.

'Mario knew I had sneaked off from the salon.' The words tumbled from Carla's mouth.

Maria, realising what this could mean, inhaled sharply as her hand went to her mouth. 'Mother of God! Did he tell?'

***

Carla's mind was racing as the car made its way from Irina's salon back to the Sturla building. The outcome of Fredo finding out that she had given Mario the slip would be drastic. But she realised there was a way out. 'Your wife has just given birth, Mario. If Fredo knows I gave you the slip and I tell him it isn't the first time, he will throw you and your family out of the building. If he lets you live, that is…' Mario got the message. But the reality of what would happen if he had told Fredo made her wake in a sweat during the night, fearing that if even a whisper of what she intended leaked out; Fredo would either kill her or throw her out. Either way, she would never see Giancarlo again. Heart heavy, she knew that being married to Fredo Sturla she would have to bear all the pain that life brought if she wanted to keep her son.

***

'No, he didn't. Living with a monster, you learn a thing or two.'

Maria took a deep breath. 'Carla, darling, I've given it some thought. Better you forget about running. It's too dangerous.' She expected Carla to protest, but instead she nodded in agreement.

'I know Nonna. I wasn't in my right mind. Just the threat of Mario telling him made me realise how drastic the consequences would be.' She hesitated before asking, 'Did you speak to Enzo about the boat?'

'Of course not. You think I don't know when you are out of your mind? Besides, he has a mouth the size of the Vesuvius crater. The entire city would have known. All the old hags in Antonio's café would have been asking if I was having a goodbye party.'

Carla let out a sigh of relief as she gave Maria's hand a squeeze.

Chapter 20

Joseph watched as Carla and her son were driven away before his eyes went to the 'ROOMS TO LET' sign in Maria's window. Having failed to find a place to rent for his family, most landlords believing that Africans overcrowd their living quarters and cause disruption with their neighbours, Maria was his last option. The overcrowding was true because it was hard for them to rent places, and by splitting the rent, they could save money to send home. As for disrupting the neighbours, the people in the barrios complained about the least thing. It was the same in most poverty-stricken areas, in whatever country – the people protective of the little they had looked at any foreign intruder with deep suspicion, often blaming them for their ills.

Maria, checking through her bills, frowned. Things were tight. She catered to mainly regular customers, but, knowing people could not afford more, she had kept her prices steady despite the price of fresh goods having risen so much in the past year. She was surprised to see Joseph walk into her café.

'Over a year on my pavement, and only now do you want to buy a coffee?'

'You make good coffee.'

'It's arabica. We Italians know how to make a decent coffee.'

He didn't tell her that arabica came from Uganda, where, in most homes, the coffee beans are roasted fresh and boiled for some time until the flavour is perfect.

'Is that what you want?'

Joseph shook his head. 'I want to rent the rooms.'

Maria's mouth dropped open. 'You? You want to rent *my* rooms?'

'Yes.'

'So you can fill it with ten Africans. No, thank you,' she huffed.

'It's not for them, it's for me.'

It was obvious to Joseph that the idea of an African man living so close did not appeal to Maria. But then he didn't relish the idea of living close to her, and hated asking her to rent him the rooms, but he didn't have much choice.

'It's five hundred and fifty euros a month, plus a month in advance and a month's deposit.' She assumed that was the end of it and carried on checking her bills.

'And it's extra for electricity and water,' she added.

'Agreed.' He put the money down in front of her. 'Three months' rent in advance and one month's deposit,' he confirmed, nodding at the pile of euros.

Maria hid her surprise well. 'Huh! I see it's good business on the streets. Maybe I should do that instead of slaving all day to feed people.'

'Good business if you work sixteen hours a day and are prepared to starve.'

She studied him. He was a hard worker, something she admired in a man. It was also true that €2,500 was very tempting and would pay off a few debts. Sighing, she reached out and picked up the money, muttering, 'I must be crazy doing this.'

Maria opened the door next to the café entrance, and he followed her down a hallway, which led into rooms backing onto the café. The small apartment, comprising a living room, bedroom, a well-equipped kitchen and a decent-sized bathroom was a vast improvement on where he had lived for the last year. The furniture, once belonging to Maria's parents, was old but well-looked after, and the rug looked new. There were no curtains at the windows, which looked out onto the inner well of the building, where washing hung from lines outside of the upper apartment windows.

'I want no sub-letting, no noise, and you must keep it clean. You understand?'

'I understand.'

'If you break the rules, you leave, and you lose your deposit.' She handed him a key. 'The neighbours will think I've gone loco.'

'Maybe you have,' he suggested.

She nearly smiled, but the sound of gunfire coming from the street made her gasp in alarm. 'At my age, I want a peaceful life, and this is what I get. Another war between those greedy Camorra pigs.'

Joseph frowned, grateful that it wasn't a war he had to fight. He looked at his hands, which were still hard and calloused after years of holding and firing a gun. *Never again.*

Back on the street, with Maria observing from the café window, Joseph watched as the Carabinieri surrounded a Black Gianelli SUV, in which there were four dead men. One of them was Guido from the warehouse, with a hole in his head and his mouth agape. Surprise? Shock? Fear? Whatever it was, Joseph had seen many soldiers with the same look etched on their dead faces.

Chapter 21

'What do we do if we can't work? They attack people every day and take their stuff,' complained Benjamin as they all ate. 'We've been lucky so far.'

Bolo nodded. 'They both want us to buy from them and threaten us if we don't. What choice do we have?'

'And where do we get our gear now they've bombed the warehouse?'

'They make the goods here, so they will find ways to distribute. We have to wait until they do,' added Joseph.

There was a sharp knock on the door. Always alert to danger, every man's head turned toward the sound. The knocking became louder, more insistent. Bolo opened the door to Joe Donato, a weasel of a man who was supposed to do repairs in the building but was never available when needed.

'Well, look who's here. Slow Joe, finally come to mend the water heater.'

'Your rent is going up. It's now a thousand a month. It's due in one week.'

Bolo was stunned. 'No fucking way! This is a shithole, and the electrics are dodgy. You're ripping us off, man. We'll complain to Mr Gianelli.'

Joe Donato snorted his derision. 'It may have escaped your notice, but the Gianelli clan don't own this building anymore. It belongs to Alfredo Sturla.'

Sturla had bought up lots of the slum properties six months earlier, through an untraceable company based in Panama. Sergio Gianelli, who owned several slum buildings, but didn't care to do the extensive repair work, wanted rid of them, and called Fredo a fool for buying them at the price had had asked. But Fredo had plans for the buildings, which, with no thought for the tenants, he intended to demolish when he could bribe permission from the council to build a hotel.

'If I were you, I would consider who you buy your shit from. It might help keep your rent down.' Donato left with an obnoxious grin on his face.

Angry, Bolo faced everyone, who looked even more depressed.

'Fucking Sturla. He's ruining our lives. How can we pay when we're not working?'

'You're right, and no one else will rent to us,' said Big Moses. 'Look how many times we tried to move from this dump.'

'The Gianelli clan does nothing to protect us. Why should we stick with them? If Sturla offers us goods cheaper, we should take them.'

Everyone looked at Abdi.

'They might not protect us, Abdi, but they will hurt us,' said Benjamin.

'It's not our war,' said Joseph. 'Whoever wins will need us to sell their goods. We should sit tight until it's over.'

Abdi turned to Joseph, ' Yeah, Joseph, good idea. Let's sit tight until we starve to death,' he sneered, making everyone feel uncomfortable.

Joseph, knowing Abdi was angry with the world, ignored him. 'Changing sides will change nothing else and will only benefit the Sturla clan. Their stuff might be cheaper, but for how long? If they get control, the prices will shoot up, including the rent. Buying from Sturla will bring the Gianelli mob to your door. Is that what you want?'

'It's already at our door, Joseph. We're in the middle, and there is bad feeling everywhere,' Jacob said, quietly.

Since the war between the clans started, there was a stronger sense of underlying aggression in the city. Even the vibrant morning market in Garibaldi Square had transformed into a ghost town as stallholders stayed away in fear, refusing to open their businesses. Joseph inwardly cursed Sergio Gianelli, who did nothing to protect them. One thing he was sure of was that when mad men were at each other's throats, the innocent suffered.

Chapter 22

The shattering of glass terrified Saba, who snatched Sami from his cot and took refuge, crouching in a corner of the room, holding him close. Outside, a gang of hooligans shouted abuse and banged on the wooden boards nailed across the broken shop window.

'Call the police, Jamal!' Saba begged.

'I've called twice! Don't fret, they will be here soon.' The smell of smoke reached his nostrils. Alarmed, he ran downstairs to discover a flaming rag had been pushed into the shop below. Afraid more for their lives than of the thugs, Jamal yanked open the door, yelling that the police were coming.

The ruffians drove off on their Vespas, which sounded like angry hornets, laughing and making crude gestures.

Using an ancient fire extinguisher from behind the counter in the shop, Jamal doused the flames before the fire took hold.

Holding Sami tightly in her arms, Saba whimpered with fear. 'Have they gone?'

Too incensed to talk, he nodded.

A police car arrived and pulled up in front of the shop. There were two cops. One looked bored and remained behind the wheel as the other got out. It was a humid night, and as he opened the door of the vehicle, a blast of freezing air came out with him. Jamal explained what had happened and pointed out that this was a second attack. Seeing the damage, the cop shrugged. 'Can you identify them?'

'Maybe if you put them in a line-up.'

'It's not a murder case,' the cop smirked, already eager to leave. His shift was about to end and the last thing he wanted to do was write up a report sheet. 'So, what do you want us to do? You can't identify anyone, and there is no one to be seen.'

Jamal choked back the rage he could feel ready to erupt, and took a deep breath. He refrained from saying that if they had bothered turning up earlier, they would have caught them in the act. He told the cop that the thugs had tried to set fire to the place and they could have died, but the cop was paying more attention to his radio, calling in to report that it was nothing serious.

Jamal wanted to scream at him but knew it would get him nowhere.

The cop's parting words were, 'If you're bothered again, call us. But they're kids. I doubt they'll be back.'

Watching them drive off and wiping the sweat from his forehead, Jamal knew the 'kids,' as the cop called them, would be back. He put his arms around Saba and his son and held them close.

Jamal was twenty years old and working as a sales attendant in a Naples tailoring shop owned by an Iraqi immigrant when his father, missing his roots and a familiar way of life, returned home to Iraq. Fariq had heard through the grapevine that the people who had been a threat to him and his family were all dead, and the Americans would soon pull out after a disastrous war, that had left his country in ruins. Even if it took the US army a few years to leave, Fariq was sure returning was the right thing to do, as there could be many opportunities for him. However, Jamal had met Saba and knew he wanted to marry her, so, against his father's advice, he stayed in Naples. He worked two jobs to raise the money to rent his shop. With a small business, a wife and a child, he had been a contented man. Now, feeling Saba's fear, he asked himself if he had made the wrong decision by staying in a country where he wasn't welcome.

Chapter 23

Joseph put on a cotton jacket and pulled up the hood. Apart from some gentle snores coming from the sleeping men, all was quiet in the apartment until an explosion, thunderous and close enough to make the building shudder with the aftershock, startled everyone awake. From the window, Joseph saw a fire burning near the port. *Another bombing.*

A feeling of depressed resignation settled on the men. What they had escaped, had followed them. They settled back into their beds without speaking. Trembling with anxiety, Big Moses locked himself in the bathroom. Jacob stood behind Joseph at the window, shaking his head. 'Dogs at each other's throats.'

'So long as they're not at ours. I'm going away for a couple of days, Jacob. Watch out for Big Moses.'

Jacob nodded. Although curious about where Joseph was going, he didn't ask.

Joseph made his way to the seafront. In the near distance, he could see police vehicles and fire trucks in the port area. Passing the shop selling African antiques and seeing two elephant tusks mounted on ivory bases, he stopped in his tracks. *Kony's white gold.*

***

UGANDA 1998

White Gold. Elephant tusks. To the Messiah, the ton of meat on an elephant needed to feed his army was worth nothing compared to the ivory tusks of the animals when sold on the black market. Trafficked across the border into the Congo, the poached haul of ivory made its way to the coast and was sold to Far Eastern countries for vast amounts of money, which was then spent on ammunition and supplies bought by the Messiah from the Sudanese.

Reaching the top of a cliff in the mountainous area on the borders of Sudan, Odango and his rebels attacked sleeping government soldiers, outnumbering them three to one. It was slaughter by gunfire. It sickened Joseph to see bodies hurled from the clifftop to the rocks below. Reclaiming the twenty elephant tusks seized by the government soldiers from a rebel convoy crossing the border, Odango and his men also found large amounts of alcohol.

Transporting a large tusk on his blistering shoulders back to their base, the only thing on Joseph's mind was when and how he could escape with Kizza.

Once back in the camp, Odango and his bodyguards drank to excess, celebrating their victory. Joseph didn't like the effects alcohol had on him. At best, it made him feel fuzzy, unable to concentrate, and at worst, it turned him into a drooling idiot, as had once happened when Odango, not trusting anyone close to him being sober when he was not, poured it down his throat. Now, he pretended to be drunk and bided his time until they were all inebriated and unconscious before he went into action.

After he had done what needed to be done, he made his way stealthily through the sleeping camp, darting from one hut to another, out of sight of the guards perched high in the teak trees. From experience, he knew their shifts were too long, and tedium often set in. Most of them fell asleep during the night, but he could take no chances.

Awakened by a hand clamped over her mouth, Kizza struggled, overwhelmed with panic. But seeing Joseph with a finger to his lips, warning her to be quiet, she relaxed a little and scrambled quickly to her feet, taking care not to stir the other women asleep in the hut as she left.

The whispered words, 'It's time, Kizza,' made her shake with anxiety. To escape via the river was dangerous, as the crocodiles were most active at night. If they didn't get you, the rapids would. The only viable route out was through the dense forest area, which, at night, was alive with animal predators. Fearing failure, Kizza hesitated, urging him to go without her as he would have more chance alone. But Joseph, who had had many chances in the past to escape without her, was adamant that they leave together. He took her hand firmly in his.

'If we don't go now, you will die here.'

She did not recognise the eyes of the boy she had known, in the man he had become. He seemed older than his sixteen years. The strength in his calloused hand enveloping hers felt powerful. But since her father died, no man had touched her without menace, and it was all she could do not to yank her hand away.

'Trust me, Kizza,' he urged, pulling her behind him.

Without further hesitation, she followed.

They crossed the deep ditch that encircled the camp by the latrines, an area the guards avoided because of the very real threat of catching typhoid, and disappeared into the forest.

With a panga gripped in his hand, Joseph was alert to sounds and movement around them as they made their way stealthily through the jungle. No way did he want Kizza or himself to become supper for the cubs of a hungry leopard, which liked to hunt at night. His gun was strapped over his shoulder, but to use it would alarm any troops nearby. Despite its faded appearance, wearing the rebel uniform would be a red flag to government troops, who might shoot them on sight. The rebel soldiers would react the same way, knowing they were deserting, so they had to move quickly and cautiously, which they did.

After a twelve-hour trek through dense vegetation, they were fatigued and in desperate need of water. With escape in mind, Joseph had mentally mapped out the area when out on raids and felt sure there was a water hole close by, but was now wondering if he had miscalculated. Kizza looked ready to drop, but he urged her to keep going. He felt immense relief when he heard the trickling of water. Without speaking, they ran towards the rocky crevice from where the sound was coming and discovered a small waterfall running down the rock face, which had formed a pool around the base. They fell into it and drank until they could drink no more. Their bodies were used to being without food, but water was essential to keep them alive. Kizza squealed with delight as she washed away the sweat and dirt accumulated on their journey. Joseph joined in, laughing and splashing her. The pain of what they had endured was briefly forgotten; they were children again.

Kizza's laughter was infectious. He wasn't sure if she had yet forgiven him for killing her mother, so an overwhelming desire to kiss her was pushed out of his mind. Catching her foot on a mossy stone, Kizza slipped. He reached out and caught her by the arm to steady her, but she pulled away from his touch.

'Don't,' she snapped, looking away from him. Childhood perished again in a single touch, and only an abused girl remained, her arms hugged around herself.

'You don't have to be afraid of me, Kizza.' he said, as he moved away.

She shook her head. 'I…I'm not afraid…of you.'

Eager to change the subject as he didn't have the words to comfort her, he looked around. 'We need to find food'

Ariya not only educated Kizza on the healing properties of plants in the bush, but also which ones were harmless to consume. Searching out the leaves of shrubs growing close to the water, and knowing they were edible, Kizza stuffed them into her mouth, encouraging Joseph to do the same. He did so and grimaced. They were bitter to the taste but life-giving, so he kept eating. With only escape on his mind, they had walked a long way south with no determined destination. Where they were headed and where they would be safe, was a decision Joseph still had to make.

Before Joseph's father met and married his mother, she had worked as a travelling teacher, moving from village to village, educating children the best she could. She would often point south, to Kampala, where she was born, advising Joseph that when he was grown, he would be wise to move to that city, where there was no threat of falling into the clutches of the rebel army.

'Kampala. In the south. We will go there,' he decided.

'Kampala? But what if the Messiah is there?' Kizza asked, eyes wide with consternation.

'He's not there. It's where the government soldiers come from.'

'They kill people too.'

'Only rebels.'

'They will think we are rebels.'

'We will tell them what happened to us.'

'It's a long way.'

'So we have to keep moving.'

'But I'm tired, Joseph. We have to rest.'

Despite the invigorating water, she sounded weary. He looked at her, realising that he had pushed her too hard into doing something a soldier would do.

'Yes, but not here. It's too dangerous to sleep here. We will find a safer place.'

She nodded, knowing it would be a watering hole for predatory animals. 'Just one last dip,' she begged, reluctant to leave, and sinking again into the coolness of the bubbling water, her eyes closed and a look of contentment on her face. Joseph watched her and the feeling of love enveloped him.

The short time she had spent here was the closest to what Kizza remembered her life had been before the onset of the nightmare. It wasn't Joseph's fault her mother died; she accepted that now and knew she should tell him so. As she stepped out of the water, she disturbed a snake. With a lightning strike, it sank its fangs into her ankle before slithering off into the undergrowth.

Chapter 24

Her cry alarmed Joseph, who was relieving himself in the bushes. He returned, gun ready to fire, fearing soldiers had Kizza, and was relieved to see her alone. The relief didn't last long. Kizza gasped, 'Snake,' before collapsing to the ground.

He ripped a sleeve off his shirt to use as a tourniquet, which he tied above the wound. His hands were shaking with concern for her life. She was already delirious. If he didn't get help, he feared she could die. Having avoided contact with any villagers for fear of them reporting them to the soldiers, he now had no choice.

Carrying Kizza, who was burning up with fever and barely conscious, he made his way to the nearest village. The people, seeing his uniform, were filled with dread. With a cry of outrage, a woman picked up a rock and threw it, hitting him on the head, causing a gash that bled. With blood running into his eyes, he cried out that he wasn't an enemy. Others, deaf to his cries, picked up rocks from the ground, intent on the same action. Joseph feared they would stone them to death when a stern voice rang out above the outcry, demanding everyone's attention. Everything came to a sudden halt.

The village elder recognised Joseph as the boy who had saved them during an LRA attack. It was Mabu village where Joseph had killed the rebel soldiers and given their weapons over to the villagers to defend themselves. Ashamed to discover they had attacked their saviour the villagers quickly took action. A man lifted Kizza from Joseph's weary arms and ran with her to the hut of Umar, the healer.

Umar warned Joseph that if she had been bitten by a dreaded black mamba, she would not survive without the anti-venom. The nearest hospital was in Gulu, some fifty miles away, and she would be dead before they reached it. Hoping it was a bite from a snake less dangerous, he treated the wound with a paste of herbs and roots to draw out the venom in her system, followed by a potion of mixed herbs to cool her blood.

Joseph hoped Umar knew what he was doing.

After enjoying the best meal he had eaten in a long time, comprised of mashed banana, beans and rice, the villagers gave him a pallet outside to lie on. Despite his insides churning with worry about Kizza, exhaustion overtook him, and his eyes drooped and closed. His sleep, the first in two days, ended abruptly with the cold steel of a gun nudging his temple.

***

When government soldiers patrolling the area arrived in the village at dawn they had discovered Joseph in his LRA uniform. Ignoring the vehement protests from the villagers, explaining how Joseph had saved them from the rebels, they threw him into the back of an army vehicle and transported him 171 miles south to Kampala, where, to his frustration, they put him in a holding centre to be processed. It took a month before they were convinced he had been kidnapped and could be trusted. Turning a blind eye to his age, knowing an ex-child soldier had the skills they required, they encouraged him to sign up. But more soldiering was the last thing on Joseph's mind; he had to find Kizza.

Set free, and with no means to return to Mabu village hundreds of miles away, he tried relentlessly to find employment – without success. He slept on the streets with thousands of other homeless children, who carried bundles of sacking on their backs that served as beds and struggled daily to find enough food to keep themselves alive. After a few months, reduced to stealing scraps of food and, near starvation, Joseph eventually took the only job open to him. At sixteen years of age, he reluctantly joined the government army. The training was more physical than mental, and Joseph survived where others didn't. His first posting was in the south, taking him still further from Kizza, and he had no option but to obey. But they soon agreed to his request to fight the rebels in the north.

Transported north in the same army vehicle he recognised as the one that had taken him south, and at the first opportunity, he made his way to Mabu, where he hoped Kizza had survived the snake bite, only to find the village abandoned. Persistent in his search, he soon discovered that the people of the village had moved to the Pabo refugee camp. Begging leave from his commanding officer, he trekked to Pabo. There he located Umar sitting among the ashes of the fire, which three days prior had raged, burning down most of the huts and killing many people.

Umar informed him that Kizza had survived the snakebite but had disappeared on the night of the fire. Bodies were burned beyond recognition; they assumed Kizza was one of them as she had not been seen since. Grief settling into a hard lump in his chest, Joseph threw himself wholeheartedly into fighting against the Messiah. The man responsible for taking all that he loved

NAPLES 2019

As the sun rose, casting a golden glow on the sea and heralding a hot day to come, Joseph sat on the deserted pebble beach, patiently waiting. Three years was a long time to be away. He had missed those formative years in his son's life, but he was determined to make up for it. A boat appeared in the distance. Scrambling to his feet, he made his way to the water's edge, alert for any sign of border patrols, and watched as the vessel sailed closer and dropped anchor. They lowered a dinghy into the water. A crewman climbed into it and started up the outboard engine. An immense feeling of relief washed over Joseph when he could make out Gennaro Bianchi helping a woman and child into the waiting dingy, followed by four North African men.

The dinghy approached the shore, bumping over the waves until it hit the sand. The men scrambled out and ran through the shallow water towards land. Joseph ran into the water past them until he reached his wife and boy. He swept Mussa up in his arms and carried him to the shore, followed by his wife, lugging a bundle of belongings wrapped in a colourful patterned fabric.

Kizza, standing tall on the beach, looked anxiously around her. Joseph smiled. 'Welcome to Europe.' She made no move to embrace him. Mussa stared at him with big, brown eyes. The crew member started up the outboard engine of the dinghy, making a sudden noise. Her nerves on edge, Kizza was startled, pulling Mussa close.

'It's okay. It's just the boat. You're safe,' said Joseph, touching her arm and pulling his son into a hug. 'We are all safe.' As he spoke, he looked at Kizza, holding out his hand to her. She hesitated before giving him a small smile as she took it.

'It was a long journey. You must be tired.'

'Life has been a long journey, but here we are.'

'Yes. Here we are,' echoed Joseph.

Chapter 25

Wanting to see Maria and escape her prison, Carla told Fredo that she had unwanted boys' clothes to take to the refuge for the homeless. Fredo, taking advantage of the war, had prevented her from leaving their apartment, 'for her security,' told her to send them with Mario. Determined to stand her ground, Carla insisted it was necessary for the wife of a don to be seen spending a little time at the charity outlet when times were hard.

'It's about respect, Fredo. Seeing me there is like seeing you there and knowing you care. The people look up to a benefactor like you, especially with mad Sergio Gianelli threatening their everyday lives.' *God, forgive me for the lies.*

Fredo made donations to charities for the poor and liked to think of himself as some sort of philanthropist. It never occurred to him that he was giving back what he had stolen. But liking the image of himself she had painted, he smiled. 'Good idea. I would go myself if I weren't so busy,' he lied.

***

Arriving at Joseph's apartment, Carla, pleased at her little victory over Fredo, filled the closet with the boy' clothes she had made Mario carry in, her arms being full of fresh flowers. Putting the blooms into jugs of water, she noticed the snowy white voile curtains hanging at the window and a colourful cover draped over the sofa that had seen better days, improving its appearance. The kitchen cupboards were stocked with provisions, and the beds were neatly made.

Satisfied that it looked inviting, she made her way into Maria's café, arriving at the same moment as Joseph holding Mussa by the hand. Kizza followed, holding tightly onto her bundle.

'I thought you should meet who's going to live next door,' he said. 'This is my wife, Kizza,' he nudged Kizza forward a little towards Carla, who smiled at the beautiful, statuesque Ugandan woman. 'And my son, Mussa.'

'Welcome Kizza. I'm Carla, and this is my Nonna, Maria.'

Maria came out from behind the counter, holding a small plate of pastries, and glared at Carla. 'Signora Rinaldi, if you don't mind.'

Ignoring Maria, Carla bent down to Mussa's height and looked into two large chocolate-brown eyes. 'And this is Mussa.'

Mussa grinned, showing that he was missing two front baby teeth. It gave him an endearing look and Carla would have liked to hug him, but Kizza pulled Mussa closer.

'They don't understand Italian,' Joseph said in an apologetic voice.

'Oh! Of course. Excuse my ignorance. Please tell Kizza and Mussa that we are pleased to meet them.'

Joseph nodded and translated. Kizza nodded her head but kept her eyes down.

Maria put the plate of pastries in Mussa's hands. 'The child looks hungry. Take them with you and bring the plate back. Here's the key.' Taking both, Joseph thanked her, and they left the café.

From the window, the two women watched Joseph and his family enter the door leading into the apartment.

'She's a beautiful woman,' said Carla.

Maria looked critical. 'Why do they have those barbaric marks on their faces? And why doesn't she have a suitcase? Carrying her stuff around like a bundle of rags.'

'Maybe she couldn't afford one, Nonna. The boy looks very sweet.'

'He'll be inviting all of Africa here soon,' Maria grumbled.

'If you feel like that, why did you put up new curtains for them, make the beds, fill the fridge, bake them pastries?' Carla said it with a teasing half smile.

'Because I don't want her to think all Neapolitans are barbarians.'

The black Mercedes, driven by Mario, arrived outside. It amused Carla that, despite it being an uneasy alliance, her position with Mario had been reversed. Instead of her fearing his reporting to Fredo, he was now relying on her to keep her mouth shut. Today, Mario would report that she had taken the clothes to the homeless charity and spent the time there as a volunteer. She had dropped off a large donation to the shelter on her way to Maria's, appeasing her conscience. But she never forgot that Mario's first allegiance was to Fredo, and she would never trust him or consider him a friend. There was no such thing in Fredo's world. A world she would desperately like to escape from with her son.

Chapter 26

The heady perfume of fresh flowers was the first thing Kizza noticed as she entered the apartment. A calmness, which she hadn't felt since her journey began, enveloped her when she saw the full-blown roses in a vase that Carla had placed on the table.

Is this an omen? she asked herself.

As a nurse, she had hung a print of similar roses, the original painted by an Englishwoman, on the wall of the small room where she slept, and she had often wondered what such beautiful flowers smelled like. One of the few possessions she had treasured, the rose print was left behind in favour of more essential things. But here they were, welcoming her.

Touching a pale pink bloom, she marvelled at the beauty and the delicacy of its colour, the velvet touch of its petals, its pleasing scent. Joseph spoke, startling her. Her hand jerked, causing petals to fall from the flower. She hastily gathered them together, as if guilty of having hurt them.

'Look around,' he encouraged.

She did, and she liked what she saw. Once married, she and Joseph had lived in shared army quarters for a few years, which were designed to be practical. Before Joseph left for Europe, he moved them out of harm's way into two small rooms on the edge of the city. Kizza tried to make them homely, but she never felt she had succeeded. Here, it already felt comfortable.

'It has a good feeling. It's ours? Just for us?' she asked, walking into the bedroom.

'Yes. This is our home now.' Joseph followed her into the bedroom.

Mussa, exhausted from the journey, succumbed to sleep the moment his head touched the pillow on the small truckle bed Maria had provided when she learnt a child was coming. He was still holding a half-eaten pastry, which Kizza removed from his sticky fingers.

The small bedside table held more flowers, which she couldn't identify, but their perfume was also very pleasing to her. She opened a cupboard and frowned.

'Whose are these clothes?' she asked in a quiet voice so as not to wake Mussa.

'For Mussa. They were no longer needed. Carla asked if it was okay to bring them, and I said yes. I knew you couldn't carry much on your journey.'

'Why is she doing this?'

'She's a good person, Kizza.'

She knitted her brows and pouted a little, wondering what else she had given Joseph.

'Is that the only reason?'

'Yes, it's the only reason.'

Joseph, hiding his bemusement at her little show of jealousy, took her hand. With it, he touched the scar on his cheek. 'K for Kizza. It's your mark. I am yours. I have always been yours.'

In the evening twilight, Joseph and Kizza lay side by side in bed. Together, but apart. She ran her fingers gently over his chest until they found a small, round scar just above his heart, and let out a deep sigh. *Yes, our lives have been a long and dangerous journey.*

UGANDA 1998

Bitten by a rhombic night adder, a species that enjoyed lingering in damp areas, Kizza suffered from delirium and pain, but the bite was not deadly. Recovering to find Joseph gone, she feared for his life and her own safety, and, being destitute, there was nowhere for her to go and no family to run to. She was relieved when they encouraged her to stay in the village and assist the ageing Umar, who was glad of the help. Day after day, she kept watching and hoping that Joseph would appear. Joseph, who had protected her when he could and had rescued her from the camp, where she would have surely died. She berated herself for blaming him for the death of Ariya, knowing it wasn't his fault, and for losing the chance to tell him. 'Please come back,' she prayed.

Days ran into weeks, weeks into months. She kept to herself, knowing that, as a kidnapped child, some villagers didn't trust her. Despite this, they treated her well, and she would have stayed in the comfort of its security, knowing it was a place where Joseph could find her – and would have done, if the bush war hadn't escalated. After another rebel attack on Mabu, when the men used the weapons Joseph had given them to defend themselves, and fearing the next onslaught would overpower them, they made the decision to abandon the village for a place of safety.

With no belongings other than a cup and a bowl, Kizza was once again eaten by fear. Dreading the thought of being dragged back to the LRA camp, where they would execute her for running off, she was glad to leave the village.

Like thousands of Northern Ugandans, they made their way on foot to the Pabo concentration camp provided by the government to keep them safe from the rebels. Located twelve miles north of the city of Gulu, it was a densely packed settlement of mud huts and people in despair.

Once there, Kizza worked alongside Umar as she had done in the village, following his example and learning from him all he had to teach. Competently treating minor injuries, scabies, dysentery and hepatitis, endemic because of the scarcity of clean water in the camp, she often despaired at the overwhelming task and the unending queues of people desperate for help. Medical supplies came once a month, but they were never enough.

After a long and arduous day, she shivered in the freezing night air as she made her way to the small hut that she shared with two others. People lit open fires to stay warm, and many men had gathered around them. Despite the biting cold, she didn't dare venture close. Because of the congestion and boredom that camp life created, the danger of sexual abuse ran high. Kizza, growing into a beautiful young woman, feared it was only a matter of time before someone bad laid eyes on her. And now it had happened.

He was the braggart in a small group that congregated close to where she lived. With the swagger of a bully, he followed her to work that morning, and she knew it was only a matter of days before he would make his move. Once alone in the safety of her hut, her mind racing, sleep evaded her. Feeling like a trapped animal, she lay clutching her stomach, knowing she had no choice but to run. But to where? The bush was dangerous, and she had no family to come to her rescue. As always, her thoughts went to Joseph, wondering where he was and if he would ever find her. As she wrestled with these thoughts, a more imminent danger alerted her senses.

A raging fire took hold in the compound as the wind carried cinders to a thatched roof. During the ensuing chaos, Kizza's instincts for self-preservation drove her to find a way out. As bad as she felt about leaving Umar, she made her way, coughing and choking, through the smoke-filled area to a small building where government deliveries were kept before distribution. There, she found who she was looking for. The driver of an army truck, who had arrived to deliver canned food to the camp that day, and was about to return to Kampala. He recognised her as the girl who earlier had treated a badly infected wound on his hand, inflicted on himself while fixing a problem with his engine. She pleaded with him to take her with him.

The father of two daughters, Daniel was all too aware of the perils she faced; however, he was not allowed to take civilian passengers in his military truck. Then again, he was grateful to her for treating his hand. He looked around nervously. Everyone's attention was on dousing the flames with the little water they had, and he realised it was unlikely anyone would see her getting into the truck and report him. He made the decision to take her, but warned her that if they met an army convoy or soldiers on the way, she would have to get out or he would be in big trouble.

Grateful to escape her predator and to make her way to Kampala, where Umar told her they had taken Joseph, Kizza didn't look back as they drove away from the inferno enveloping the camp, but prayed the Mabu villagers were safe.

It was her first time inside a vehicle, and she held onto the dashboard for part of the journey until, overcome with tiredness; she fell into a fitful sleep only to be woken by Daniel nudging her, letting her know they had arrived in the city.

Kampala overwhelmed her. She gaped wide-eyed at the monumental buildings, chaotic traffic and crowds of people going about their business. It was far from anything she could have imagined and she feared that she would never find Joseph in the human mass swarming the city.

Daniel stopped outside a centre known to help kidnapped children. 'Go inside. Tell them who you are,' he urged. 'Where you come from. Tell them everything.'

Kizza, looking fearful, didn't move.

'Girl, I took a chance bringing you here. People will see you in my truck. You have to get out.' Still she didn't move. Daniel sighed. She was a country girl, and he was aware, from its reputation, that the place he had brought her to and which was run by well-meaning volunteers, was perpetually short of funds to provide for so many kids in need. Chances were they would turn her away, and she would end up on the streets of Kampala begging for food, sleeping rough, vulnerable to abuse. He parked the truck. 'Get out, child. I'll come with you.' She hesitated, but did as she was told and they entered the building.

'Please help this girl,' he begged the woman in reception, relating how Kizza had saved his hand with her healing and the lives of many others. And they did.

Able to read and write – taught by Joseph's mother, Dembe, the village teacher – and clearly intelligent, they sent Kizza to a government-funded boarding school in Kampala to further her education.

As a rural child who had been in the hands of the rebels, it made the superstitious staff and pupils at the school wary of her. She made no friends, but it suited her. Apart from Joseph, she trusted no one, anyway.

The discipline in the school was very strict, but compared to what she had endured, she found it easy to adapt to. She marvelled at running water that came from taps, liking the sensation of it flowing through her fingers; the flushing toilet, a clean bed at night, food in her stomach. She was grateful for all of it. Books were a wonder to her, and hungry for knowledge, she pored over them, absorbing all they could teach her. Joseph was never far from her mind. Never wanting to accept that he could be dead, and allowing more grief to slip under her skin, each night she would mentally relate to him what she had learned and how her day had gone. At seventeen, she applied for a job as a trainee nurse in the city hospital, and was accepted.

'Nurse Okello, can you check the stats in the ICU, please?' It was more of an order than a request. Kizza, bone weary from her twelve-hour shift in the Central Hospital, Kampala, nodded her head and sighed. Her working days were getting longer, and the influx of patients was never-ending. Medication was free and people swarmed into the massive hospital from all parts of the country. Her shift should have ended two hours ago. She could refuse, but she knew all the staff were under the same pressure; besides, there was no one waiting for her in the small room she called home. No one to appease the deep sense of loneliness she felt.

'We have one gunshot victim. Operated on this morning. Touch and go. Stats have been up and down all day. Could need a clean dressing.'

Kizza sighed. Another man shot by rebels. 'Patient's name?' She asked.

'One moment. Yes, here it is. Patient in for gunshot wound…Name is Joseph Amaru. Twenty-one years of age.'

Kizza's breath caught in her throat. Her heart thumped against her breast. 'Did you say Amaru? Joseph Amaru?'

'That's what I said. What are you waiting for? Get to work.'

Joseph is alive! She hadn't seen him in five years, and here he was. Head spinning, she walked towards the emergency ward situated at the far side of the vast hospital. Her pace quickened until she was running. Stopping outside of the unit, she hesitated, almost afraid to go in. Her mind was on fire. *Don't get your hopes up. There could be more than one Joseph Amaru…Dear God, please let me be wrong,* she prayed. But there was only one way to find out. She took a deep breath and stepped into the ward. The intensive care patients were always situated near the door, close to where the nurses were stationed. She located him at once. Joseph was unconscious and intubated. The machines surrounding him beeped at a steady pace. She stepped closer to the bed, aware that she was holding her breath. She recognised him and could see the boy had become a handsome man. She exhaled, her shoulders relaxing as she touched his forehead tenderly. 'Joseph, it's really you.' Overcome with emotion, love filled her heart.

Despite the oxygen mask, his breathing sounded laboured. She took the information board at the bottom of the bed and read that the bullet had missed his heart by a fraction, destroying an artery, which had caused internal bleeding. They had replaced the vein with one taken from his leg. Kizza, telling the busy staff she would take care of him, stayed by his bedside all night, afraid that if she left he would somehow disappear, maybe this time forever. Fate had brought him back, and she had no intention of losing him again.

There was confusion in his eyes when he first opened them and saw her. She took his hand and held it firmly to let him know she was real. 'It's me, Joseph. Kizza.' The beeping of the heart machine beat faster. 'It's okay. You're safe, but did you really need to get shot to find me?' She chided him with a smile. Before sinking back into unconsciousness, he let out a deep sigh, as if his life were ebbing away. For a moment, hearing this, alarm gripped her, but it was just a sigh of relief.

***

'Why? You never told me why,' she said in a quiet voice so as not to wake Mussa.

Joseph turned his head and looked at her questioningly.

'All those years ago, why did you look for me? Why save me from the camp, from Odango? From it all?'

'Because you look like my mother,' he teased.

'I don't look like your mother. Was it pity? Was it the promise you made?'

A silence hung between them.

'I rescued you because of the promise I made when I took your mother's life.'

'She forgave you; I forgave you. You owed me nothing. Is that why you married me?'

'No. The ugliness and pain we both suffered tied us together, Kizza. It was fate. I recognised that my attachment to you was something else.'

'What? What else?'

'You know what else.'

'I want you to say it.'

'Kizza, when I close my eyes at night, I think of you. When I wake up in the morning, I think of you. You are always with me.'

'And…What does that mean?'

'I love you, Kizza.'

Tears ran down her face. 'And I you. I love you, Joseph Amaru.' They were words never spoken before. Maybe, each fearing that by revealing themselves, they would be tempting fate, which they both knew could be cruel. She took his hand in hers, and they lay quietly with each other. When he slept, Kizza slipped from the bed. In the bathroom, using a razor blade, she flinched as she cut the inch-long straight scar on her face into the letter 'J.'

Chapter 27

Dressed in his new clothes, Mussa stood proudly next to Joseph as he sold his fake designer bags supplied by the Gianelli clan, who had devised a way to distribute directly from their underground factories. The word on the street was that they had halted their European deliveries, fearing the hijacking of their trucks. The war was escalating. Politicians and the police were powerless in their efforts to stop it.

Big Moses and Jacob worked close by, as did other African men. A whistle of alarm came too late for them to escape with their stuff. Ten of Sturla's gangsters in green SUVs led by Luigi Ricci pulled into Garibaldi Square and were upon them. People scattered in all directions, while tourists visiting the market stood in terror at the sight of drawn guns. The men, including Joseph, knew it would be useless to protest. Suppressing their anger, they stood back as the thugs swept up all their goods and piled them into a mound in the middle of the road.

Maria appeared, surprising Joseph by taking Mussa's hand and ushering him into the café. 'Where's his mother?' she called over her shoulder to Joseph, 'He should be with her, not out here around those thugs.'

He couldn't tell her that Kizza, feeling alien in this place where she didn't speak the language, hadn't found the courage to leave the apartment since their arrival two weeks earlier. Standing with his father was Mussa's only chance to get outdoors. But he knew she was right; he should have moved Mussa away from the violence.

Watched by the scowling Africans, who were helpless to fight back, a Sturla thug poured petrol over the piled-up goods before throwing on a lighter. The goods burst into flames, sending dark, foul-smelling smoke into the air. 'This is your last warning,' Luigi yelled before they climbed into the green SUVs and sped off.

The police arrived, sirens wailing. Maria came out of the café, leaving Mussa seated at the table near the window, eating a piece of cake.

'Too late, as usual,' she shouted at them. 'Look at this mess,' she yelled, pointing at the blazing fire. 'There is enough garbage on the streets without this.'

A cop looked at her and shrugged. She answered with a hand gesture, showing just what she thought of him.

***

Unaware of the turmoil on the street, Kizza finished her tasks and sat quietly in the apartment, holding a rose. She breathed in its perfume. The fragrance filled her with calm. It had been a surprise when Joseph replaced the flowers, knowing she got pleasure from them. Thinking back over the years in Kampala, many spent apart when he was away fighting for the government, she remembered how he'd revealed the caring and tender side of himself. Accepting that she was afraid of being intimate, he had never pressed her, and for a long time they had existed like brother and sister. If he visited other women, she never knew, but she'd felt a niggling pain in her heart at the thought, when he sometimes went missing at night. She later discovered that he was out helping to feed the kids on the streets of the city.

When they eventually joined together as man and wife, it was at her instigation. For a long time, she thought that the continual raping by Odango and his men had damaged her so much that she had little hope of bearing a child, so she believed it was a miracle when she became pregnant. Mussa brought enormous joy to their lives. But he was a baby who suffered from colic. His cries of pain often left Kizza feeling helpless and in tears. Joseph, stationed in Kampala at the time, would often sit through the night holding him so she could get some rest. It also gave him pleasure to bathe and feed his son. She felt contentment when she watched them together, but always at the back of her mind was the niggling anxiety that it could all go wrong. It did.

Like her, the people in Uganda were sick of war and growing angrier by the day with the corruption that riddled the government. She wasn't shocked when they turned on the men who ruled, but was alarmed when they misdirected their anger towards the men who protected them. Outbreaks of violence against soldiers and their families ignited in Kampala. Menace was once again on her doorstep.

It surprised her when Joseph announced he was leaving for Europe to find a safer way of life for her and Mussa. Never questioning how he handled their finances, she discovered he had been very prudent, planning for a day that had now come.

Europe was a fantasy world to Kizza. She had read about London, Paris and Rome, but they had never seemed real to her. Dreading that circumstances would part them forever, she did not want him to leave. But she came to accept that the journey was not over for them or their son, and he must go to prepare the way. Now she was here in this strange land, where people spoke a strange language, and though curious when seeing her,

they were not aggressive or unfriendly, so she wondered why she
didn't feel more at ease.

'It happened again?' she asked Joseph when he and Mussa
returned earlier than usual.

'Yes, it happened again,' Joseph answered as he put a forkful
of the food she had put before them into his mouth and smiled.
'It's good.'

'Yes, Mamma, it's good,' said Mussa as he pushed food into
his hungry mouth, a big smile on his face.

Kizza touched his head affectionately, her eyes on Joseph.

'You keep telling me not to worry, but I don't like this,
Joseph.'

'It's not our war. You shouldn't worry.'

'But I do. It follows us everywhere.'

'It's not the same.'

'How is it different? You must stop selling the bags.'

'And do what? How do I pay the rent? Food?'

'Apply for papers. Get a proper job. I'll learn the language. I
could be a nurse here.'

'We will never get papers. Not while the syndicates run the
city.'

'Then we move somewhere else.'

'No. No more running. It ends here.'

Kizza sighed. 'It's your choice. It's always been your choice,
and I've always trusted you. But here in this foreign country, tell
me, when do we start living?'

'What's war, pappy?' Mussa asked.

'Nothing good,' Kizza answered before Joseph could.

Perhaps she is right, he thought as he lay awake that night.
Perhaps I should stop selling the bags for a while and keep the danger from

our door. The day after Kizza and Mussa arrived, he had been back at work on the streets. Time he should have spent with her, showing her how grateful he was to have her and their beloved son here with him. Always frugal with his money, he knew he could provide for a short while, but the war between Gianelli and Sturla may go on indefinitely. What then? He remembered that his father, when overburdened, would sit outside and look at the sunset. As the sun went down, he would take a deep breath as if lifting a heavy weight from his shoulders and say, 'Whatever comes, comes.'

He decided his father was right. It was time to take a deep breath.

Chapter 28

The next morning, he suggested something that made Mussa jump up and down with excitement. After breakfast, they left their apartment along with Big Moses, whom Joseph had persuaded to join them, and who smiled like a kid, holding Mussa's hand. When they passed Maria, cleaning the pavement outside her café, she looked mildly curious as to where they were off to.

Kizza, in her long Ugandan-style dress, walked very close to Joseph. Everything was foreign to her. Her eyes darting from one thing to another, she realised Naples had many faces as she took in the grandeur of each monumental building they passed, and peered down long, narrow, upward-sloping streets that ran alongside them, bursting with pungent aromas and bustling with people scraping a living and gesticulating with their hands in animated conversation. Despite all the war and chaos the city had suffered throughout history, which she knew from the research she had done in Uganda, Kizza felt Naples exuded a sense of proud defiance.

Entering the Stazione Nationali, they had to make their way to the underground railway Napoli Gianturco. There, they took the N2 train to Rotunda Diaz. Mussa spent all of the thirty-minute journey with his face pressed against the window. Overawed by the sheer size, strength and speed of the train, he decided instantly to become a train driver. Joseph smiled, knowing that if he had been lucky enough to ride a train as a boy, he would have made the same decision.

Mappatella Beach on the city's waterfront, known locally as the *Lungomare*, is the most centrally situated stretch of sand in Naples. Not known for its cleanliness, being so close to a port, it is nonetheless the nearest place for Neapolitans to cool down in the summer heat.

Mussa and Big Moses took no time to kick off their shoes and strip to their shorts. The burning sensation of the hot sand on their feet made them yelp as they ran hand in hand into the water. Moses picked up Mussa and threw him into the air, letting him fall with a big splash into the sea. Mussa squealed with delight, repeatedly crying, 'Again! Again!'

Joseph, sitting on the sand with Kizza, laughed, a low, throaty sound. It warmed his heart to see his son so happy. Kizza nearly laughed, but stopped herself. Joseph frowned.

She smiles, but…?

'It was at the waterfall,' he said.

'What was?'

'The last time I heard you laugh. You smile a lot, and it's beautiful, but laughter?'

Kizza looked away from him. 'You remember the laughter? I remember the snake.'

'You must put the past behind you, Kizza.'

She chewed on her lip and shook her head. 'I know it's stupid, but I feel that if I laugh, someone will come and steal it away. I try, Joseph, I do, but I can't forget.'

He put his arm around her and pulled her close. 'Be a river. Don't look back. It's not the direction we're going, woman.'

'And you? Don't you look back? The cruelty of Odango, the LRA and those years of believing one politician after another would change things and stop the violence? But no matter how hard you tried, nothing changed. Each one brought more pain. Can you forget the pain, Joseph? Can you forget what they made you into? What they made us into?'

He thought about this and sighed.

'I am what I am, Kizza.'

'But do you ever wonder what life would have been like if Odango never happened?'

'No. What happened, happened. We can't change that. We have a new life now. It's different here. We're safe, and so is our son.'

'But the gangsters here are crazy.'

'They are crazy, but they are gangsters, not the government. Not a rebel army, not crazy as we know it. They are none of our business.'

'They're at war.'

'With each other. It's not our war.'

'You say that but they are attacking and burning your stuff.'

'We just have to stay out of their way until they are done fighting each other.'

Kizza stared at him and shook her head. 'Be a river, you say, but an ocean swallows a river. Maybe violence is what the world is about, and we are longing for something that doesn't exist.'

'A peaceful life does exist, woman. Remember Cobo, our village? How happy we were as children? The things we used to dream about?'

'And where is Cobo, now? Burnt to the ground with the dreams we had.'

'We have new dreams. Be positive, woman. You're in Italy now. We have nothing to fear. *You* have nothing to fear.' He pulled her close, and she relaxed against him as he gently ran a finger over the keloid scar forming the letter 'J' on her face. It should have marred her looks, but in fact, it took nothing away from her beauty. She closed her eyes, savouring the love in his touch. Joseph felt the desire to kiss her, but not in public. He respected that Kizza, being a private person, would not like that.

Mussa came running towards them. 'Mamma, come with me!,' he demanded, yanking on her hand. She stood, and he pulled her towards the sea.

Sitting on the beach with Big Moses, Joseph watched with pleasure as they paddled in up to their knees, Kizza holding up the skirt of her dress in a failed effort to keep it dry.

Looking out over the sea, Big Moses sighed. 'My family is dead; their spirits are across the water in Africa.'

'Mine too,' replied Joseph, feeling a sharp stab of pain pierce his heart, before he pushed it away.

'Here, I feel I can reach them.'

'We're your family now, Moses.'

'Is that why Mussa calls me Uncle?'

'Yes. Now you are his uncle. All boys need an uncle as much as they need a father, right?'

Big Moses smiled at hearing this. 'Right. We all need family and Jesus,' he declared.

'Yes, Moses, and Jesus,' Joseph answered, not wanting to deny it, knowing it would upset his friend.

'Jesus takes care of us,' Moses said with a smile.

Joseph looked away. Jesus hasn't been doing a very good job.

Kizza suddenly squealed with fright and, holding her dress up to her thighs, ran splashing through the water to the shore. Mussa laughed as Kizza did a little dance on the sand, as if shaking something off her. 'Ugh!' Running out of the water, his son called to Joseph. 'Mamma is frightened of a fish!' Kizza relaxed and suddenly laughed. Her eyes went to Joseph.

'It was a big one,' she protested, and she surprised herself by laughing out loud.

Joseph felt his heart soar when he heard the sound, suppressed for so long. Getting to his feet, he took Mussa's hand and ran with him back into the water, where Mussa climbed onto his shoulders before falling with a big splash. Joseph laughed as he hauled Mussa out of the water, coughing and spluttering.

Happy, exhausted and hungry from their time at the beach, they stopped at a café for something to eat. They ordered two Margherita pizzas, which originated in Naples in 1890 when pizza was a street food that had been sold in the area as far back as the 16th century.

Mussa watched wide-eyed as the man in the kitchen opened the iron doors of the oven and, using a paddle, popped the uncooked pizzas in. When he opened the oven door and lifted the pizzas out, smelling of melted cheese and basil, his face broke into a wide grin of delight. Kizza, tasting it and finding it delicious, nodded her head in agreement with Mussa and declared she could eat a lot more pizza. Big Moses, who could have eaten the two pizzas himself, surprised them by insisting on paying the bill for his new family. Joseph had never seen Kizza so content.

Chapter 29

After a quick trip to China to ensure the deal he had made was still in force, Fredo, holding a spotless white linen handkerchief over his mouth and accompanied by Luigi Ricci and two alert bodyguards, came out of a large, dust covered building. They were in Bagnoli, a deserted area the size of a small town in the west of Naples, where disused factories stood like forlorn, crumbling monoliths. A world steel crisis had led to the progressive closure and decommissioning of the steel plants once located there. Because of the high levels of pollution and toxic waste that had been spewed into the sea and surrounding land for a hundred years, the industrial site was now condemned.

As a safeguard against possible duplicity by the Chinese, Fredo had chosen the area to reinstate his cement business when his war with Gianelli was over. Volcanic activity meant that underground thermal waters – an essential element in the production of cement – flowed from behind the building; it was the perfect location.

The area was dangerous to the health of anyone who worked there, but Fredo couldn't have cared less for the well-being of his employers. Aware it was illegal on so many levels – pouring more waste onto the land and into the heavily polluted sea went counter to the government's revitalisation program – he decided the site suited his needs perfectly. It had taken months to gain permission to open the industrial unit again, something that should never have been permitted, but this was a city where money talked, and he had done a lot of talking, along with a few death threats.

With a disdainful look at the dust on his highly polished handmade shoes, he vowed never to visit the place again as he climbed into the dark green SUV and took his place in the back of the vehicle next to Marco. As Luigi drove off, the force from a deafening explosion hurled the vehicle into the air. Metal crunched and screeched against the ground as the SUV landed on its side. Chunks of concrete gouged huge dents in its bodywork, and the bulletproof windows shattered.

***

Sergio, seated at the ludicrously long dining table, eating a large plate of pasta tossed in garlic oil, was jubilant.

'Let's hope that's the end of him. That fucking punk, thinking he could outsmart me,' he crowed. He had learned of Fredo's plan to re-start his cement business in Bagnoli from a contact in city hall who was on his payroll. The informer alerted him three days before that the license was going to be granted. Before the conflict, it wouldn't have concerned him, but he had seized this chance to strike at his enemy. On his orders, Frankie and Toni had spent days at a nearby abandoned factory that stank of rat excrement and urine, waiting for Fredo to show up, waiting to press the button on the detonator that would trigger the explosives they had planted deep under the outer wall of the building.

Michael Rossi swallowed hard. He hadn't approved of the attack on Fredo Sturla's life. So far, buildings, trucks and merchandise had been the target. If the attempt failed, it would escalate the war to a far more dangerous level. But Sergio was becoming more erratic by the hour and would not take advice. *The damned soap operas are screwing his brain.*

'But someone will take Fredo's place, and the war will go on.' *Do I always have to state the fucking obvious?*

'Then we kill him and the one who comes after him, until they learn some fucking respect.'

The door burst open, and Gino came in. Small beads of sweat glistened on his forehead. At the sight of him, Michael's stomach tightened into a cramp, waiting for the bad news.

'The timer jammed; he had left the building, when it detonated. It took the building down and flipped his car, but Sturla got away.'

'Useless fucking idiot.' Sergio snarled at Gino.

Knowing there would be huge repercussions for the attempt on Fredo's life, Michael thought this might unnerve Sergio, but he was wrong. Sergio, ignoring them both, walked into the main area and turned on the television.

Gino shrugged. 'We've got to get Sturla before he retaliates.'

Michael wondered just how he proposed to do it. 'Now, more than ever, Fredo will have an army of protection around him. We've crossed the line, Gino. All hell will break loose. None of us is safe now.'

***

Secure in the safety of the penthouse, but covered in cuts and scratches, Fredo Sturla seethed with rage as he pulled off his heavily soiled jacket and threw it across the room. 'If we hadn't left when we did, I would be dead! Dead! Luigi, you were supposed to make sure the place was clear?'

159

The attack had left Luigi off balance. 'Don Fredo, I led the inspection myself, and the place was clean. I don't understand how the bomb got into the building.'

'Perhaps it didn't,' said Marco.

Fredo turned his eyes on him. 'Explain.'

'They could have buried it in the ground close to an outside wall. The building was old and any explosion would have been strong enough to bring it down.'

Luigi shrugged and nodded.

Fredo glowered at him. 'You didn't take that into account? You didn't check the outside? What the fuck am I paying you for?'

'Don Fredo, we checked everything, outside and in. We found nothing, and I left two guards in the building. They must have planted it days before and connected it to a remote-controlled detonator. If it was buried deep enough we wouldn't have picked it up on the sensor.'

Marco nodded in agreement. 'Sergio must have someone in the city council office to know we were planning to set up again, and where. What Luigi says makes sense.'

Fredo looked at Luigi coldly. 'Or maybe the two fucking idiots you left there were working for Gianelli?'

'If they were, they would have left before the bomb went off,' Luigi pointed out.

'They're both dead.'

'Saves you a job,' Fredo scowled. When Fredo was in this mood, it was useless to argue that unless they had dug up all the land around the building, they had no way of knowing a bomb was there.

'Don Fredo, come to some arrangement with Gianelli,' urged Marco, hands in a placatory gesture. 'This war has been going on for too long. He won't stop until you do. His business in Europe has taken a massive blow. Once he realises that his attempt on your life failed, he will expect you to go after him, so he'll be prepared to come to an arrangement. Demand a share in the fake business, big enough to satisfy the Chinese: maybe France or Spain, for a share in the bank, and if he agrees, we can move forward.'

Since the war between them had begun, the chances of them owning a Chinese bank had diminished by the day. If the conflict didn't end soon, the chances of their bank ownership would slip away completely. But Fredo was now hellbent on revenge against Sergio and wouldn't listen to reason. It was something that Marco had witnessed before, when he was a young man in the service of the Clementi family, before Fredo talked him into betraying them with a promise of change. Carlo Clementi, like Sergio Gianelli, thought violence resolved everything. It had ended with his death and the deaths of many of his men. Marco knew that if Fredo travelled further down the same road and did not think logically, it could have a bad ending for them all.

'No arrangement! No fucking arrangement! I'll kill the old bastard. First we must cut off his legs, Gino and Rossi. Then we get Sergio,' Fredo replied. 'Luigi, you do it. And don't screw it up.'

Marco paled. 'Killing Gianelli will turn the syndicate against you.'

'They tried to kill me!' Fredo sneered. 'The syndicate might shout and scream about it, but ultimately they'll all want a slice of his business. As for the Chinese, it's a better deal for them if Gianelli is out of the picture. Then there is no one to stand in their way and no one to stand in mine.'

Chapter 30

'Stay close,' Kizza called to Mussa, who was lingering behind as they took their early morning walk to the market. Once there, Kizza would examine the vegetables, indicating to Joseph which she wanted. Bit by bit, she was growing more secure in this land, where people spoke with their hands. She liked the sound of the Italian language. It was like music to her ears, and she was determined to learn it. Walking home, they passed Arturo's and saw Maria sitting outside enjoying a coffee. She managed a tight smile and a nod of the head as they went by; Kizza nodded back. *She's like my grandmother, who would have treated strangers from another land just the same. But she made the apartment nice for us and made the cake for Mussa, so there is a heart behind the barbed wire.*

Later that day, while preparing food in the small kitchen, she listened to Joseph encouraging Mussa to speak Italian.

'Say it, Mussa, say 'Buongiorno.'

'Bon…Gorno.'

'Again. Buuuon…geeee…orno.'

'Bon Geeeno.'

Joseph smiled and caught Kizza's eye. She was also smiling.

'Now you must learn the moves.' Shrugging his shoulders and using his hands like an Italian, Joseph showed him how. 'Buon Geee…orno Mussa.'

Mussa tried to imitate his moves. 'Bon Gornc Mussa.' Kizza joined in doing the movements. 'Bongeee…orno…Joseph.'

Joseph applauded. 'I have such a clever family!'

Mussa answered with a big smile.

'He will soon pick it up when he starts school,' Joseph said, smiling at Kizza.

'Yes. I want to. I want to talk to Giancarlo. When can I go to school?' Mussa demanded.

Kizza looked at Joseph, also wondering what the answer to this question was.

'It's closed now. When the summer is over.'

'Go wash your hands, Mussa. Food is nearly ready,' said Kizza, nudging him towards the bathroom.

'Is it pissa?'

'No. It's something better than pizza. Do as Mamma says.'

Mussa went into the bathroom, and they could hear the tap running.

'Will he be okay in school?' Kizza asked anxiously. 'Not knowing the language.'

'He has to learn to survive here, Kizza, as we do.'

As she was about to walk into the kitchen, she stopped and faced Joseph.

'Thank you, husband.'

'For what?' Joseph asked, looking a little puzzled.

'For this. For everything. I realise how hard you must have worked to get us here.'

Joseph stood and pulled her close. 'Does that mean you're happy here?'

'My child is happy, so I am happy.' She hesitated before saying more. 'I am happy to be with you.'

They stayed quietly locked in the embrace.

'Mamma, where's the food?' Mussa interrupted, doing an Italian shrug, making them smile. They broke apart, and Kizza hurried into the kitchen with a smile on her face.

'It's coming, child, it's coming.'

In Uganda, women don't encourage men and boys to be in the kitchen, and it applied to Joseph and Mussa in Italy. Kizza loved to cook and would strive to produce dishes from home. Mussa loved a 'rolex,' which was an omelette wrapped in a chapati. Joseph liked to eat 'chickennat,' a chicken and onion stew served with peanut butter. Today she had cooked 'matoke,' knowing it was one of Joseph's favourites. Like a beef stew, but with mashed plantains, peanut sauce, beans, garlic, ginger, chilli and cumin simmered together and served with chunks of warm bread. It was a meal that left their stomachs gurgling with satisfaction. Joseph, enjoying contentment with his family, believed in no God, but if he did, he would have thanked Him, believing that all was well in his world.

Chapter 31

Abdi and a reluctant Big Moses knocked on the door of a small house near the docks, set in a terrace of small, two-storey buildings, once the homes of fishermen and their families. The windows were blacked out, and with no sign of life within, Big Moses was agitated. Abdi had talked him into coming and he was now feeling anxious about his decision.

'It doesn't look right Abdi, lets go home.' As the words left his mouth one of Sturla's men opened the door and invited them in.

Once inside, and finding no weapons on them, the man showed them through a long warehouse, which had been created by removing the inner walls of the terraced houses, opening them up into each other.

Row upon row of shelves crammed to the ceiling with fake designer goods, packed the place. A couple of Camorrista, sitting at a table playing cards, viewed them with suspicion.

'I'm Danny. You'll be dealing with me from now on,' the man who had opened the door said, waving an arm at the merchandise. 'Check it out. It's much better gear than the crap Gianelli sells.'

To them, it looked just the same, apart from a couple of

different brand names, but who were they to argue? They chose what they wanted and paid for their bags and sunglasses.

'Deal with us, and we will take care of you. Tell the others and come back soon,'. Danny said, all smiles.

At least we don't get threatened or insulted here, Big Moses thought; but the situation made him nervous. Already, he was regretting it.

'Probably the same stuff the bastards stole from us,' grumbled Abdi as they walked away, carrying the large bundles over their shoulders.

'Joseph says buying from them is bad,' said Big Moses with a worried face, glancing back over his shoulder.

'Is Joseph putting food in our bellies? Paying our rent? Gianelli doesn't protect us. They don't give a fuck about us. No one does.'

'Jesus does Abdi. Jesus loves you,' Big Moses protested.

'Fuck Jesus. What did he ever do for me? Where is my family? All dead. Do I have anyone? No! Do you have anyone? No! What did Jesus ever do for me or you? Nothing!'

He walked off, leaving Big Moses trailing behind, his shoulders hunched in dejection, muttering, 'Jesus loves *me*.'

***

The rent was paid for a few months, and he still had a small amount of money stashed, but ever cautious and fearing it would run out, Joseph — after a two week break with his family, and promising Kizza he would stay alert for trouble — returned to work on the streets. He laid out the bags he'd bought from Gianelli's supplier before he took a break, in his usual place. When Big Moses spread his blanket close by, Joseph saw that the stock was different.

He frowned. 'You bought from Sturla?'

'It's half the price. We have to eat, Joseph, and they said they will reduce the rent,' Moses whined.

'Until you have no choice.'

'Now that you've left, it's more difficult.'

Joseph felt bad that he had moved out just as they threatened to raise the rent, and because of the clan war, there was little money going into the house to keep them afloat.

'I know it's hard, and I'm sorry I'm not there to help, but what you've done is not a good move, Moses. It's dangerous. The Gianelli clan is dangerous. They're evil men.'

Big Moses looked guilty. 'I didn't want to, but Abdi got angry. He's always angry. He has no family.'

'He's had a bad deal in life. His anger makes him blind. Buying from Sturla could bring you both big trouble.'

'Buying from Gianelli brings trouble, too. Jesus will protect me.'

'I hope, for your sake, Jesus does a better job than he has been doing so far.'

Big Moses frowned. Seeing how unhappy this made him, Joseph immediately felt ashamed for saying it. 'But maybe there's a reason, and He has a plan for you, man.'

Big Moses grinned. 'Yes. Jesus has a plan for me. I know this.'

Bored with having nothing to do, as there were few tourists about, Joseph set about mending one of Maria's outside chairs, the leg of which was wobbly. He enjoyed working with his hands and liked the smell of wood. If given the chance, he would like to work as a carpenter. Maria, busy in the café, kept glancing out of the window, watching him suspiciously as she went about serving her customers. Feeling her eyes on him, he ignored her.

Coming out of their apartment holding Mussa's hand, Kizza saw Joseph mending the chair. 'She'll never thank you.'

'I know,' he said, testing the chair and finding it sturdy.

'So why do it?'

'Because I can. Are you going somewhere?'

'I decided it was time I walked about, explore a bit.'

Joseph, surprised and pleased, smiled. He wanted her to assimilate, and to get to know the area better. This was the first time she had shown any inclination to do so. Apart from her visits to the market with him, she had remained indoors.

'You want me to come?'

'No. I must learn. I want to learn. This is my home now. Isn't that what you said?'

'It's what I said.' He rooted in his pocket and took out a €10 note.

'I don't need money,' she protested.

'Yes, you do, Signora Amaru. You must have a coffee. Sit and watch people go by. Be Italian.'

She took the money, smiling. 'I'm not sure I can be that, but I'll try.' She shrugged like an Italian, making him laugh.

Mussa pulled his hand from Kizza's. 'I want to stay with Pappy. I don't wanna walk.'

'Mussa, you must go to take care of Mamma,' Joseph insisted.

'I don't wanna. I wanna stay!' With his lower lip pushed out, he looked determined.

'It's okay with me if it's okay with you,' said Kizza. Joseph shrugged. Kizza kissed Mussa's forehead. 'Be good,' she said. She smiled at Joseph, and with a little wave of her hand, she walked off.

He watched her go, proudly thinking what a fine woman he had. But he was concerned because she had never walked through the city alone. Naples was a maze of alleys and streets, and it was easy to lose your direction. The chair mended to his satisfaction, Joseph took Mussa's hand. 'Let's follow Mamma and make sure she finds her way back.' He called out, 'Hey! Big

Moses, watch my stuff.'

Mussa pulled his hand away. 'No, Pappy, I wanna stay with Uncle.'

Hearing Mussa call him uncle, Big Moses' face broke into a huge grin. 'He wants to stay with me, his uncle. Go. You go,' Moses urged.

'Okay. But any sign of trouble on the street, get yourselves inside. Here are the keys.'

Big Moses took the keys from him. 'Don't worry. He's safe with me.'

'Obey Uncle Moses. You hear me?'

Mussa nodded his head and stood beside Big Moses, slipping his hand in his as Joseph walked off.

Relishing the thought of joining his wife for a coffee and a stroll around the city, Joseph grinned to himself. *Now I'm becoming Italian.*

In the first shopping street off Garibaldi Square, he caught sight of Kizza ambling along. occasionally stopping to look in a window, curious about what they were selling. *One day, I will buy you whatever your heart desires,* he vowed.

Kizza, looking happy and relaxed suddenly filled him with misgiving. He had spent his life protecting her and it was a hard habit to break, but he knew it might make her crazy if she thought he didn't trust her not to get lost. After all, she had spent years alone in Kampala when he was a soldier and when he had left for Europe. About to turn back, he paused, seeing a black Gianelli SUV with two men inside pull up in front of a restaurant near the end of the street. *Trouble?*

Frankie and Toni, climbing from their vehicle, hands on guns and eyes alert for any signs of danger, scanned the area. But all they could see was an African woman walking down the street towards them.

When the yellow Maserati pulled up behind the SUV and Gino and Michael got out, Joseph's danger antenna was crackling. He didn't want Kizza anywhere near them. Hurrying towards her, he called out her name. But the roar of a powerful motorcycle engine as it screeched around a corner drowned out the sound of his voice. His mind slipped into slow motion as he took in the bike and its rider, his face hidden by his helmet as he tossed a hand grenade and sped off.

The grenade rolled under the Maserati. Acting quickly, Frankie and Toni pushed Gino and Michael into the restaurant, where they all hit the floor.

'KIZZA!' Joseph yelled.

Passing the cars and hearing her name, she stopped to look back and smiled at the very moment the grenade exploded. He watched in horror as her body was lifted in the air and flung onto the pavement, covered in glass from the shattered restaurant windows.

His heart thumping against his chest and lungs struggling for air, Joseph ran to the scene, screaming, 'No!!'

Kneeling on the pavement among the rubble, Joseph cradled Kizza's mangled body in his arms, his heart breaking. The bodyguards, first checking there was no further threat, hurried Gino and Michael out of the restaurant, pushing them toward the black SUV, standing next to the blazing Maserati. They were all in a state of panic and shock. Michael's eyes met Joseph's for a nanosecond before he followed Gino into the damaged SUV. The door slammed, and they raced off without a thought for the destruction or the dead woman.

***

In a trancelike state of stunned disbelief, Joseph returned to Garibaldi square and retrieved the key from Big Moses. Taking Mussa by the hand, he walked towards his apartment and slipped the key in the lock without saying a word.

Big Moses asked, 'Did you fight with Kizza?' His question went unheard as Joseph closed the door, shutting him out.

Inside, the first thing he noticed was the smell of the roses he had bought her. Dropping into a chair he pulled his son onto his knee and held him close as he explained that his mamma would not be coming back. He had promised her she was safe, and now she was dead.

I failed her.

Chapter 32

'To hell with what Joseph says. He's an old man.'

'But he's right, Abdi. Dealing with Sturla, you're looking for trouble. They'll come after you both,' said Abel, dishing out the food.

'And what? They'll kill me? Better than starving to death.'

'Abdi's right,' said Benjamin. 'This war could go on for a year or even longer. Who knows? What difference does it make who we buy from? If the Sturla Clan says they will protect us, what have we got to lose?'

Big Moses shook his head. 'Joseph says it's dangerous.'

'Is he here? Shut up about Joseph,' Abdi growled at him. 'We bought the stuff from them, and nothing happened. Right?'

A hard rap on the door quietened them, all fearing Abdi had spoken too soon. Jacob opened the door, not knowing what to expect. It surprised him to see Joseph with Mussa.

Joseph pushed Mussa at him. ' Keep him safe,' he said and walked off before Jacob could react.

Abdi shook his head. 'He can't leave the kid here. Who'll take care of him? Where's his mother?'

'I'll look after him. I'm his uncle. Muss, come here.' Mussa ran to Big Moses and stood close to him. He saw that the child had been crying. 'What's wrong? Why you cryin', man?'

'Mamma's gone.'

'Gone? Gone where, Muss?'

'Gone to heaven.' Fresh tears ran down his face. Everyone was stunned into silence.

'To heaven?' Big Moses lifted Mussa onto his knee, holding him tight and thinking Mussa must have it wrong. 'Maybe she got lost, and Pappy has gone to look for her.'

Jacob, searching the news app on his phone, gasped. He showed the others a report of a nameless African woman who was killed in a gang attack in Naples. They were stunned.

With Mussa held close, Big Moses rocked a little. 'But Joseph didn't buy from Sturla. Why would they hurt Kizza?'

Benjamin shrugged. 'They need no reason. You know that, man.'

'So where's Joseph gone?' Bolo asked.

In the campagna, Joseph ran like the wind until totally exhausted. Heart pounding, he dropped to his knees. Suppressed grief for his parents and Mimi, had erupted just as Vesuvius, in the distance, once had. Time does not heal, it just covers over the scars with hard tissue. Losing Kizza had ripped them open. Unable to cry, he screamed in despair. The wretched sound echoed around the area.

In the Gianelli compound, everyone was on edge after the attack. Sergio was behind closed doors and Gino was nowhere to be seen. The two men standing guard at the gates were suddenly alert, hearing Joseph's cry of anguish, which had echoed through the night.

'What the fuck was that?' one asked, his hand reaching for his gun.

'Who knows?' The other said with a shrug. 'Could be an animal or Gino having fun at someone's expense.'

'Not Gino. He's too busy pissing his pants after what happened.'

'Maybe we should take a look?' He glanced at the woodlands surrounding the compound, which were dark and menacing. 'Or let the dogs out.'

Not relishing the thought of moving beyond the gates, they were both relieved when the screams stopped.

Chapter 33

From the bedroom window of his palatial residence in Posillipo, the wealthiest area of the city, Michael Rossi checked to ensure the men guarding his house were in place. He knew deep down that if Fredo wanted to attack his house and kill him and his family, no number of guards would prevent him.

He cursed Sergio for the danger he had put them in as he climbed into bed next to his wife.

Sara, a comely woman born in Sorrento, further down the coast, kept talking and talking.

'They could have killed you. Our children without a father. What would happen to them? And me?'

He hugged her to him and sighed. 'Hush Sara. I'm here.'

'And what about tomorrow and the day after that? Will you be here then? Next time, you might not be so lucky.'

'The threat comes with the job, Sara. You've always known this from the day we were married.' He hesitated before adding, 'Sergio wants us to move into the compound. He thinks we will be safer there.'

'No. Never. I will not stay near that disgusting man.' Her reply was as he expected.

'Just tell me, Michael, why do they have to act as if it's the Middle Ages when people slaughtered each other over bits of land? For Christ's sake, it's the 21st century. When will they ever move on and leave bloodshed behind?'

Michael shook his head, a weary look on his face. 'Nothing will change with Sergio and Fredo Sturla running things. Fredo thinks he is different, educated, with a big brain, but violence is still his answer to most problems. They act like mad dogs when someone tries to take a bone from them.'

'With a bit of luck, Fredo and Sergio will kill each other.'

'Then I will have mad Gino. He's already champing at the bit to be capo.'

'But you should be the next capo, Michael! Not Gino, who hasn't got a brain in his head. Then things could change. You could stop the violence.'

He put an arm around her and pulled her closer, shaking his head. 'Me as the capo?' he snorted. 'It'll never happen.'

'Why not? You're a good man who could change things for the better. You're not like them. They're animals.'

'Yes, I would stop this killing, but Sara, it's not possible. Believe me, they will survive. They always do.'

'We could leave. Get away from here. We have enough money. We could start a new life somewhere else. A good life for our children.'

'And go where? They're everywhere. Since the age of fourteen, it's been the only life I've known. Once you're in, there's only one way out. You know that.'

She also knew of the crimes her husband helped Sergio Gianelli commit, and she enjoyed the rewards. Much as she talked of leaving to live elsewhere, she never would, and Michael knew it. His wife was greedy and ambitious, much like himself.

A small child wept as she ran into the room and climbed into the bed. Sara cuddled her.

'What is it, Cara? You had a bad dream? Mamma is here, and so is Pappa. We will chase the naughty dreams away.' The child snuggled into Sara. Sucking her thumb, she closed her eyes. 'We are all suffering from nightmares,' Sara said, gently stroking back the hair from her child's face as the tears dried up and sleep overcame her.

Michael said, 'One nightmare after another. After the attack on his life, Gino wants blood.'

'Then you'd better get Fredo before he gets you,' were her last words before her eyes closed.

He gently lifted his sleeping daughter and carried her back to her own bed. Knowing that sleep would evade him, he went downstairs and poured himself a large vodka before checking from the window again to make sure the guards were in place. Maybe he was worrying too much. Fredo had always shown him respect on the few occasions they had met to discuss business. He couldn't have known he would be with Gino in the restaurant that day. It was a last-minute thing. Francisco, the owner, had reluctantly turned away his regular lunchtime customers, so that Gino, taking no chances after the failed attempt on Fredo's life, could enjoy his birthday lunch without fear. Sergio, too cowardly to leave the compound, had insisted that Michael join Gino. Sighing, Michael knew he was deluding himself. Fredo wouldn't give a damn if he died.

Chapter 34

On the other side of the city, Carla was treading on eggshells around Fredo, expecting him to explode any second. After putting Giancarlo to bed and reading him a story about Chumly, a curious chimp, she had listened at the door to Luigi, reporting the failure. Eavesdropping was a habit she had acquired while living with Fredo. If business had gone according to plan and Fredo was happy, she was safe. If he wasn't, she would suffer. Now she feared the worst.

Never once did she hear him say Luigi was on borrowed time after his second failure. but she knew it was only a matter of time. Neither did he show any remorse for the death of the innocent woman at the scene, whom she had recognised from a news report as Kizza. *People's lives mean nothing to him. Mine included, if he didn't need me as a punch bag to convince himself that he wasn't weak. He can hide his weakness from his men, who equate viciousness and narcissism with strength, but he can't hide it from himself or me.* She shuddered, dreading the coming night.

Luigi passed her as she was closing the door to Giancarlo's room, having checked that he was asleep. He wished her a goodnight and she acknowledged it with a nod. It made her furious and deeply ashamed that Luigi and the Sturla men in the building gave her sidelong glances, but never made eye contact. Fredo thought he was being clever by hitting her where it didn't show, but they knew. They all knew. Especially the women in the building, many of whom suffered from the same abuse. Wife beating was endemic among gangsters who were paranoid that their women, given the slightest chance, would cuckold them. When a man was sentenced to prison, their wives served a similar sentence in their home, watched over by fathers and brothers making sure she didn't step out of line. Luigi's wife was a small, pale. timid woman who didn't speak unless spoken to – and then always with a glance at her husband, as if asking permission. But Carla had never seen a bruise on her. Luigi ruled by fear.

Damned hypocrite. You would kill me without blinking if Fredo gave the order, she thought as she watched him enter the lift.

They ate supper late, as was Fredo's wish. She had cooked his favourite – a rare, almost blue, steak with pasta, tossed in black garlic-infused oil. He drank from a crystal glass with a half empty bottle of his favourite Scotch close to hand. Holding up the glass, he smiled at her. 'To my beautiful wife on our tenth anniversary.'

He never forgot. She would rather not remember, but she knew that if she failed to acknowledge it, she would be accused of being ungrateful and would suffer. She had put on a black dress that was perfectly cut to her figure, one he liked her to wear. *Keep him happy, and he keeps his fists to himself.*

But what could you buy a man who really had everything and saw sentimental value in nothing? She passed him a beautifully wrapped package. He took it, looking bemused. 'What is this?'

'Happy anniversary, Fredo,' she said with a forced smile. He ripped away the wrapping paper to reveal a beautiful silver-framed photo of him showing interest in the small metal toy car Gianni was playing with.

'Me and my son. Grazie mille, Carla, but where are you in this photograph?'

Nothing is ever enough. Greedy for more. Even in a photo. 'I didn't want to give you a set photo of the three of us taken by a professional. I thought it was better for me to catch an intimate moment, with you both unawares. More natural, Fredo. In the photo, you can see how much you love your boy.'

He looked at her and smiled. 'True, but I will never tire of looking at you.'

Or punching me. 'Or I you, Fredo.' Appealing to his ego sometimes worked. He was vain, as handsome men often were, and always dressed to perfection. His power gave him a certain charisma, which fooled many people into thinking he was human. Women lusted after handsome Fredo Sturla, something he revelled in, but it made Carla want to puke.

'Put on that blue dress I like so much, and let's have drinks on the terrace.'

'But I put on this one because you said it was your favourite.'

'Change the dress, Carla.'

Control, control, control. Fuck you, Fredo. 'Si, Fredo, of course. It will be nice on the terrace with just the two of us.' *Liar, liar.* The last thing she wanted was to be alone with him. She forced another smile and went to her bedroom, stopping to look in on Giancarlo to check that he was still asleep.

Putting on the blue dress, she gave a wry smile. *The colour of bruises. Probably why he likes it.* Grabbing a glass of wine and drinking half of it quickly to calm her nerves, she joined him on the terrace where he was standing, looking over the city. Seeing her, he smiled and held out a slim red Cartier box to her.

'To match your eyes.' He liked the fact that she had blue eyes, unlike most Italian women.

She took the box and tried to show some enthusiasm.

'Thank you.'

Inside was a beautiful necklace of blue sapphires, which had obviously cost a fortune. It had little impact on her, but she managed to look awed. 'It's exquisite, Fredo. Did you choose this?' She knew the answer. He had, because he liked to impress people with how much money he spent on his wife.

'Of course. An anniversary gift to you is a gift from me,' he answered as he kissed her on the forehead.

Maybe it will be okay. He seems relaxed. She smiled at the thought. He smiled back, thinking it was for him.

'Here, let me help you,' he said, taking the gorgeous jewels from the box. She turned and lifted her long hair, which he had forbidden her to cut, as he hung the necklace around her neck. The stones felt cold against her skin. It made her shudder slightly. Using the necklace, he suddenly pulled her into a choke hold. Her head snapped back. His face pressed next to hers as he spoke in a quiet, menacing voice: 'Carla, help me with a slight problem. Why is it that I can't trust anyone to do the right thing?'

'Things go wrong, Fredo. It happens,' she gasped, knowing that struggling would make things worse.

'That's not what I want to hear.'

She shuddered inwardly.

'Do you do the right thing, Carla?'

'I try to, Fredo. I always want to please you.'

'Really? Is that why you make eyes at the African trash selling the Gianelli garbage on the streets?' He sneered.

What? 'As you say, they're trash. I feel insulted that you would think such a thing.'

'Giancarlo told me you spoke to one.'

Her mind raced. 'Yes. Yes, I did. I was examining the bags he was selling. Checking the quality. I know you are going into the fake business, and I want to help. I could do quality control for you. It's so boring, doing nothing.'

Her voice was rasping, and her throat hurt, but he increased the pressure of the chokehold. Black spots danced before her eyes; it was difficult to breathe. Close to losing consciousness, she felt sure that this was the day she would die. But the pressure was too much. The necklace snapped. Carla gasped in relief, her hand going to her throat as she gulped air into her lungs. The sapphires scattered noisily as they bounced on the marble floor. He spun her around, his face close to hers. She could see spittle at the corners of his mouth and thought of a rabid animal.

'I wish I could believe you. I want to believe you.'

She knew there was nothing to say that would stop the onslaught. *Fight or die.*

'No, you don't,' Carla, filled with fury, spat out, screaming and pushing him away. 'You just want an excuse to beat the life out of me again.' As it was unexpected, she took him by surprise, and he took a step back.

'Couldn't kill Gino, so you attack a woman? You're a fucking coward, Fredo. A fucking coward! You get others to do your dirty work because you haven't got the guts to do it yourself, and your men know it,' she shrieked.

'That's not true!' Losing his usual control, he twitched.

'No. It's not,' she scoffed. 'I forgot. You killed Toni Clementi, who treated you like a son. And your father? The doctors said he was making a good recovery. Was he standing in the way too? Two old men who couldn't fight back?' she sneered.

The first blow knocked her to the floor.

Chapter 35

The humidity hung over the city like an invisible fog. Maria, sweeping the pavement in front of her café, was worried because she had not seen or heard from Carla. *God knows what's going on in that household; nothing good, that's for sure.*

Looking at the space where Joseph usually sold his stuff, she sighed. She had been shocked to see a report on the local TV news reporting the death of Kizza. But she hadn't had sight nor sign of him to offer her condolences. Her eyes went to Mussa, standing by the station, looking sad and fearful as he clung to Big Moses' hand. *Poor child.*

With a screech of brakes, a black Gianelli SUV appeared and drove onto the pavement, running over Abdi and Big Moses's merchandise. Jacob grabbed Mussa, pulling him out of Frankie and Toni's path as they jumped from the car and bundled Abdi and a terrified Moses into the SUV at gunpoint.

'Let this be a goddamn warning,' Frankie yelled at them all before they drove off.

'And they call this civilisation,' Maria muttered as she watched the car disappear in the distance.

***

The SUV made its way to the outskirts and across a wasteland towards a black dot in the distance. Gino Gianelli leaned against Sergio's Ferrari. To his mind, it was a car wasted on an old man who liked to ride around in a custom-made Rolls-Royce. Sergio had a collection of expensive cars that never saw the light of day. Gino smiled to himself, knowing that one day they would all be his without 'fucking Sergio' looking over his shoulder and carping all the time. Killing him would be easy enough for him, but crafty Sergio trusted no one, especially those close to him. Having killed his own father and brother to inherit their wealth and status, he couldn't take the chance that Gino wouldn't do the same. Sergio delighted in telling Gino that he had arranged to have him executed if he should die by his hand. So much for family love.

Gino watched the SUV pull up in a cloud of dust rising from the parched earth. Frankie and Luca jumped out of the vehicle and dragged Big Moses and Abdi after them, sending them sprawling on the ground.

Abdi's eyes opened wide with dread when he saw Gino holding a gun. 'They threatened to throw us onto the street. What else could we do?' They were to be his last words. Gino coldly shot him in the head.

'How many times must you fucking apes be told? You-do-what-we-tell-you-to-do.' With each word, he struck Big Moses with the butt of his gun and viciously kicked him. 'I will kill you all if you buy from Sturla. You understand? You fucking Black ape,' he sneered, looking down at Big Moses curled up in the foetal position. With a last act of violence, kicking his face and head, Gino got in the Ferrari and, followed by Frankie and Toni, drove off, leaving Big Moses unconscious and Abdi dead.

***

Wracked with grief and having fallen into a fitful sleep, Joseph woke from his fractured dreams with a start. He felt the pain of his aching bones, caused by lying on the hard ground for so long and thought of the rebel camp, where sleeping rough was the norm…and of a fateful night, so long ago.

***

UGANDA 1981

After a successful raid to recover the ivory, Joseph and others, shoulders bruised and bleeding with the effort, hauled the heavy tusks back to the rebel camp.

Once there, not having eaten more than a starvation diet for days, they ate greedily from tins of compressed meat, food supplied by the government for their now-dead troops. Odango and his protectors drank the alcohol they had looted, becoming more inebriated by the minute. By midnight, the whole camp was asleep, apart from Joseph and the sentries posted on the periphery.

Seizing the moment, Joseph made his way stealthily past Odango's bodyguards, who were lying outside his hut snoring away their excess alcohol, and entered the hut, where the tyrant lay in a drunken stupor. Without hesitation, he sliced Odango's throat open with his panga. 'For my family and Ariya.' He raised the panga again and sliced through the monster's genitals. 'For what you did to Kizza.' Dispassionately, he watched the blood drain from Odango, whose eyes were wide with terror and disbelief. He tried to cry for help, but only a guttural gurgle came out as the blood flooded into his throat and lungs, drowning him. The pain Odango had so often inflicted on others was now his. 'For all the children,' Joseph muttered as he left, vowing to himself that never again would he let anyone hurt the people he loved.

185

Kizza had never asked him about Odango, and he had never spoken of it. He could hear her words spoken long ago, echoing in his head. *Will you kill him?'* Joseph's face hardened. He struggled to his feet and turned his eyes, which glittered with grim determination and vengeance, towards the city of Naples. 'Yes, I will kill him.'

Chapter 36

The atmosphere was heavy with despondency as Big Moses, slumped in a chair, his eyes swollen and lips cut, cried like a baby, recounting to the others what had happened.

'They'll kill us all. Kizza is dead. Abdi is dead,' he wailed, rocking back and forth, clutching his Bible.

Mussa, sitting at the kitchen table, listened with a solemn expression. Jacob, who was cooking food for him, was concerned by what he was hearing, but reasoned that he had not been much older than Mussa when he had first killed a soldier. *Where the hell is Joseph? If he's dead too, what should I do with Mussa?* But even as he thought this, he knew that somehow they would take care of him. He put a dish of scrambled eggs in front of the child.

'Don't listen to them, Mussa. Eat up.'

'What do we do? We can't fight back. We're powerless to defend ourselves,' said Benjamin, controlling his anger.

'We can't go back on the streets; end of,' said Bolo, whose turn it was to do the laundry. Stripping the sheets off the beds, he paused at Abdi's bed, mentally saying a brief prayer for him. The bed was to be used by Mussa for as long as the boy was with them. He turned over the mattress, revealing all the money that

Abdi had squirreled away. Seeing it, the others gasped. It was around €2,000, and would help them through the rough patch, but no one found any joy in it.

'Why didn't he have his fucking steak?' asked Bolo. 'Stashing his money for what?'

No one answered because they knew that, like all of them, Abdi suffered from the trauma of his childhood. His complaining and squirreling away money were walls built against his mental pain.

Jacob shrugged, 'Good for us that he didn't. At least we can pay the rent this month.'

'Let's hope the Sturla and the Gianelli clans will kill each other soon,' muttered Benjamin, who had got hold of an old electric fan that had needed repairing. He was good with electrics, so the others had left him to it. Plugging it in, the fan whirred into life, sending out gusts of welcome cool air.

Mussa ran from the kitchen, climbed on Big Moses' knee, and hugged him. 'Will they kill you? Will they kill Pappy?' Big Moses tried to put on a positive face for the child and hugged him close. 'No. Your Pappy is a superhero. He saved my life. He pulled me out of the sea when I was drowning. No one will hurt Joseph Amaru.' But he didn't believe what he was saying. What had happened to Abdi and Kizza had left him hollow, wondering what life was about when it was so full of hurt and pain. Joseph was right.

Jesus is not doing a very good job. There are too many devils.

***

Under the cover of darkness and unaware of what had happened to Abdi and Big Moses, Joseph, having sworn never to pick up a gun again, smashed the window of the African antique shop and grabbed the panga. It felt familiar in his hand as he slid it through his belt and pulled his shirt down, obscuring it from view. After buying a bottle of water and a loaf of bread from a twenty-four-hour shop, he stealthily made his way through the back streets and out of the city. His mind totally focused, he headed south down the coast, where he eventually found the destination he was looking for.

He perched himself high in a tree, staking out the infamous Sturla building.

There was a balcony to each apartment at the front, as well the apartments located at the back. There were no back entrances or low windows. Armed men patrolled the lower part of the building and its entrance. Two security cameras were visible: one situated at the main entrance, pointed at the road, monitoring anyone entering or leaving by the main door or the garage; the other was at the rear of the building. Both cameras swung 180 degrees from side to side, scoping the area. He counted the seconds they took before they changed direction and noted the one-minute lapse between the garage doors' opening and closing. At night, the patrolling guards followed the same routine: every thirty minutes, they checked around the building with large flashlights, their guns ready to fire.

The place appeared impenetrable. Joseph's eyes landed on the penthouse apartment. *Patience,* he thought, as he settled into his vantage point, hidden by the leafy branches of the tree, and cat napped during the night.

Waking the next morning to the sound of an engine as a car left the garage, he drank water and munched on some bread before patiently spending the day watching vehicles come and go from the building. His patience was rewarded when, at precisely 7.30 pm the garage doors rumbled into action and a motorcycle came roaring out.

Chapter 37

Marco, heart racing with the news he had to deliver, knocked once and walked into the room where Fredo brooded over their failure to kill Gino and Rossi. Fredo was a great believer in the Machiavellian saying, 'If an injury has to be done to a man, it should be so severe that his vengeance need not be feared.'.

Aged thirty-six, Marco had never married. People assumed that his wealthy bachelor lifestyle, mixing with beautiful women, was that of a playboy, but it was a façade. Marco Falco was gay and had lived with the secret all his life, hiding it first from his parents and then from the clans. He knew that even the hint of a rumour that he was homosexual could end badly for him. The son of the head of the Ndrangheta Mafia group was a drag queen, and the talk was that they were going soft on homosexual men, even allowing them to become foot soldiers, but clan bosses in Naples had scoffed that no one would even notice, as the Romans were all 'faggots' anyway.

From their school days, he knew that Fredo had suppressed tendencies. Fredo was in the year above him at school and spent most of his time with Marco's second cousin, Pietro Angeli, a shy, handsome boy who had confessed to Marco that he and Fredo were in love – a secret Marco could never reveal. When they found Pietro shot dead in the grounds of the school with a gun in his hand, the coroner ruled it suicide. Days later, Fredo disappeared to a boarding school in Rome, and his father made a charitable donation to the Angeli family. No one could prove Fredo had indulged in a lewd act with Pietro Angeli, which sent him into a frenzy of self-hatred powerful enough to kill.

His sadism towards Carla made Marco more aware of Fredo's loathing for who he was, which made him a threat to people like himself. Coming out or acting on his sexual impulses was not something he would ever consider doing around Fredo Sturla, who wouldn't hesitate to have him killed. He had overheard Carla accusing Fredo of being a coward, and knew she was right. Mixed with his narcissistic personality, it made him irrational and dangerous when things didn't go his way. And things were not going his way.

'We have to strike again before they hit us,' Fredo said, jabbing his knife at him, before meticulously cutting his omelette, perfectly cooked with baby garlic, into tiny pieces.

'We will never get to them again, Don Fredo. Luigi blew it. That's twice he has failed, now we are all in danger.' Knowing he was a stone-cold killer; Marco had never liked Luigi and would be happy to see him gone.

'I'll deal with him when the time is right. Tomorrow, I want Carla and Giancarlo taken to the villa in Portofino. Send men to guard them. I want my son safe.'

He's not thinking coherently. 'Don Fredo, if they are a target, they will find them. I wouldn't trust Sergio or Gino not to hurt them. This place is impregnable. They're safer here.'

Fredo didn't like to be told he was wrong, but he could see the sense in what Marco was saying and reluctantly nodded his head. 'Make sure they are. Sergio knows we expect him to retaliate, so we have to act before he does. Hit him where it hurts most – his underground factories.'

Marco hesitated before relating the news that he was about to deliver. He wondered if ancient Roman senators felt like this when giving bad news to mad emperors such as Nero and Caligula. 'He's already struck.'

Fredo glowered, turning his cold eyes on him.

'Where?'

'They bombed the Chinese storerooms. We lost the stock. The Chinese lost their buildings.'

Fredo's rage erupted, his plate smashed against a wall. The remains of his meal ran down the pristine white paint, creating a poor work of art.

'The Chinese are not happy,' Marco said, not needing to add that the bank deal was probably blown.

'And I am?' Fredo snarled. 'I want them dead! All of them. Fucking dead.' Just like I want you dead, Fredo, thought Carla, as she dabbed a cooling lotion onto the bruises around her neck and on her body.

Chapter 38

Tuesday was the day on which Maria cooked fresh lasagna, topped with a generous sprinkle of Parmesan, served with a crisp green salad. It was her mother's recipe, and she knew it was delicious. Her customers had been eating it there every week for years and always left with satisfied stomachs.

When the door opened and Big Moses walked in, face bruised and swollen, gripping Mussa by the hand, everyone stopped eating and stared. Maria, instantly irritated, moved to stop him from entering further.

'What do you want?' she demanded, nudging him back towards the door. 'If you are looking for your friend, he's not here. I haven't seen him for days.' She spoke in a low tone so the customers couldn't overhear.

Moses looked flustered. 'I have to leave Mussa here.'

Maria's eyebrows shot up. 'Oh, no you don't. I can't look after a child – I'm working.' She protested.

'He needs to be safe. Please,' he pleaded.

'Impossible.' She swept a hand toward her customers, who were all agog, wanting to know what was going on. 'I have a business to run, in case you haven't noticed.'

Ignoring this, Big Moses pushed a parcel into her hands. 'Give this to Joseph. Tell him I've gone to see my family.'

Maria could see the pain and unshed tears glistening in his eyes. Her heart softened.

'What happened to you?'

'Nothing good.' He walked out.

'No! Wait!' Maria called. But Big Moses kept walking, leaving behind the child and Maria, huffing with impatience, uttering, '*Merde.*' She couldn't chase after him, and she couldn't throw the kid out.

'Sit yourself over there,' she said, pointing to a table in the corner. Mussa, head down, went and sat as instructed. Her customers were all still staring.

'He's just a child. You haven't seen a child before?' She demanded, clearly irritated. They all averted their eyes and continued eating as she pushed a biscotti into his hand and went about attending to her customers' needs.

At least he's quiet, thought Maria, an hour later, as she finished the washing up. Apart from a young courting couple sitting outside, who seemed more interested in each other than finishing their coffee, and Mussa sitting quietly at a table, the café was empty. When everything was cleaned to her satisfaction and put away, she spooned spaghetti with a meat sauce made from her own recipe, onto a plate.

'I'm sorry about what happened to your mamma, but this is not right. Your father should be here for you,' Maria grumbled to Mussa. 'I know he's grieving, but he should remember he has a child to take care of.' She put the plate of spaghetti in front of him.

Mussa, sad and confused, didn't understand a word she was saying. He looked at the spaghetti suspiciously.

'Eat it up. It's good,' Maria said impatiently.

Mussa shook his head. Maria put a fork in his hand.

'Yes, you must eat.'

Mussa kept shaking his head, refusing to touch the food. Maria rolled her eyes.

'It's good for you. *Capisce?*' Realising that he didn't understand, she shook her head.

'In the name of the Holy Mother, what kind of language do you speak?'

Mussa pushed the plate away.

She remembered Carla saying they had come from there when they had first arrived. 'Uganda?' Pointing at him, she repeated, 'Uganda.'

He nodded his head. Maria went behind the counter and found the iPad. Not understanding her own suspicion of it, the device had remained unused. Ignoring the fact that he couldn't understand, she kept talking.

'My grandson taught me how to do this. Giancarlo is very clever. He's the same age as you,' *but with a monster for a father*, she thought. Unfortunately, as she had only been half listening, she didn't remember what Carla had taught her or even how to switch the thing on. She held it out to Mussa.

'If you're going to live here, you must speak Italian. Do you know how this thing works? Google.' She remembered that, liking the sound of the word.

He took the device and switched it on, opening the Google search page. She raised her eyebrows, impressed.

'You, Ugandan. Me Italiano. Lingo.' *Dear Mother of God, I'm talking rubbish.*

With Kizza's persistent tutelage, Mussa had been adept at reading since he was four years old, and often Big Moses let him play with his phone. Like a lot of kids, he had soon become skilled at accessing the Internet. He slowly typed in what language they spoke in Uganda. It surprised her.

'English? You speak English?' Mussa nodded.

'Why didn't you say so?' Not that it would have made a difference, because she only knew a few words of the language.

'Damned English, gets everywhere,' she muttered, watching Mussa search for the English-to-Italian translation page. He had seen the boys doing this on their phones when they didn't quite understand something in Italian. 'Hello lady' instantly became 'Ciao Signora.' Maria almost smiled. *Maybe this thing is useful after all.* He passed it to her, showing that she should write something. She took the tablet from him and slowly typed, 'Perche non mangi il tuo cibo?' It immediately translated to 'Why don't you eat your food?' Seeing the translation, she was mildly fascinated. Mussa took the iPad and typed in his response before handing it back to her.

'Oh, you're quick at this,' she said as she looked at his translated answer. 'What? You don't eat worms?' Maria looked at the spaghetti and frowned. She typed and then showed him the translation. 'Not worms. Flour, eggs and water. All good stuff. It will make you grow.'

Seeing the translation, Mussa shook his head, not convinced. Maria took his hand and led him behind the counter, where she took pasta dough from the fridge that rattled with old age. She rolled it out and held it up to show him. Then put it through the small device for making homemade pasta, and long strands of spaghetti came out.

'See? Not worms.'

She sat him back at the table. 'I don't know what kind of godforsaken country you come from that doesn't eat pasta. Here, open your mouth,' she ordered.

Mussa, still reluctant, opened his mouth, and she put a fork of pasta in it. Reluctantly, he chewed. She watched his face, and eventually he gave a small smile. Maria smiled back as she put the fork in his hand. 'Good, now eat it. Buon appetito.'

'Bon appatta,' he wrongly answered, not knowing what it meant, but he tucked into the pasta because he was hungry.

After clearing the coffee cups from the outside table once the couple had left, Maria looked anxiously around. There were no Africans to be seen and no Carla, who was not even answering her phone. It was too late in the day for her to come, but it didn't stop her from hoping. Garibaldi Square was devoid of people sitting at the pavement cafés eating or enjoying a glass of Chianti. The recent violence had frightened them away. *So bad for business. Not that the damned gangsters care, always looking out for themselves.*

Having carried in the small tables and chairs, Maria locked the door. She had closed later than usual, hoping that Joseph would appear and collect his son.

Mussa finished the lemon cake that came after the pasta.

'So? You like my cooking?'

He didn't understand, but using his hands like an Italian would, just as his father had shown him, he said, 'Bon gorno.'

'And a good day to you too,' she answered. 'But not 'buon giorno,' it's 'grazie.'

'Grazie…'

'Si. Bene…Prego.'

'Merde,' said Mussa, having heard Maria say it earlier.

'No! not that word.' Remembering that Giancarlo had played on the iPad, she held it out to him. 'Here, take it.'

He shook his head, looking lost and forlorn. His lip quivered. 'I want Mamma.'

Maria's heart melted. *His mamma, of course. What was I thinking?*

'Piccolo, your mamma has gone to heaven,' she said. 'And God only knows where your father is,' she muttered under her breath as she put an arm around him. 'Come now; you need to go to bed.'

He hesitated before he took hold of her hand and followed her upstairs to her living area. An hour later, Mussa was fast asleep on Maria's bed with the iPad next to him. She covered him with a blanket and watched as he slept. *Six years old, just a baby. Why was I so reluctant to watch over him? When did my heart grow so hard?*

But as she thought about it, bringing tears to her eyes, she knew the answer. Living in a place like Naples, it only took a moment in life to take you from an average person doing normal things like caring for your family, to facing the pain of losing them. Her son and his wife had not survived this city, and now Carla and Giancarlo were in danger. Fredo didn't fool her with his loving father façade. She knew he was a killer, and would murder his own son if he got in his way. *If anything happens to them, please, husband, come and take me.* She prayed, then became irritated with herself for thinking such things. Wiping away the tears, she looked out the window. *Joseph, where in God's name are you?*

Chapter 39

After patiently waiting and watching vehicles come and go all day, Joseph slipped unseen inside the Sturla garage and discovered what he was looking for – the motorcycle. He easily blended into the shadows where he waited. At 7:29 pm precisely, the owner of the bike again appeared. This time without the helmet. He recognised Luigi Ricci as the man he had seen watching the brutes beat up the African in the port. *So, you're the man who killed my wife.* He wanted to kill him there and then, but knew he had to first get to the one who gave the order. The electronic garage doors swung open, and Luigi left on his bike. Joseph slipped out of the garage before the doors closed.

For hours, he sat immobile in the treetop, watching the same guards circle the building every thirty minutes to check if it was secure. Two more men remained on guard at the entrance. They had been on duty for eight hours. *Too long.* Sitting high in the branches for long hours doing guard duty for the LRA, Joseph's brain would often drift into sleep mode. As an officer in the Ugandan army, he had changed shifts to four hours, which ensured the men stayed alert. Here, they called themselves foot soldiers, but they were just thugs with guns who wouldn't last as long as some kids in the bush.

Luigi returned at 10.00 pm, and the comings and goings of various vehicles ceased around midnight. Having done their checks, the guards were at the entrance, smoking and laughing at something on YouTube. As Joseph suspected, the long hours of boredom had created a dangerous lassitude. An hour after midnight, when he was sure that most of the occupants were asleep in their beds, he made his move.

Preferring to be barefoot, he slipped off his shoes, leaving them under a bush, secured the panga at his waist, and lifted the hood of his black cotton sweatshirt over his head to obscure his face from view. As the camera swung away from his direction, he ran furtively through the gardens until he reached the wall of the building, where he stood in the shadows, waiting for a reaction. None came.

To a man with Joseph's background, balconies were like stepping-stones to the roof. Sergio Gianelli's words ran through his head, asking if he had ever climbed? Assuming he hadn't, he had given Joseph no time to answer, not that he would have told him that Uganda was a land of mountains and tall trees that every soldier had to climb barefoot, without a helmet or harness like Gino wore. He smiled to himself. It was like comparing American footballers to rugby players. Rugby was a game the British had introduced to Uganda. Despite his size, in the army Joseph had been a keen and accomplished player.

Pressed against the first balcony wall, he could hear a couple inside arguing. The woman wanted her widowed mother to live with them. Her man wasn't happy, stating he had married her, not her mother, and he didn't want her living there. She was adamant. Joseph didn't doubt she would win.

He furtively scaled further up the building. His muscles were burning, reminding him that he had not used them in a long time. Halfway to the top, a Camorrista, wearing a shoulder holster, stepped outside to smoke. Joseph froze, suspended against the wall under the balcony. Not having a solid grip, he struggled to hang on. He could climb onto the balcony and kill the man, but it would raise an alarm, and he would have to give up his intended target. The security would be doubled, and his chances of hitting his target would be considerably less. A light swept below his feet. The guards, using powerful torches, swept the gardens and the building, but fortunately the beams did not reach high enough to expose him. No one could suspect that someone would climb the building, so they concentrated their attention on the ground around it, and the lower levels.

The humidity was high; perspiration ran down his brow and into his eyes, temporarily blinding him, and his hands were damp with perspiration, making his grip more precarious. He was filled with relief when the Camorrista inhaled deeply, pulling the last of the nicotine into his lungs before flicking his cigarette butt over the railing and moving inside.

Joseph hauled himself onto the balcony and, wiping the sweat from his face, sneaked a look through the window. He recognised the man as one he had seen on guard duty earlier. Before sinking into a chair, the thug took off his shoulder holster and put it and his gun on a low table. A young, attractive woman, probably his wife, massaged his shoulders before taking his hand and leading him to what Joseph assumed was the bedroom. The light went out.

Taking his time, Joseph eventually reached the top floor of the building. Being cautious, he waited just below the penthouse terrace. It was unlit. Sturla had not left the building, so given the hour, he guessed he was probably in bed.

Two heavily armed men on the roof above came to the edge and nonchalantly looked down to the gardens below, totally unaware that the danger was less than ten feet away, pressed into the shadows below them. Seeing nothing happening on the ground, the men disappeared to another part of the roof to continue their game of cards– something most foot soldiers did to take the edge off boredom. Like a snake, Joseph slithered over the wall, which was topped with ornate metal railings. There was an overhang above, so once on the terrace, there was no chance of the guards above being able to see him.

He moved cautiously to the large sliding plate-glass windows and found them unlocked. The windows ran the whole twelve metre length of the terrace and led into various rooms, all of which were in darkness with no sign of activity. Hearing a man's voice verbally abusing someone, he made his way to where the sound was coming from. The window silently slid open, and Joseph slipped between the curtains of the dimly lit bedroom.

A man on the bed was holding the long plait of a woman's hair wrapped around one fist, as he punched and slapped her with the other, blaming her for his failure to perform.

The pillow her face was pressed into stifled her screams.

As the only occupants in the apartment, Joseph didn't doubt that the man he saw on the bed was Fredo Sturla. Moving silently and as swiftly as a panther, Joseph came up behind Fredo and grabbed him by the hair. Yanking his head back, he raised the panga and deftly sliced his throat open. 'For my wife. For my family.'

The blood spurted over Carla's back. Joseph, not recognising her, quickly pressed her face deeper into the pillow.

'If you want to live, don't move or make a sound until I've gone,' he said, noticing the bruises and lacerations on her body. 'Do you understand?'

She stiffened at the strange voice and nodded her head into the pillow, which she was grasping.

He reckoned that as soon as he let go, she would scream, and he would have about twenty seconds to get out. About to release her, his heart stopped when his eyes went to her hand, clutching the pillow, and he saw the huge heart-shaped diamond ring on her finger. Stunned, he released her.

'Carla?'

Hearing her name, Carla scrambled up and quickly covered herself. Her eyes and mouth were open in shock at seeing Joseph and then Fredo, sprawled across the floor at the side of the bed with his throat cut and a quizzical look on his face.

Their eyes met. Joseph thought she would scream, but she didn't. A knock on the door made her gasp. Luigi called out, 'Don Fredo, there is a call for you from China.'

Joseph ran and dropped over the terrace rail.

Luigi, hearing her scream, 'No!' burst into the room and faltered, seeing the carnage. Carla, thinking Joseph must be dead from the fall, pointed to the window. Luigi ran out onto the terrace, his gun drawn, firing into the air to alert everyone. All hell let loose as Sturla's men reacted.

At first Luigi thought that whoever it was could not survive the drop, then looked down and glimpsed Joseph, who having experienced hundreds of conflicts from the clifftops in Uganda, was dropping from one balcony rail to the next with the ease of an acrobat, now nearing the ground. Luigi snatched an automatic weapon from a man who had come running in and took aim.

A hail of bullets raked the air around Joseph, who felt the sharp sting as one hit him in the left arm, causing him to fall the last two metres to the ground. He scrambled to his feet and, grabbing his shoes from under the bush, made a run for it.

Armed men swarmed out of the building, shooting at the dark figure running in the distance. The garage doors swung open and

SUVs came roaring out, headlights on full beam. No one glanced twice at the now seemingly homeless African hunkered down in a nearby doorway.

Chapter 40

'What the fuck, Luigi?' Marco said angrily. 'A man kills Fredo at the top of a heavily guarded building and gets away? What kind of idiots are we employing?'

Carla gasped. 'He's still alive? But he jumped from the terrace. He can't be alive!' *Thank God.* Knowing that everything she said now and how she reacted would be vital, she faked hysteria. 'They tried to kill him before. You should have been more alert! It's your fault! How could you let this happen?' She screamed at Luigi, who was speechless after his spectacular failure to protect his boss.

'He didn't get past the guards on the door, so he must have climbed the building,' he protested.

'*Calmati* Carla,' Marco urged. 'We will find whoever did this, and they will be punished.' His eyes going to the huge clotting gap in Fredo's severed throat and the congealing blood pooling around him, Marco grimaced. He collected a towel from the bathroom and passed it to Carla. She used it to wipe her face and to wrap around her blood-soaked hair.

'Who was it, Carla? Did you see him?' Marco urgently asked.

'Yes…I saw him. His face was black – a black mask. He was wearing a black mask. "For my family." That's what he said.'

Marco nodded. 'For his family …? There's only one family I know of that has someone who could do that climb.'

'Of course! Gino Gianelli. That bastard climbs mountains,' said Luigi.

'Gino? Yes! He was small like Gino, and he sounded like him,' lied Carla, taking the opportunity to protect Joseph. Aware that she was in a vulnerable situation, she knew she had to play the game with them. 'Thank God you came in time, Luigi. God knows what he would have done to me.'

Luigi looked relieved that he might have done something right.

'Mamma?' They were all startled to see Giancarlo standing in the doorway, rubbing his eyes. The commotion of yelling and shooting had woken him up. Carla quickly ran to him,

'Mi caro.' She enveloped him in her arms, thankful that Fredo's body sprawled on the other side of the bed was hidden from Giancarlo's view, and ushered him quickly from the room, grateful to escape.

Neither man would voice that they were relieved at the death of Fredo Sturla. Luigi had escaped a death sentence, and Marco too, if Fredo had ever discovered he was gay.

'So, what happens now?' Luigi asked Marco.

'We end this war.'

Chapter 41

Joseph had suffered from gunshots before, but he had been younger, and this one hurt like hell. The SUVs in search of Fredo's killer had disappeared, but he was still cautious as he made his way back to the old city.

Close to home, he stopped in the shadows when he saw Jamal and Saba with their child leaving the shop with their suitcases. Hooligans had sprayed TERRORIST PIGS across the shop front. He shook his head. As in Uganda, it was hard to survive next to human animals passed over by evolution.

Jamal and his family would move to another city, or another town, but Joseph knew he would always encounter racism. It existed everywhere, between Italians, and even between the villages in his own country. He was sad to see them go. Another loss from the little family he had built around himself.

*****

With a loud sigh and unable to sleep, Maria sat on the edge of the bed. Mussa was sleeping soundly next to her. *What if his father never comes back? What will I do with the kid? He can't even speak Italian. It's not right to put me in this predicament.*

A sound from outside broke into her worried thoughts. She jumped up to look out of the window. What she saw made her sigh with relief. He was back. She grabbed a jacket, pulled it on over her nightdress, and made for the door, determined to give him a piece of her mind.

She stormed into his apartment, demanding, 'Where have you been? Your son is sleeping in my bed. I am not a nursemaid or a babysitter!'

'Why is my son with you?'

Before she could answer, Joseph clutched his arm and dropped into a chair, exhausted. Maria saw the blood and crossed herself.

'Mother of God. What have you been up to?'

'Nothing for you to concern yourself with, old woman,' he said.

'Old woman, is it?' she said outraged, leaving the apartment and slamming the door behind her.

Relieved that she had gone, Joseph removed his jacket and shirt to check the damage. *A flesh wound. Not too bad.* He searched the bathroom for something to disinfect the wound but came up empty-handed. Hearing the door open and close, he thought Maria had brought Mussa, but he was wrong. Maria stood in front of him, holding antiseptic lotion and bandages.

'It's my furniture you're bleeding on,' she huffed, seeing the surprise on his face. 'Sit down while I clean that mess up.'

Reluctantly, suppressing the urge to tell her to mind her own business, he sat in a chair.

She poured the yellow antiseptic onto a cloth and wiped the blood away. 'I don't want trouble on my doorstep. I've got enough problems without you bringing more. Look for somewhere else to live when your rent is due.'

'Why do you hate us so much?' he asked quietly.

'I don't hate you. You just don't belong here.'

'What determines where we belong, Maria? The floor we were

born on? Forever tied to that bit of earth, no matter how harsh and brutal? For us, moving is a matter of survival.'

'And this is how you survive – nearly getting yourself killed?' Maria said, as she bandaged his arm.

'I would rather die than let my son live a life like mine. Forced to watch my family murdered, forced to kill or be killed, at thirteen. Kizza, kidnapped as a child, used and abused until her insides gave up.'

Maria, stunned, crossed herself. 'Dear God.'

'All we are looking for is a decent way of life and some peace. Is that too much to ask?' What he was telling her horrified her, but Maria was Maria. 'Peace? Ha! You could have chosen a better place than this, with its never-ending gang wars. Your wife is dead, and I'm sorry about that, but here *you* are, nearly getting yourself killed, and whatever the reason, I don't want to know.'

Maria's phone rang, startling them both. She answered, her face going from annoyed with Joseph to shocked at what she was hearing.

'Mother of God. I'm coming.' She ended the call and turned to Joseph.

'Carla needs me, and your son needs you. You can leave him upstairs for tonight. Better he doesn't see you like this.'

He let out a huge sigh of relief when she left.

Chapter 42

Maria drove her old Fiat, which Enrico had bought thirty years before, and it was still going strong. She hardly left her neighbourhood these days, preferring to walk, but had been reluctant to sell the car because Enrico had loved it. Most of the time, it just sat in a nearby garage with a full tank of petrol. Tonight, she was grateful that she had kept it. She was lucky there were no police around, as she never stuck to the speed limit when she was in a hurry, and Maria was always in a hurry. Given the hour, there were few cars on the road. It took no time to arrive at the Sturla building, which she had vowed never to enter. Parking in front of the main door, she got out of the car and walked to the entrance. A guard, very much alert, stopped her to carry out a search. Maria slapped his hands away and scoffed, 'I'm the mother of Carla Sturla, idiot.'

Seated in the penthouse, still reeling from the shock of what had happened, Marco, having told them to speak their minds, listened to the Sturla top men express their opinions.

'Fredo did a foolish thing by taking on Gianelli. He knew it would be war,' said Roberto de Luca, an older member of the clan who spoke his mind with a shrug of his shoulders.

Paulo Gargiulo nodded in agreement. 'Things may have been slow in construction, but they were recovering before the trouble started.'

'And we had a fair share of the drugs,' Donato Cozzolio stated. He ran the narcotics side of the operations and had done so since Fredo took the Clementi clan down. 'The talk of a bank brought nothing but trouble,' he added.

Marco didn't respond. He had no intention of giving up the idea of the bank. For him, it was the only way forward.

Roberto nodded in agreement with Donato. 'It's bad business. With all the killing, we now have the bastard politicos breathing down our necks.'

Paulo snorted, 'No doubt with their fucking hands out.'

'The war has cost us a lot of revenue,' Marco said, nodding and looking thoughtful. 'Now that Fredo has gone, I think we should draw up a peace plan with Gianelli. If he agrees to leave us alone, we agree to leave his fake business alone.' *But I will offer him a fair share of the banking business for it,* he thought.

'Marco, killing a capo is no small matter. If you don't act, the clans will be all over our business like vultures.' The men murmured their agreement with Luigi. Marco sighed. He had hoped they would agree with him and put an end to it, but he wasn't in a strong enough position yet to disagree with them. To run the business, which he intended to do, Marco could show no sign of weakness.

'Agreed,' he said. 'If Gianelli wants to accept our terms of peace, he must hand over the man who killed Fredo.'

'He will never hand over Gino, he …'

Donato never got to finish, as Maria pushed past the two guards at the door. 'Get your hands off me,' she snorted as she elbowed the guards away and walked into the room. Seeing her, the men shifted in their seats a little. Old women made them uncomfortable, maybe because they had seen and knew too much. Maria, aware of their discomfort, looked at Marco, sitting at the head of the table, and sneered.

'Huh! Marco Falco. So you're the new capo? You didn't waste much time.' She looked around the room at them all. 'Here you all are, planning what? More war, more fighting, more killing? And you, Luigi Ricci, I knew your mother. You should be ashamed of the things you do. She would turn in her grave,' she scolded.

Luigi shifted in his chair.

'You too, Roberto de Luca. You should all be ashamed,' she sneered.

Marco looked relieved when Carla, having showered Fredo's blood off her body and dressed, stepped into the room and took Maria by the arm.

'Nonna, please,' she said, turning to Marco. 'Apologies Marco. She's upset. She's an old lady.'

Marco nodded as Carla gently led Maria out of the room.

Once the bedroom door was closed behind them, Maria took in the bloodstained bed and floor, with a sigh of relief. 'He's really dead?' she whispered to Carla.

'Si. He's really dead.'

Maria crossed herself. Seeing the bruise marks on Carla's throat made by the necklace, she groaned and pulled her into a hug. 'Thank God. I hope he goes straight to hell.'

'There's no doubt about that, Nonna.'

'Was it Gianelli?'

Checking that no one could hear, Carla whispered to Maria, 'It was Joseph.' Maria's mouth dropped open in shock. She answered, mouthing the words, 'Joseph? Why? What? I don't believe it.' Confusion clouded her face. 'Are you sure?'

'Yes, I saw him. They must *never* find out,' Carla's voice was barely a murmur.

'So that's why he was shot.'

'He was shot?' Carla said, alarmed.

'It's not serious. He'll live. But why? Why would he do it? He's not a clan member.'

'Fredo was responsible for Kizza's death.'

Maria nodded. 'A good enough reason.' She sighed with relief. 'Mother of God, Carla, you're free at last.'

'Free of him,' Carla answered, nodding towards the room where the men were in conference. 'Now I have to be free of them.' She pulled at her long, damp hair. 'And this.'

'Your beautiful hair?'

'The plait he made me wear to bed was easy to grab hold of when the mood took him.'

Maria spat on the floor. 'The pig. I wish I'd had the courage to kill him years ago. But better late than never. Joseph, huh?'

Chapter 43

Mussa was sitting quietly playing with the iPad, as Maria applied a clean dressing to Joseph's wound. The plates on the table held the remains of the food she had brought for their breakfast.

'She was twenty when she married him, believing he was just an accountant. It was good for a few months, but then the real Fredo revealed himself. When he became Don Fredo, his head grew like a watermelon, and the violence towards her escalated,' Maria said to Joseph as she bandaged him up.

'Why did she stay?'

'Married to a capo, it's stay or die. Even if he let her go, which he never would, he would never let her take Giancarlo. You've seen the way they're guarded. And she would never leave without her child. He was the only reason she stayed and endured what that pig inflicted on her.'

Joseph nodded, sadly remembering how Kizza had been so protective of Mussa.

'We never thought there would be children when we married,' he said. 'They told Kizza it wasn't possible after what she had suffered as a girl. It was many years before Mussa came.' He looked at his son. 'He's a miracle child.'

'Well, it's good to know miracles happen sometimes, but not enough if you ask me,' Maria grumbled. Finishing the dressing, she tied the bandage neatly, snipping the ends with scissors. 'If they find out it was you, they'll kill you and every African here,' she said, speaking in a low voice so Mussa wouldn't overhear. She need not have worried. A video about killer whales held all his attention.

'Are you sure that thing is good for him?' she asked.

'Anything that takes his mind away from his mother is good for him. Thank you for letting him use it.'

'Well, it's nothing I would use.' A sharp, rapid banging on the door made Maria freeze and cross herself. 'God help us; it's them.'

Joseph motioned to her to be calm as he put on a clean shirt to cover the dressing. Maria quickly dumped his blood-stained dressings from the night before out of sight in the garbage.

Opening the door, Joseph was relieved to see Jacob standing there. He took him by the arm and pulled him into the apartment. Seeing the African, whom she recognised, Maria let out a sigh of relief.

'Is Big Moses here?' Jacob asked.

Sensing the worry and tension in his friend, Joseph frowned. 'No. What is it, Jacob? What's wrong?'

Jacob could barely get the words out. 'Gino Gianelli shot Abdi. He's dead, and they beat up Big Moses.'

'Moses? Is he okay?'

'He left with Mussa yesterday and didn't come back. I was hoping he was with you. That's why I came here.'

Joseph frowned. 'I haven't seen him.'

'The big one?' Maria asked. 'He was here. He brought your kid.'

With so much going on, Joseph had not thought to ask who had brought Mussa to Maria, assuming it was Jacob in whose care he had left him.

'He left something,' Maria added.

'What?'

'How would I know? It's in my café, where I should be.'

Telling Mussa to stay put, Joseph and Jacob followed Maria. Before entering the café, Joseph scanned the street for trouble, but all was quiet, not a Camorrista in sight.

Maria reached under the counter for the package that Big Moses had left and handed it to Joseph. He opened it, dreading to discover that it was what he thought: Big Moses' Bible.

'Why leave his Bible?' Jacob asked.

'He said to tell you he's gone to see his family,' said Maria.

'But he's got no family. Joseph, man, what does it mean?' Jacob asked, bewildered.

A coldness gripped Joseph. 'I know where he's gone. Pray we are not too late. Maria, can you please watch Mussa? We have to take a train as soon as possible. It's a matter of life or death.'

Maria, seeing the urgency in his face, felt she owed him after he had been instrumental in freeing Carla. 'Train? I've got a better idea – we'll take my car. It's quicker.'

'What about the café? And Mussa?'

'The city can survive for one afternoon without my café. I'll keep Mussa with me while you do what you have to do.' She took off the apron she wore when working and quickly went and collected the car keys from her apartment. 'Where are we going?' she asked Joseph, who had readied Mussa.

On the road, Joseph, his knuckles white from holding onto the dashboard, was thinking they would be lucky to make it alive. It seemed to him that it was the way of the Italians: drive to kill, shoot to kill. Eventually arriving at their destination, he witnessed afresh the threat of death when someone tried to take the parking place Maria had spotted first.

It was a weekday, so Mappatella Beach wasn't as crowded as when Joseph was last there. Telling Mussa to stay in the car with Maria, he got out with Jacob and ran past people sitting at pavement cafés, enjoying a glass of wine with their lunch.

Maria, who was curious about what was going on, followed them after warning Mussa to stay put or else. He sulked, wanting to follow too, but by running a finger across her throat, he got the message. With the iPad in his hand, he settled back into his seat and soon became fascinated with a short film about ocean creatures.

Joseph, followed by Jacob, ran onto the beach where such a short time ago, he had spent one of the happiest days of his life.

'Why would he be here?' Jacob asked with a puzzled frown.

Joseph had no time to answer. In the near distance, he could see men hauling something from the sea. He raced across the sand, through the surf, and reached them in time to help them pull Big Moses onto dry land. Jacob, following, stopped in his tracks, seeing the gentle giant dead in the copy sneakers he had been so proud of.

'Oh, this is bad, man,' he whimpered as he wiped away tears. 'This is so bad, man. So bad.'

Joseph stifled the icy rage he could feel building in him at the sight of Moses' body, and the brutal damage done to his dead friend's face.

Maria arrived. Seeing the dead African, she crossed herself, murmuring a prayer. 'Eternal rest, give unto him, oh Lord, and let him rest in peace.' She looked at Joseph, who was staring into the middle distance, his face stony. 'You should say a prayer,' she urged.

'To who? Who's listening?' Jacob asked. 'The only gods we know are the bastards who decide if we live or die.'

'God is not the clans.'

'Who beat him up, Jacob?' asked Joseph.

'Gino Gianelli and his goons.'

'They'll pay for this. They all will.'

Maria, seeing the hard look of determination on Joseph's face as he looked at Big Moses' body, frowned.

'And what? You'll stop them? Are you *pazzo*? Yes, you are crazy! You might just get away with what you've done so far, but no one – no one – wins against them. Kill one, and there are a thousand waiting to take their place. They'll kill you. All of you. You have a son to live for. Are you forgetting that?'

Joseph turned and walked away. She was saying nothing he wanted to hear.

Maria shouted after him, 'You are talking suicide! You're a crazy man!' She then realised that everyone around was looking at her, thinking she was the crazy one. 'You have nothing better to do than look at me?' she yelled. People diverted their eyes as she walked across the sand, trying to look dignified. As she left the beach, she passed an ambulance, which was just arriving, followed by a police car. 'Too late, as usual!' she shouted.

A feeling of impending doom hung on her shoulders like a weight, and her heart felt heavy. A tear ran down her face as she thought about how sad and forlorn Moses had looked. *Why do I care? I didn't even know him,* she thought. Back at the car, there was no sign of Joseph or Jacob. Opening the door, she sighed, seeing Mussa smiling at her.

Don't smile at me. You're not my responsibility! But she knew in her heart that somehow it was precisely what he had become. Getting into the car, she ruffled his hair.

'Take revenge, you dig two graves,' she muttered under her breath to herself. Unaware that digging two graves was precisely what Joseph intended to do.

Chapter 44

Marco, flanked by Luigi and Donato, spoke directly to Sergio.

Gianelli sat facing him in the restaurant they had chosen as neutral ground, along with Gino and Michael and two of his foot soldiers,.

'Your underground factories were next, but now that Fredo has gone, I can guarantee there will be no more assaults on you, your family, or your business if we can agree on a peace deal.' He slid a document across the table. 'Our conditions.'

Sergio ignored the document. 'So, you're Il Capo now. Another ambitious lawyer.' His eyes slid towards Michael, who didn't react.

Marco shrugged. 'One advantage to being a lawyer is that we learn to recognise when we've lost.' He wanted to choke on his words, which let the old bastard think he had won. But he had no choice if they were to survive and move forward.

Sergio nodding his head. 'I like a man who can admit defeat.'

'If you agree to the terms, we can call a halt to this conflict and get on with business.'

Sergio ignored the papers. 'If there are any terms to be set, I will be the one to make them.'

The old villain is going to squeeze every drop out of us, but it's not over yet. Marco looked him directly in the eye. 'Before any decision is made, there is a matter we have to clear up. Fredo Sturla. Someone must pay for that.'

Luigi nodded in agreement.

Sergio shrugged. 'Not my doing. The punk obviously had other enemies.'

'We say it was Gino.'

'Gino? Why Gino?'

'Who else with a grudge against us could scale the building without a rope?'

Sergio, looking unperturbed, shook his head. He had heard how the attack had gone down and knew Gino would be a suspect, so he had come prepared. Michael pushed a newspaper across the table to Marco, showing a press photo of Gino with a beautiful actress on his arm.

'Gino was at a film premiere in Venice that night. Check the date.'

'Yeah, with Vera Valente. She's mad for me,' Gino smirked.

Marco was stunned. He had been so sure it was Gino, and so had Carla.

'Whoever it was, we want him,' said Marco.

Sergio, standing, leaned across the table and looked Marco in the eye. 'If I did it, he would have deserved it. He tried to kill Gino, but I did not order it.'

'If not you, who did? None of the other clans had a problem with Fredo.'

Sergio leant closer, so close that Marco could see the red veins in his eyes and smell the garlic on his breath. 'It's not my problem.' With a withering look and without another word, Sergio, followed by a smirking Gino, Michael, and the two guards, left the restaurant, leaving the food uneaten.

Luigi looked at Marco with a puzzled expression. 'If it wasn't Gino…?'

Marco looked pensive. *Did Carla lie?*

Later that day, Michael informed Marco that Sergio had Michael Rossi draw up their own terms for a peace pact, which they had now delivered. The demands were what they expected, but if agreed upon, would cease any further conflict. It was a start, and once it was settled he would approach Gianelli and try to convince him that the Chinese bank deal was bigger than his control of the fake goods business. But first, he needed to work out who had killed Fredo.

***

Confident that Mussa was safe with Maria, Joseph made his way down the Via Monteoliveto to a large hardware store. He searched until he found what he was looking for: a reel of stainless-steel wire one sixteenth of an inch thick, which, in the right place, would be almost invisible. Steel clips, wire cutters, a broom, a metal toolbox and green workmen's overalls were next on his list. Handing over €80, he asked if the store had a cubicle. The assistant was happy to direct him to the staff toilet. Ignoring the rank smell from the badly stained toilet basin, he pulled on the overalls, put the reel of steel wire and the rest of the tools into the metal box and left the store. It was four in the afternoon. He knew the walk would take him the best part of an hour. *Plenty of time.*

Focused on where he was going, Joseph rarely lifted his eyes above street level, not even as he passed the many luxurious blocks of apartments and magnificent public buildings to be seen on the road to Chiaia. How the wealthy middle class survived alongside the gangster clans wasn't a question he would ask

222

himself. Where and how people lived their lives, even those in the crammed apartments in his own barrio was of no interest to him. He had never lusted after wealth, nor what other people had. Life had taught him to need, not to want. Passing the Castel dell'Ovo, a fortress built by the Normans, and one of seven imposing castles in Naples, he was not impressed. *Another house built at the time to protect a rich, power-crazy psychopath and his gold. Nothing changes, just the architecture.*

Once outside the Sturla building, he surveyed the only road leading to and from the edifice. Apart from the odd car and bicycle, it was quiet until two SUVs appeared, making their way to the building. They stopped while the electronic garage doors opened. Joseph recognised Luigi Ricci at the wheel of the lead car with a man seated in the back. He could kill Luigi anywhere with a home-made bomb, so he would die like Kizza, but he wanted it to be more personal. They could easily blame a bomb on the other side: but that did not serve Joseph's purpose. He wanted the gangsters to feel as vulnerable as their victims did. Two hours later, the car with Luigi at the wheel returned and disappeared into the garage.

Luigi Ricci was a man of habit. Each day at the same time, he left the building on his powerful, two-wheel machine. Joseph didn't know where he went and didn't care. His destination was of no importance. Attaching the end of the steel wire around a streetlight post a hundred yards from the building, he secured it with a strong metal clip. Crossing the narrow road, the cable snaking loosely behind him, he waited, hidden by the trees. As he had thought, he had gone unnoticed by the men guarding the building, and the women returning with shopping. It was no surprise, he knew that the last person they would look for as a threat was an African maintenance worker.

At precisely 7.29 pm Joseph lifted the end of the cable and secured it around a tree trunk with a second strong steel clip, forming a barely discernible chest-high barrier across the road, and waited. As expected, at 7.30 pm, the garage doors opened, and the motorbike roared out. Joseph watched the bike gain speed as it hurtled its way towards him and the wire. When it hit, the force lifted Luigi into the air. He landed in a heap in the middle of the road. The bike continued moving until it veered into a wall and fell on its side, the engine roaring in protest. Joseph looked down at the prostrate, twitching form of Luigi Ricci with a gash across his throat. The steel wire had done the job for him. 'For Kizza,' he said, before he slipped out of sight, as the guards, alarmed by the sound of the bike's engine, came to investigate.

Chapter 45

The site of the Gianelli house had once been the home of a Roman general not rich enough to have lived in nearby Stabiae, where Roman Emperors such as Tiberius, Nero and their governments spent their summers. Like most of the historic villas in the area, it had been a ruin for hundreds of years. Apart from its secluded location, just fifteen kilometres from Naples, it was the history of it that had appealed to Sergio, who fancied himself as the reincarnation of an emperor when he had bought and rebuilt it forty years earlier.

Sergio had called a meeting of all his head men to discuss the deaths of Sturla and Luigi Ricci. They were all baffled by who was responsible, .but even more concerned that other clan bosses would take advantage of the situation, which meant Sergio's clan could be in jeopardy. This wasn't the real reason Sergio had gathered his men together; he wanted to judge if he had a Brutus among his men capable of the killings and if he himself was the target in the long term. But, after a lengthy discussion he decided there was no one strong enough or cunning enough. However he decided to keep them all at a distance, just in case.

As Sergio snored in front of the television, Gino ranted at Michael. 'I don't trust the fucking son of a *puta*.'

Michael sighed. Nothing would convince Gino that it hadn't been Marco Falco's ambition to take over the Sturla clan, or that he had killed Fredo Sturla and Luigi Ricci.

'If Falco wanted to continue Sturla's war, he wouldn't have approached us,' Michael reasoned.

Gino wasn't listening as he paced up and down. 'Why doesn't the old fuck listen to me? He's senile. His head's gone with watching soaps all day long. It's time this family had a proper leader. One who would stick it to Falco.'

Michael stifled his exasperation with Gino's ranting. 'Fredo has gone. There is a treaty on the table. We have no reason yet to distrust Falco.'

Gino sneered. 'We have no reason to trust him, either. And if he didn't kill them, who did?'

'Whoever, it doesn't matter.' Michael shrugged. 'They saved us the job. They're no threat to us. It's the Sturlas they're attacking.' Michael watched a light go on in Gino's brain and thought, *Moron. God forbid you ever become capo.*

Gino grinned. 'You're right. There's no danger to us,' he said, unaware of how wrong he was.

The open space around the compound was bordered by a tangle of vegetation, towering leafy beech trees, junipers, cluster pines and even some European oak, all grown wild over many years. Joseph had found the perfect cover by climbing a towering beech close to the clearing. There he waited for his opportunity to strike terror into the capo and his thugs. The same terror that Abdi and Moses had suffered.

The gates to the compound swung open to reveal Frankie and Tony, who appeared to be conducting a routine search. Frankie stopped at the gate to answer a call from his wife, complaining about their kids, while Toni, an automatic weapon slung over his shoulder, checked the area encircling the property. Unaware of the danger, he strolled into the wooded area to urinate.

Again, it amazed Joseph that people acting as security guards, pretending to be soldiers, rarely searched above eye-level. He silently dropped to the ground with his panga in hand.

For Moses and Abdi, who suffered much in their lives and did you no harm.

Toni's blood spurted out, turning the trunk of a tree crimson as his body dropped to the ground, convulsing in its death throes.

Quickly shinning back up the tree and disappearing into the thick foliage, Joseph waited.

Frankie, having finished the call from his nagging wife by assuring her he would spend more time at home now that the war was over, spoke into a walkie-talkie.

'Toni? All clear?' Getting no response, he tried again. 'Toni, can you hear me? Over.' Frowning, he pressed another button and spoke to Gino. 'Gino, Toni is not answering. He was checking the outside area. I'm going to look.'

Gun in hand, Frankie walked into the trees, calling to his brother. He hesitated, hearing the static on Luca's radio nearby. 'Hey man, you okay?' Walking towards the sound, he saw Luca on the ground, his blood sinking into the earth. 'What the fuck?'

Gino, peeved at being disturbed during his gym time, came out of the gates with a couple of men, speaking into the walkie-talkie.

'Frankie? Frankie?' He turned to the men. 'Where the fuck are they?'

They made their way cautiously through the trees and discovered Frankie and Toni, both dead. Gino, stunned, shouted, 'Spread out! Find who did this!'

As he scarpered back to the house, Joseph heard him yell into his phone, 'Michael, get back here. Now!'

Chapter 46

Maria smiled as she took in her granddaughter's new look. Carla's hair had been cut by Irina to shoulder length, and she was wearing a crisp white shirt with blue jeans and white sneakers. Gone was the ultra-sophisticated couture look that Fredo had imposed on her, and she looked years younger. She was also driving herself about in a car that Fredo had bought her after the birth of Giancarlo, but because of his restrictions, she had hardly used it.

'So tell me what happened?' urged Carla, who, since the death of Fredo, was now free to come and go as she pleased.

Maria glanced at the children before answering. Mussa sat with Giancarlo at a table, playing a game on the iPad. Despite the language difference, they communicated as only children can, by Giancarlo picking up words in English and Mussa picking up words in Italian. She answered quietly, so the children would not hear.

'He disappeared. Left the kid with me…What could I do? I couldn't leave the child on his own. He returned last night, but not a word about where he'd been.'

'Nonna, he got Luigi Ricci, another candidate for hell.'

'Good riddance, I say.'

'Marco is freaking out. Gianelli claims he didn't do it. Everyone is jumpy. They don't know where it's coming from.' Their eyes went to the window where Joseph stood on the pavement, selling his fake handbags.

'Now he's after the ones who killed his friend, may he rest in peace,' Maria said, crossing herself. 'He's determined to get Gianelli. Nothing will stop him. I've told him it's suicide.'

Carla looked thoughtful. 'If we can't stop him, maybe we should help him.'

Maria's mouth dropped open. 'Help him? Now you're the one talking crazy.'

'Maybe, but is it crazy to want to get rid of them? Think about it, Nonna,' she urged. Maria thought for precisely one second and shook her head.

'More will follow. Just as bad. I've seen too much of it happen over the years. They've been operating since the 17th century, for God's sake.'

'I know, but maybe things are changing. Marco wants to move into legitimate business, away from drugs and stuff. They want the money without the aggravation. Sergio is standing in the way of change.'

'That snake is not the only one.'

'True, but the others are decrepit, they can't last much longer.'

Maria chewed on her lip as she thought about this and again shook her head. 'Carla, they killed your father and mother, and God knows who else. I don't want them killing you.'

'They're evil men, Nonna, murderers. All of them. Yes, they killed my parents, and God knows how many others. And wouldn't hesitate to kill you, me, and Giancarlo if it came to it.'

Maria shuddered at the thought. 'Mother of God, don't even think such a thing.'

'But you know it's true, so why not help Joseph?' Carla urged. 'If you were Sophia Loren in a movie, you would tell Marcello Mastroianni to go get the guns,' she teased.

Maria gave a wry smile. 'But there's an army guarding Gianelli in his fortress. Huff! They call this the city of castles. Nothing has changed. Probably gangsters then and gangsters now. It's impossible to get near him.'

Carla snorted. 'Like it was impossible to get near Fredo? And Luigi, who threw the bomb that killed Joseph's wife? Believe me, Nonna, I don't know Joseph's background, but he's no ordinary man.'

'But why get involved, *tesoro*? Fredo has gone. You're out of danger, and now you want to put yourself back in the lion's mouth? It's crazy! *Pazza*!'

'As you said, Nonna, he will do it regardless, and I owe him.

***

'It was fucking Falco. I warned you. He hit Frankie and Toni. I will fucking kill him.'

'Kill him, Gino? Falco swears they didn't do it. Just like we didn't order Fredo or Luigi Ricci to be taken out,' said Michael.

'So if it wasn't him, who did? The syndicate?'

'It's not the syndicate,' Sergio said. 'They assured me they're not involved.'

'So if it wasn't them and it wasn't Marco Falco, it only leaves the Chinks,' said Gino.

Sergio, looking pensive, shook his head. 'Attacking us would destroy their business in Europe, and they know it. It's not them.'

'So who, a fucking ghost?'

'Never heard of a ghost wielding a knife or climbing buildings and laying traps in the road. Someone has a grudge against us,' Michael said. *And that could be the whole damn country*, he thought.

'Michael's right. It's a ghost that will bleed when we rip out his fucking heart,' Sergio sneered at Gino. 'Do your job. Double the guards and find who's doing this.'

Michael refrained from rolling his eyes at the thought of Gino succeeding at any task apart from inflicting pain. 'Don Sergio, we have to arrange for the funerals and take care of Frankie and Toni's families.'

'Responsible for them even when they're dead,' Sergio grumbled, unconcerned by the deaths of his two loyal foot soldiers. He had a hundred men ready to take their place, all willing to follow orders and kill when instructed. 'Do what you have to. Nothing more.'

'Si. In the meantime, I advise you to take care, Don Sergio. Your life could be at risk.'

Looking at his gold Rolex with its diamond-studded bezel, Sergio growled. 'Look at the time: I'm missing my program.' Ignoring Gino and Michael, he turned on the television.

Gino, who thought this was a sign of the old man's senility, looked at Michael and shrugged. It was the small tic at the side of his eye that let Michael know that Sergio Gianelli was afraid.

Chapter 47

Carla drove her car through the enormous gates, which opened onto a grand house with a marbled portico. The windows were opaque with years of dirt and the overgrown gardens were neglected. It looked like an abandoned hotel. She parked in front of the porticoed door and turned to Joseph. 'It belonged to Fredo's father. We lived in it for a while, but once he became the capo, Fredo never felt safe here, so he bought the Sturla building and filled it with his men, thinking he had made it impregnable.' She rooted in her bag and brought out a key fob. 'I still have a set of keys.'

Joseph ran his eyes over the place and frowned. 'Why are you bringing me here?'

'You'll see.'

They entered through the main door, the lock of which was well oiled, as were the hinges. Opening the shutters of the salon, dust dancing in the sunbeams made Carla sneeze. Joseph saw that the neglect was all external. Despite the furniture being covered in white sheets, which gave the place a ghostly appearance, it was evidently a rich man's house. The money spent on the heavy silk drapes at the windows alone would have fed a family for months. As if speaking would wake the ghosts of the past, she beckoned him to follow her through the kitchen with its Calacatta marble tops and brass fittings into a larder of sorts, which had a door leading down narrow stone stairs into a vast, musty smelling wine cellar. 'Fredo wasn't a connoisseur of wine. Even though it's worth a fortune, he wanted nothing to do with it or the house, after his father died.'

Joseph looked around at the hundreds of wine bottles housed in metal racks. 'Is this house yours now? If you're trying to rent it, I can't afford it,' he joked.

Carla smiled, her new haircut making her look like a teenager. 'No. Nothing is ever yours with the clans. If Giancarlo claimed it, he would belong to them. That will never happen, not as long as I live.'

Joseph watched as she searched around until she found what she was looking for. 'Got it,' she said, as she pulled a hidden lever. The bottles clinked in protest as the shelving slid to one side. It was slow, but it eventually revealed a steel door with two keypads next to it.

'One is an alarm system and the other is the lock to the door. If anyone tries to open the door lock without deactivating the alarm, it would alert them and they would have someone here within minutes.' She tapped in the codes, and the door, with a loud click, was unlocked.

Smiling in triumph, she looked at Joseph. 'Fredo was clever, but arrogant; it made him underestimate me.' She clicked a switch, and a bright light revealed more stone stairs.

He followed her down four flights, curious about where they were leading. It became darker as they reached the bottom, and he had trouble seeing until Carla pulled another switch. Joseph gasped at the sight of a massive underground cavern housing a cache of every imaginable weapon.

'The Sturla arsenal,' Carla said, sweeping her arm around the mountain of armaments: boxes of explosives, grenades, Kalashnikovs, M16s, AR-15s, and shoulder-mounted missile launchers that could take down an aircraft. 'No one outside of the top echelon of the family knows it exists. I discovered it by chance when I saw Fredo coming down here.'

Joseph was too stunned to say anything more than, 'Incredible.'

'Yes. And to think it lies below the city,' said Carla with a wry smile.

'They don't have guards?'

'It would send signals to the wrong people. Also, people in the neighbourhood know the house belongs to the clan, so it would take a brave person to break in.'

'And the Gianelli arsenal, is that underground too?' he asked.

'I don't know. Fredo suspected it was in their compound, but having it that close to his home would be crazy.' She looked at him and shrugged. 'But who knows? Sergio is more than crazy.'

'But why here in the city? If this lot ignited …'

'You think they care?' she scoffed. 'There are hundreds of caverns like this below Naples. Some stretch for entire streets, but this one runs only under this house and its grounds. It was the reason why it was built in 1890. Its sole purpose was to be an armoury. Fredo's father took up residence here when he was appointed caretaker. Fredo never appointed anyone in his place. I'd like to think it was because he couldn't stand the idea of someone living in his father's house,' she snorted before continuing, 'but I know that was not the reason. His father haunted him, as he should.'

'There are enough weapons here for an army.'

'They are an army. Never forget it. Take what you want, but do it quickly just in case Marco sends someone here to check.'

Joseph ran his hand over a missile launcher. It would be easy to blow the Gianelli compound to hell with it, but it would be dangerous, as they could trace it back to the clans, and if there was an inventory, it could lead them to Carla. Besides, it wasn't his style.

Carla, surprised by the small amount he had chosen, watched anxiously as Joseph quickly gathered everything he needed and loaded it into the boot of her car. The high oleander bushes secluded them from the road, making it unlikely anyone would see them leaving, but to be sure, she had prepared a story: she was thinking of using the house and wanted a gardener to assess the work needed to restore the gardens. But if they discovered what she had really done, Marco would have no choice but to kill her. A sigh of relief left her lips as they drove away.

Driving in silence, they soon reached the outskirts. Joseph had spent several days surveying the lie of the land, so he knew the safest and most secluded place to be dropped off. It was at the beginning of the forest area, out of sight of those guarding the Gianelli compound. Joseph scanned the area to make sure no one was watching, before he unloaded the large metal box, heavy bag and garden spade, from the boot of the car. He noticed Carla's worried expression; she was obviously fearing the outcome and having misgivings about what he was going to do, but there was nothing he could say to put her mind at ease. When you go to war, you cannot predict the outcome.

'Thank you, Carla.'

'For what? Helping you kill yourself? You're no match for these men. They're brutal, unforgiving killers, all of them.'

'I've known many men like them. Don't worry.'

'I don't doubt it. I don't know who you really are or what you have been through. Maybe it's better I don't know. Perhaps you can do this, but on reflection, I would rather you change your mind. Come back with me,' she pleaded.

'I can't do that.'

'But you can't kill them all! Maria is right – kill Gianelli, and tomorrow there will be another Gianelli and another after him. You would have to blow up the entire country.'

'Don't tempt me,' he teased, smiling at her.

Despite the tension, Carla managed a small smile back, then sighed. 'You've made the world a better place for me and my son.'

'It wasn't my intention.'

'I know. But it happened.' She hesitated and laid a hand on his arm. 'If you don't come back…I'll take Mussa as my own and care for him,' she said, before getting in the car and rolling down the window. 'If you get Sergio, you must get Gino, too. He's a mad dog with no brain. If he lives, lots of innocent people will suffer.' She didn't wait for him to reply.

Joseph watched as she drove off before he hitched the strap of the bag onto his shoulder, picked up the spade and metal box, and carried his load into the forest.

Chapter 48

Hidden by the density of the trees, Joseph dug a hole deep enough for a grave. Dripping with perspiration from strenuous work and heat, he dropped the box and bag into it, leaving room to slide in when he needed sleep or cover. He felt confident that they would not be able to trace him to the dugout unless they had an experienced tracker, which he doubted, but not being a man to take chances, he scaled trees, cutting branches from way up high where they wouldn't be noticed, and used them to lay over the hole. Satisfied that everything was in place, he sat with his back to a tree. He felt a familiar comfort being surrounded by trees, an abundance of which was lacking in the city area where he lived. He inhaled, savouring the musty smell of the earth and welcomed the sweet, pungent sting in the air, a sign of coming rain, that could be used to his advantage. Not having eaten all day, he attacked a salami panino, one of a few that Maria had wrapped in tinfoil and pushed into his hand as he was leaving. Alone with his thoughts, he wondered if Maria was right. Was he insane with grief, wanting revenge? *Is that what has driven me all these years – using my pain as a means to survive? Kizza, always nervous and on her guard, never came to terms with the cruelty inflicted on her. Have I? Did I focus my entire world on protecting her to avoid dealing with my own trauma? Always looking forward, never looking back?* Her voice echoed in his head: *An ocean can swallow a river, Joseph.* His mind troubled by these thoughts – the crocodiles swimming in his river – he closed his eyes to rest, half asleep but alert, and waited for nightfall.

With the onset of night, Joseph stripped naked and coated his body with menthol, a simple enough trick that often worked to repel dogs. He donned the green camouflage fatigues he had taken from the Sturla armoury. With his dark skin, they made him almost invisible in the trees. Making his way slowly, careful not to leave a trail of broken branches, he reached the clearing surrounding the compound.

Using powerful night binoculars, he surveyed the movement of the armed men stationed at the gates. They were alert and nervous, the way he wanted them. As with the Sturla thugs, routine checks left them open to attack. There were dogs, but no cameras. *Too much faith in their guns.* Timing the guards and knowing he had fifteen minutes to act, he moved swiftly towards the compound, where he would gather the information he needed. Reaching the outer wall, he climbed it with ease and lay flat on top, his camouflage suit blending in with the darkness of the surrounding trees. The branches overhanging the wall from the garden trees also provided coverage. Lying still, he watched as the two armed men passed below, their entire focus on the outside of the compound. Once they were safely out of sight, Joseph scanned the house, locating each man posted around it.

Dropping into the garden, he made his way unseen to the long, low outbuilding situated against the west wall and concealed from the main building by high shrubs. A man stood guard by it. Needing confirmation, he deliberately stepped on a water sprinkler. It burst into life, alerting the dogs. The frantic barking alarmed everyone.

Gino came from the house, shouting out orders, and ran past Joseph, who had blended into the bushes. Making his way to the outhouse, and unlocking the huge security locks, Gino pushed past the guard, entered, and returned holding an automatic weapon, confirming to Joseph it was as he suspected: the building was the armoury.

Floodlights illuminated the area, and the snarling dogs were set loose. They came close to Joseph, but confused by the strong smell of menthol, they moved off.

Thinking the house and grounds were secure, Gino yelled, 'Outside! Check outside!' He stood inside the opened iron gates, watching as his armed men moved into the clearing. Taking him out would have been easy for Joseph, who was hidden just metres away from him, but it wasn't what he had in mind. After silently downing the armed man guarding the outhouse, he moved rapidly, climbing the wall and lying prone, again concealed by the overhanging branches. He watched as the guards on the outside, having found nothing, made their way back into the compound.

Gino's lower lip pouted with annoyance until he heard someone cry out.

'What the fuck…?' He exclaimed, standing over the body of the armoury guard.

Angelo, who had replaced Frankie, shrugged, looking nonplussed. 'The dogs are out, Gino. We searched everywhere.'

'Obviously not everywhere, you fucking idiot. He was in here and could have killed me!' Gino looked toward the house. 'Search again. I want whoever did this to be found. Now! If anything has happened to Sergio, you will all pay,' he snarled, as he made a hasty retreat towards the house, hoping that something *had* happened to Sergio.

The man was his uncle, but he detested him. He enjoyed putting him down in front of people, making him feel like a child. Sergio had taken Gino in when his father, Sergio's older brother, and his wife had died in a plane crash. Gino rightly suspected Sergio had arranged their deaths in the private plane so that he could take over the clan. Now, he was itching to do the same thing to Sergio.

Twenty men armed with automatic weapons and accompanied by dogs, searched the grounds and the area around the compound. Entering the wooded area, they walked slightly apart. A foot soldier trailing behind didn't hear the soft thud as Joseph dropped behind him.

Following in the rear, another guard recoiled in shock at the sight of the dead body and called out. Angelo and the men ran back. Knowing the attacker was still close by, but not knowing which direction the assault was coming from. It had everyone on edge.

'Get back to the compound!' Angelo ordered.

A rustling in the undergrowth startled him. He turned his automatic weapon in its direction and let rip, it was a small creature. Joseph was safely nestled high above them.

Michael knew better than to speak when Sergio was ranting.

'How did they get in? How? Twenty fucking guards, and they still get in. What the fuck are we paying them for? If they can get into the grounds, the cunts can get in here! Who the fuck are they?' he screamed, slamming his fist down on the desk, making Gino flinch. 'Whoever it is, find them and crucify them. You hear me? Fucking crucify them!' He paced the room, seething, one eye twitching, his mind ticking over. 'Are you sure it's not Falco?' he asked Michael.

'He says not. He's not organised enough to carry this out so quickly. This is coming from the outside. Someone wants to take us all down.'

'Tio, maybe you should move away from here for a while. Go to Rome or Venice. You have houses there,' suggested Gino.

'If I'm not safe here with twenty fucking armed men, I am not safe anywhere,' he raged, picking up a jug of water from the table and flinging it across the room.

A Camorrista entered the room and whispered urgently to Gino, who ran from the room.

Sergio snarled at Michael. 'Another one? I'm surrounded by useless fucking morons!'

Michael left the room quickly before he became the object of Sergio's wrath.

The air was electric with tension as Michael looked at the dead body of the guard lying in the dust, thinking there was something primitive about the way the men were dying. Bombs and guns were what they understood, it was business, this was something else. It felt personal. *What the hell is going on?*

Thunder rumbled in the distance and the heavens opened. Ignoring the torrential rain and surrounded by armed men, Gino came running from the outhouse holding a flamethrower, which he aimed at the trees in front of the compound. Brittle from the dry, hot summer, they exploded into flames.

'I'll kill the bastards! Shoot anything that moves!' he yelled.

Too distracted to keep a watch on the grounds, the sound of breaking glass and the alarm going off in the house caused Gino to swing around, mouth agape.

Joseph, having thrown a rock through a window, and confident that they were now in a state of panic and focused on the house, dropped down from the wall, and ran for cover, half-hidden by the now torrential rain that had reduced visibility. Once out of sight, he watched through his night binoculars as the guards locked the gates. He nodded, satisfied that everyone was inside, precisely the result he wanted. They were now his prisoners.

The fire had destroyed a good few trees, but the heavy downpour dampened the flames down before they took a fierce hold. The smoke and smell of the smouldering vegetation enveloped Joseph, reminding him of battles fought at a tender age, when fate had robbed him of his choices and forced him down a path he had never wanted but had made him who he was; a man who refused to be swallowed by an ocean.

Back at his base, he slipped into the dugout, which had gathered inches of rain, and pulled the tree branches over him. Knowing that no one would look for him in the forest tonight, he ate the last of Maria's sandwiches and slept.

Chapter 49

With Joseph on her mind, Maria took off her apron and collected her purse.

'Put that away. We're going out,' she said to Mussa, pointing at the iPad in his hand.

'Where's Pappy?' Mussa asked, not taking his attention away from what he was watching.

'I don't know.' *But I think I know someone who might.* 'Come on, we're going to the market.' She indicated they were leaving by pointing towards the door.

Mussa, engrossed with what was on the screen, wasn't listening. She looked over his shoulder, wondering what could be so interesting, and saw that it was the life of an octopus that captivated him.

'I like very much to eat *pulpo*,' she said, pointing at the octopus on the screen and then at her mouth.

Mussa looked horrified. 'No eat!'

'Your Italian is improving, child. Why not?'

He showed her how clever they are, with their nine brains, three hearts, extensive communication skills, and the ability to change shape to fool predators or catch food. Maria became fascinated. It amazed her to learn that and octopus can befriend humans, and that some scientists think they come from another planet, maybe originating from atoms carried here on an asteroid.

'Well, I never. I didn't know any of that. I just knew they tasted good cooked in white wine, drizzled with a little olive oil and lemon. You're very smart for a six-year-old. Now we must go. Leave that thing here. You don't want to lose it.'

Mussa reluctantly put down the iPad.

They made their way through the neighbourhood streets to the Porta Nolana market, where Maria, buying fresh fish, thought she might find the answer to Mussa's question. She held her head high as she walked past the stalls manned by fishermen she had known for years but ignored, as any woman would.

'No one walks like you, Maria!' one called out.

'Why? Haven't they got legs?' she answered, hiding a smile and swinging her hips a little more. She stopped at Enzo Baldacci's stall.

'Buongiorno Enzo.'

The man gutting a fish looked up and beamed.

'Maria, a sight for sore eyes.' He gave a pretend soulful look, seeing Mussa. 'My heart, you have a new boyfriend? But he's a little young for you, isn't he?'

Maria huffed and said, 'At least he has his own teeth and doesn't creak when he walks, like some people I know. I want some fresh fish today, Enzo, so don't try fobbing me off with yesterday's catch.'

'Ahh. Maria, so dominant. You drive me wild when you talk sexy,' he teased, grinning at her, revealing perfect teeth for his age.

'Is Mussa short for Mussolini?'

'That pig? Damned fascist. I should hope not.'

'My father wanted to name me Benito after him, but my mamma, God rest her soul, said no.'

'Well, you can thank the Holy Virgin that your mother had some sense.'

Mussa tugged on her coat.

'What child? What do you want? '

He pointed at a bucket that contained a small octopus. Maria immediately turned to Enzo. 'You have a live *pulpo*?'

'Si Maria, for you, a good price.'

'A good price?' she said, outraged. 'It has nine brains and its own language. It's more intelligent than you, with your half-brain. They're not for eating.'

'But you always like pulpo,' Enzo said, looking nonplussed.

'I like them in the sea. You shouldn't eat them. And you're upsetting my friend.'

'Maria, Maria, I don't tell you not to eat meat, like me.'

'Since when did you not eat meat?'

'Every Friday.'

Maria huffed, remembering the old church rule that Catholics could not eat meat on a Friday. 'That's because you are still frightened of going to hell.'

Mussa put his hand in the bucket, and the octopus wrapped its tentacles around it. He gave Maria a pleading look.

'How much is it?' she asked with a sigh.

'For you? Twenty euros.'

'Twenty? *Pazzo*!'

'Not crazy. It's very fresh.'

'Of course it's fresh. It's still alive.'

Mussa stepped forward, and to Maria's amusement, took charge. 'Fifteen.' He said, in perfect Italian.

Maria was surprised. 'You heard him, Enzo, fifteen. No more.'

'You want me to starve? What about my wife and six kids?'

'You haven't got six kids. They've all left home and your wife hates you. Fifteen, it is. And you can throw in the bucket. Take it or leave it.'

'For you? Anything,' he said with an exaggerated sigh. Smiling, he lowered his voice. 'You could have it free for just one night, Maria.'

'If you think I would trade my wonderful body for an octopus, it's the reason it will never happen.' The fishermen around laughed and jeered at Enzo, who held up his palms and shrugged. 'What else can I do? I offered her a free *pulpo*, and she still turned me down.'

With the octopus in a small plastic bucket, Maria took Mussa by the hand to Arturo's café nearby, where she ordered a cappuccino and chocolate milk. She ignored the curious looks from the old women gathered there, all wondering what she was doing with an African child. *Like it's any of their business.* She didn't have long to wait before she saw three African men leaving the building where Joseph had lived. Mussa, excited, waved and ran to them. They each fussed over him and showed interest in the pulpo. Maria, recognising Jacob, approached him, asking if he had heard anything from Joseph. He said he hadn't; none of them had.

'If you want us to take Mussa, we will,' Jacob offered.

'Did I say that? Do I look like I'm not capable of looking after a child?' huffed Maria as she took Mussa by the hand. 'We have to go if you want to free that thing.' She looked at Jacob. 'If you hear from him, let me know.' It sounded more like an order than a request. Jacob nodded as she walked off with Mussa who was gripping the handle of the plastic bucket.

Once they reached the sea, he lifted the octopus out of the bucket and put it on the ground.

'Better to put it in the water,' Maria suggested.

Mussa shook his head. To her surprise, the octopus started moving toward the water itself. Before slipping into the sea, it stopped; for a moment, Maria felt it was looking back at her as if to say thank you. *This kid is making me crazy.*

'We have to go. I've wasted enough time. I have a business to run,' she scolded, annoyed with herself for feeling good about setting the *pulpo* free. Mussa gave a gap-toothed smile and a little wave to the octopus as it slipped out of sight under the waves.

Chapter 50

'We go see Nonna. Yes?' Carla said to Gianni, buttoning up his shirt.

'And Mussa?'

'Yes, and Mussa.'

It was the first time since Fredo had died that she had seen him smile as he nodded his head. She hugged him close. 'I know you are missing Papa, Gianni. I'm sorry for your pain, but I will love you enough for two people. I promise.'

'Mamma, are you missing him too?'

'Yes, of course.' *God, forgive me for the lie.*

He pulled away from her, his eyes on the floor. 'He hurt you.'

Carla gasped. 'No…I…'

'I saw him. He hit you to the floor.'

'No, Gianni, I fell,' she protested. She thought she had taken precautions to prevent her son from ever knowing of the violence Fredo had inflicted on her, but like most parents, she had underestimated her child.

'I'm not a baby, Mamma.'

Putting a hand to her mouth, and with tears in her eyes, Carla didn't know what to say. He took her hand and pulled her towards the door as Marco Falco walked into the room. Carla frowned her disapproval.

'You can enter my rooms now, without knocking?'

Marco held his hands up. 'Apologies, Carla, but they tell me you're going out with Giancarlo.'

'Gianni, go wait by the elevator.' Giancarlo left the room, and Carla turned on Marco.

'So, you are now Fredo? I'm not allowed out alone with my son?'

'*Calmati* Carla. I am just concerned about your welfare. For you both. Bad things are happening.'

'Bad things are always happening here, Marco. I can take care of myself and my child.' She was about to leave when Marco caught her arm.

'People are dying. You could be at risk.'

She pulled her arm away. 'Why would Gianelli want to hurt me? Fredo is dead.'

'But that's it, Carla…I don't think it is Gianelli. Someone attacked their compound again last night. It wasn't us.'

With a small intake of breath, Carla stopped in her tracks. 'Do they know who it was?'

'No, and neither do I.'

'Probably the clans.'

'They say not.'

'And Sergio?'

'Unhurt.'

Damn.

'I spoke with Michael Rossi an hour ago and had to convince him it wasn't us. Someone is going after both families. That's why I'm concerned for you both.'

'Marco, I'm no threat to anyone.'

'True. But if you insist on going out, you must have a bodyguard.'

Carla looked him in the eyes. 'To protect me or spy on me?'

'I'm not Fredo, Carla, and I have no wish to be. Your life and your son's are your own concern, but I want you to be safe.'

He looked sincere, and, not wanting him to become suspicious by her refusal to be protected, Carla pleaded. 'Please, Marco, just let me be free for a little while. I've been living like a prisoner for so long.'

After consideration, he held up his hands in surrender. 'Have it your way. But be careful and stay alert.'

'I will.'

As she was leaving, Marco asked, 'Carla, why were you so sure that it was Gino who killed Fredo?'

She turned to look at him, her heart missing a beat.

'I just know. His size and his voice.'

'But it wasn't him. He was at the Venice film festival that night.'

Carla swallowed hard. *Merde. Think, Carla, think.*

'It was him, Marco.' As she was about to walk away, she stopped. 'Have you checked when he left the festival? It only takes ninety minutes to get back from Venice on a private jet. It was well after midnight when Fredo died.' She left, leaving Marco looking thoughtful. It was only when she was outside that she realised she was holding her breath.

***

Maria's face lit up as they entered the café, where she was busy baking in her small oven. Giancarlo ran over and hugged her. Mussa, sitting at a table playing with the iPad, watched them.

'My beautiful boy. I have made your favourite cake today,' Maria said, hugging him back.

'Grazie, Nonna Maria.'

Maria cut two slices of cake and put them on small plates. Handing them to Giancarlo, with a smile, 'For you and Mussa. Go eat while I talk to your mamma.'

Giancarlo slipped into the seat next to Mussa. They quickly attacked the cake, and they were soon involved together in a computer game.

'You're cooking late, Nonna,' said Carla, sitting at the table by the window.

'Yes, well, I've been busy all morning setting a *pulpo* free.'

Carla's eyebrows shot up. 'What?'

'Did you know that they have nine brains? Scientists say they could be aliens. They come here all the way from another planet, and what do people do? They eat them.'

'You set one free?' Carla looked bemused.

'Yes. Well, it was the kid's idea.' Maria's face dissolved into worried concern. 'Have you heard anything?'

'The Gianelli compound was attacked again, but they didn't catch him.'

Maria crossed herself. 'Thank God. And Marco?'

'He's confused. They don't know where it's coming from. They're looking at everyone.'

'But not at the man who sells their shitty handbags. If I wasn't so afraid for him, I would laugh,' said Maria.

'If they discover it was Joseph, Gianelli and Marco will kill them all. There will be nothing we can do to stop them.'

'Then he mustn't get caught, right?'

Carla, picking up a pastry and taking a bite, smiled. 'Right.'

The two boys whooped out loud. They had scored a win. Both children had suffered the loss of a parent but found comfort in each other's company and were at ease, playing together. Carla looked at them fondly. 'Why can't we all live like this? No racism, no tribalism.'

'Tribalism? What has that African nonsense got to do with us?'

'It's not just Africans, Nonna, it's all of us.'

'What are you saying?' Maria asked as she moved into the kitchen area and picked up an old wire brush, practically worn away from constant use, and, opening the oven door, started scrubbing the inside.

'Well, some Italians only want to mix with Italians…'

'Nothing wrong with that.'

Carla held back a smile. The answer from Maria was typical. 'But some want to mix only with the people from their town, from their district, or even just the people on the street where they live. The Napolitans hate the Romans, the Romans hate the Venetians and the Venetians don't like the people from Genoa. That's tribalism.'

'We all have our own problems. It doesn't stop foreign people from coming here,' Maria said with a huff.

'No, it doesn't, which makes you wonder what sort of hell they come from.'

Maria shuddered, wiping her hands on her apron and sat down next to Carla, dropping her voice so the kids couldn't hear. 'It's not for me to tell, but his poor wife was repeatedly raped as a child.'

Carla was appalled and filled with sadness. 'Poor woman, and then gets blown to pieces in what is supposed to be a civilised country.'

'Yes, God rest her soul.'

'That's why we must give people a chance, Nonna. And think about it, if Joseph hadn't come, I would still be Fredo's punchbag.'

'True. But they're not like us.'

Carla understood that Maria's prejudice came not from the colour of a person's skin but from the fear of losing her way of life. What she knew and loved was ingrained in every fibre of her being, and with the arrival of so many immigrants, she felt another culture was threatening her space. But she knew Maria was more bark than bite, and had a big heart, would always do the right thing. After all, here she was, taking care of Mussa and worrying about Joseph.

Chapter 51

Fearing betrayal, Sergio had dismissed all the house staff, and now scowled at the offering of bread and cheese Gino had rustled up for supper.

'…and I say it isn't. If we focus on him, it stops us from looking elsewhere,' insisted Michael.

'It makes no sense. It must be Falco,' argued Gino.

'Sturla employs apes. You think fucking apes could get past my guards?' snarled Sergio, 'Could it be an inside job? One of our own with ambitions.' His eyes sliding in Gino's direction made Gino twitch.

'There is no one here with the brain or the cojones, Don Sergio. And if that was the case, what would they benefit from taking out Sturla and Luigi Ricci?'

Sergio glanced at Gino. 'No one with a brain, you say. You're right. It would take an idiot to go against me and survive,' he snarled. 'But we have plenty of those. I don't want the men in the house.'

He's getting paranoid. 'But, Don Sergio, you must have protection. Now more than ever.'

But Sergio was adamant. 'One man, that's all. The rest outside.'

'Could it be coming from Rome?' asked Gino.

'I keep telling you, it's not Rome!' snapped Sergio. 'When disagreements happen between us, they warn us of the outcome. It's the way things are done.'

'So it's not them. Marco probably killed Fredo and got his own men to make it look like someone's attacking both clans,' insisted Gino. 'None of his soldiers have died. Just Fredo and Luigi Ricci. Very convenient for a takeover.'

Michael shook his head. 'Why would he need to cover it up by attacking us? What does he get from that? And no guns. Who operates like that? It's like something out of a fucking assassin movie.'

Sergio frowned. 'One thing puzzles me. When Fredo Sturla got it, why did they let Carla live? Why leave a witness?'

'Maybe the bitch is in it with Falco,' suggested Gino. It was a long shot, but even Michael, running out of patience with them, thought it was worth looking into, as maybe Carla had seen more than she had said.

'We should have a little talk with Carla Sturla,' said Sergio, looking pensive.

'I know how to get to her,' answered Gino. 'I'll do it first thing.'

Michael's eyes went to the window. The gardens were illuminated, and men were patrolling the grounds continuously. Sergio had demanded he stay; he hoped there would be no more alarms and they would get some sleep.

Foot soldiers were always at the lowest level of alertness just before dawn broke. Something the generals had used to their advantage in past battles. Joseph was about to do the same. With tools in hand, he made his way cautiously to the west side of the wall surrounding the compound.

Safe in the knowledge that he had successfully spooked the men enough, ensuring they stayed behind locked gates, it amused him to think he could make a fortune teaching them warfare, but he had worked for enough devils. *Never again.*

Laying explosives along the west wall was slow work, time consuming, as he had to be constantly alert and careful not to be seen. The rain had cut down the humidity and the sky was clear. The forest area around him was in deep shadow, despite the sun, as he made his way to the area in front of the gates. His finger hovered over the remote control button, ready to blow them all to hell, when the gates suddenly swung open. He retreated back into the cover of the trees, as the black Ferrari, with Gino at the wheel, came roaring out. It was followed by a black SUV with four men inside.

Damn.

Carla's voice rang in his ears. *'You have to get Gino, too, or lots of innocent people will suffer.* Disappointed, knowing he couldn't strike until Gino was back inside, he returned to his place high in the trees and waited.

***

Carla, preferring not to spend time in the penthouse, was again breakfasting in Maria's café with Gianni and Mussa. Hearing the low rumbling sound of a powerful engine, she looked from the window and saw a black Ferrari pulling up outside, followed by a black SUV. Gino got out of the car, followed by four henchmen, their eyes searching the street for danger. Her heart thumped against her chest and her mouth went dry with fear, thinking that maybe Marco was right and she was a target.

'Nonna, it's Gino Gianelli! Move the boys,' she said urgently.

Maria grabbed the two boys, and not having time to take them to her apartment, she shoved them out of sight behind the counter, warning them to lie low and be quiet.

Gino and two of the goons walked into the café. The other two stood on watch outside.

Maria pushed in front of Carla, confronting them with a sneer. 'What have we got here? Poor little Gino needs four men to protect him from two women?'

Highly sensitive about being called small, Gino wanted to lash out at her, but kept himself under control. It wouldn't go well if Sergio came to know he had struck an old woman. Not that Sergio would mind him striking her, but he would mind knowing she had gotten to him.

'Buongiorno Signora. We require a word with Carla,' he said, with a fake smile.

'My granddaughter doesn't want a word with you. You're not welcome here.'

'Like I want to be in this dump?' Gino sneered. Ignoring Maria, he faced Carla.

'How lucky for us that you visit your Nonna every day, now that Fredo has gone.'

Carla scoffed, 'So, you have nothing else to do but stalk me? They have a name for men who do that. You heard my grandmother. You're not welcome here.'

'Then we talk elsewhere.'

A goon grabbed Carla, who slapped his face and struggled. 'Get your hands off me!'

Maria attacked Gino, hitting him with her wet dishcloth. 'Pig! Leave my granddaughter alone.'

Gino pushed Maria, who fell backward onto the floor. Carla screamed and kicked, but they hauled her outside and forced her into the Ferrari.

The two boys, fearful for Maria, helped her to her feet. She hugged them. Tears ran down her face. 'It's okay, Nonna Maria, I will protect you,' said Gianni, wrapping his arms tightly around her.

'I protect you, Nonna Maria,' Mussa said, as he too hugged her.

Hearing this, Maria looked at Mussa, shaking her head.

'I'm not …' She stopped herself, looking at his small, earnest face, and forced a smile through her tears. 'Thank God I have you both here. My brave little soldiers. I don't know what I would do without you.'

'Will they hurt Mamma?' Giancarlo asked with a fearful look.

'No! They wouldn't dare.' *Dear God, I hope not.*

She hugged them both closer, her face full of anxiety for Carla, wondering if they had discovered Joseph and the part she had played. As much as she hated to do it she knew she had no choice, but to turn to Marco Falco for help.

Chapter 52

Carla, trying to calm herself with the thought that they would not bring her car if they intended to kill her, sat as far away from Gino as she possibly could in a Ferrari. His closeness gave her the creeps.

'You're a looker, I'll give you that …I bet Marco Falco thinks so too,' Gino sneered, glancing at her sideways.

'Go to hell, Gino.'

'Were you fucking him when Fredo caught it? Is that what happened?'

Carla looked at him with disgust. 'I was in my husband's bed when you murdered him.'

'I didn't kill him, and you know it, bitch, but killing you will give me a high, when we find out who did.'

So that's what they want me for, she thought. *They're running scared because of Joseph.*

She glanced from the window, wondering where Joseph could be; it was a waste of time hoping he'd given up.

As the black Ferrari made its way to the compound, Joseph, holding the detonator in one hand, used the other to train his binoculars on the cars as they approached. Within minutes, they would be through the gate, and he would press the button. Focused on the Ferrari to ensure it was Gino inside the car, he was alarmed to see a female sitting beside him. *A woman, what the hell?* As the vehicles entered the compound, he was stunned to recognise the car following behind. *He has Carla!*

Aware it wasn't a social visit and immediately concerned for her safety, Joseph laid the detonator gently on the ground next to his panga. Carla was in danger because of him. There was only one thing to do.

As he approached the gates of the compound, the guards came rushing out, brandishing their automatic weapons. The men on the roof and prowling the grounds immediately alerted, pinpointed him in their sights.

'What are you doing here? *Vaffanculo*, before I blow your head off,' one threatened.

Joseph remained calm.

Another looked him over with disdain. 'He's nothing. Just a fucking monkey.'

'I want to see Don Gianelli,' Joseph said.

The guards laughed. 'Just like that? You want to see the Don? Get the fuck outta here.'

'Tell him I know who killed Alfredo Sturla.' The guards looked at each other, amused.

'What? You?' one asked with a grin. Joseph stared at him. The grin died on the man's face and he twitched a little, obviously feeling the power coming from the man standing before him. 'Get Michael Rossi,' he told his partner.

***

Inside the compound, Carla was about to be searched when Gino pushed the guard away.

'I'll do the job myself,' he said, leering at her.

Carla gritted her teeth with disgust as he ran his hands over her body, lingering on her breasts. Carla spat in his face. 'Is this how you get your kicks, Gino? Sexually assaulting helpless women?'

He slapped her and pushed her into the house, walked her past Michael and down the long hallway lined with priceless artwork. If she hadn't been feeling apprehensive about what was to come, she would have been impressed. Michael followed them both to the main living area, where Sergio was waiting. As Michael was about to enter behind them, Gino, a grin on his face, closed the door, shutting him out.

The patio doors leading into the garden were open, and there was a light breeze in the room. Sergio, seated in a comfortable armchair, didn't take his eyes off the television screen. 'Can you believe it?' he said, looking impressed. 'Tina Marie got away with murder. What a woman.'

It took a moment for Carla to realise he was talking about a character in the soap opera he was watching. *Don't show him you're scared.* 'This is outrageous, Sergio. Your nephew sexually assaulting me and now you're kidnapping women?'

He turned the television off and faced her. 'Sit down, Carla. You're looking as beautiful as ever.'

'A little old for your taste, I hear. By the way, how is Lucia these days?' A nerve at the side of Sergio's eye twitched, proving to her that the rumours he had killed her were true.

Gino pushed Carla roughly onto a chair opposite Sergio, who laughed without humour.

'So, the chicken has claws. Interesting …Lucia left, and good riddance to her. It's what happens when women step out of line. You know that, Carla. And yes, it's true…I like my chickens young and fresh. You…are tainted meat,' he sneered.

'If you mean I was a married woman, yes, but now I'm a widow, thanks to you.'

Sergio shook his head. 'Not thanks to me, but maybe someone closer to you. Someone you know.'

Carla had a quick intake of breath. If they had information about Joseph, then both she and he were doomed.

'Someone you're fucking, Carla. What happened? He get ambitious?'

Fucking?

'What? Who? That's ludicrous. If any man looked at me, Fredo would have killed him, and me.' She pointed to the fading bruises on her neck. 'See these? They were for saying thank you to a man who opened a door for me.'

'I believe it,' said Sergio, nodding his head, 'But some people like to live dangerously. After all, you married Fredo Sturla. I'm curious, Carla, tell me about the night Fredo died.'

Carla hesitated.

'Does Gino have to encourage you?' Sergio smiled as he threatened.

Carla swallowed hard. 'I was lying on my stomach as we …so I didn't see him cut Fredo, but I heard him say it was for his family. I only glimpsed him as he escaped. He was wearing a black mask. That's all I know, Sergio, I swear.'

Sergio looked hard at her. 'So, enlighten me, Carla. Who do you think did it?'

Gino leaned close. 'If you hold anything back, I will kill you, but first I will hurt you, then I will hurt your Nonna and your kid. *Capisce?*'

Sergio nodded his approval.

Damned monsters, she thought, as the words burst out of her mouth. 'Gino! Gino did it! He wanted Fredo's cement business. Gino wanted him dead. He wants you all dead. He wants to take over your clan, Sergio! Everyone knows it. I recognised his voice and his size.'

'Fucking bitch. It wasn't me! I was in Venice!' Gino screamed.

'But you came back at midnight by private jet. Marco checked. You were here when Fredo died, Gino. It was you!'

Sergio scowled at him. 'You came back?'

'With a woman. I brought her back with me. I was in a hotel in the city,' he protested.

'Who was she?'

'I don't know, just a woman gagging for it.'

Carla was pleased to see how defensive he had become.

Sergio sighed, a disdainful look in his eyes. 'You don't know who you were fucking, Gino? Where did you meet this woman, on the streets?'

Before Gino could answer, there was an urgent knock on the door. Michael walked in.

'Scusi, Don Sergio, but there is a man here who says that he knows who killed Fredo Sturla.'

Carla's heart thudded in her chest.

'See *Tio*? I told you.' Turning to Michael, Gino asked, 'Is it one of Sturla's men?'

'No, Gino. It's one of the Africans.'

Gino grinned. 'What the fuck? A fucking eggplant? It's a joke, yes?'

'No joke. He's adamant he saw the person leaving the building that night.'

'Anyone can say that. He's looking for a handout. Get rid of him.'

'Don Sergio, he said the man was injured. Marco told me they thought they had clipped him with a bullet. No one else knows that.'

'See *Tio*? They shot him. Have I been shot? No!'

It puzzled Carla as to who it could be. Had Joseph told one of his co-workers who was about to betray him? If so, she was now in serious danger. So was Joseph, and everyone connected to them. A ripple of fear ran down her spine.

Michael, holding his phone, said, 'Also, Don Sergio, Falco has been on, asking why you have taken Carla, and if he is to understand that you have resumed hostilities.'

Sergio bristled, 'Hostilities? I just need a small talk with her. Tell him if I resume hostilities, he will soon know about it.' Irritated, he nodded his head at Michael. 'So, ask the mulignan.'

'He refuses to tell anyone but you, Don Sergio.'

'Kick it out of him!' Gino suggested.

Michael ignored Gino's typically immature response, and looked only at Sergio, who, now curious, shrugged. 'Okay, I'll see him.' Michael left as Sergio pointed at Carla and told Gino, 'Get her outta here. Fuckin' hostilities,' he grumbled.

'But what if she was part of it?' Gino protested.

'If he says he saw someone leaving the building and was shot, then it wasn't an inside job, you dumb shit. But if it was, we know where to find her. Now get her outta here.'

Carla swallowed hard as Gino pushed her through the door. He marched her down the long hallway, holding her firmly by the arm, his face close.

'You bitch, I'll be coming for you and yours.'

'You and whose army, Gino?' she sneered, determined not to show any fear.

But Carla didn't doubt that he would hurt her and her family, given the chance. If Joseph failed, she would have to turn to Marco to protect Giancarlo. Maria must have called him for him to make the call to Sergio, which maybe had made Sergio think twice about harming her, but the last thing that she wanted was to put herself and her son in debt to them. Marco was different compared to Fredo, but who knew what a man becomes once he's in power? Leaving the house, she had a sudden intake of breath when she saw Joseph walking towards them, flanked by two guards and Michael Rossi. *Mother of God! What are you doing?*

Chapter 53

Joseph was relieved to see that Carla was alive and unhurt. As they passed him, Gino grimaced at Joseph, sneering, 'Fucking ape.'

Where are they taking her? Joseph wondered.

As if reading his thoughts, Carla yanked her arm away from Gino, shouting. 'I can drive myself back to the city, thank you.'

Michael, with an armed man, walked Joseph through the house and into the main area, where Sergio was seated at a desk big enough to be a dining table.

Joseph quickly scanned the room. Open window, with no visible guard outside.

Sergio Gianelli wrinkled his nose, as if there were a foul smell in the place.

'Him? The one with the scar?'

'Si, Don Sergio. His name is Joseph,' said Michael.

A car engine fired up and Joseph heard the scraping of the gates as they opened.

She's leaving. Good.

Sergio looked at Joseph, his eyes narrowing to small slits as he weighed him up. 'So, talk.'

Joseph looked at Michael and the guard, indicating he wanted them to leave.

After mentally assessing the situation, Sergio decided there was no danger. 'Wait outside,' he instructed them.

'But Don Sergio…' Michael protested.

'He's a fucking eggplant. What can he do?' As he spoke, he reached into a desk drawer, and took out a gun, which he laid on the table in front of him.

'We'll wait by the door,' Michael said, as he reluctantly left the room with the armed thug, closing the door behind them.

Joseph mentally measured the room, counting how many steps were needed to reach what he needed.

'So out with it, who killed Alfredo Sturla?'

Playing for time to ensure that Carla was safely away, and knowing from experience that psychopaths, which he didn't doubt Sergio was, were vain, he said, 'I would like to ask you a question.'

'What? What question? Irritated, Sergio shifted in his chair. 'I'm the one who asks the questions.' His hand settled on the gun.

'What is it like to feel like an emperor?'

Taken by surprise, Sergio relaxed and grinned. 'An emperor, heh? You got that right.' His grin widened. 'Better than being lion shit. As you will be if you don't answer me. Who killed Sturla?'

Before he could blink, Joseph took two rapid paces, ripped the Roman gladius from the wall, and before Sergio had time to register what was happening, Joseph opened his throat with one slash.

'I did.'

Sergio, clutching his neck, a look of incredulity on his face, fell to the ground. His blood oozed out, bright red, staining the marble floor. He had the same look as Odango and Fredo Sturla – stunned to discover he was mortal.

Sergio's chair, clattering to the floor, brought the thug stationed outside the door bursting in, gun drawn. Momentarily shocked by the sight of Sergio's body, it gave Joseph time to cut him down before he could fire. However, Michael Rossi was in his wake, with his gun in hand.

'Put the sword down,' he ordered.

Joseph let the sword fall from his hand. It clanged against the marble floor.

'Kick it away.'

He did.

Michael glanced at Sergio's dead body with a look of total bewilderment. 'Who the fuck are you? What has anything got to do with you?'

'Gianelli and Sturla killed my family.'

'What…?' He then remembered. 'The black women who died in the car bombing – yes, you were there. I saw you.'

'She was my wife.'

'Jesus Christ! I don't believe this. That was Alfredo Sturla's doing, not us.'

'And the Gianelli killed my friends. Funny thing about friends…know them long enough, they become family.'

Michael still couldn't take it in. 'It was you…Sturla, all of it? One man? A fucking looky-looky boy?'

Joseph looked at him with cold eyes. 'I stopped being a boy a long time ago.'

'You killed two Camorra Dons.'

'Who killed hundreds with drugs and guns. What's a few more?'

Fuck, thought Michael, *thanks to this goon, I'm now saddled with idiot Gino as a boss*. His eyes had a mean look. 'Prepare yourself for hell.'

Before Michael could shoot, Gino burst into the room brandishing a gun. Seeing the carnage, and Michael with his gun trained on Joseph, he stopped in his tracks.

'What the fuck? He did this? That fucking monkey?'

'He did it all, Gino. Sturla as well. A one-man fucking army,' said Michael.

Gino let out a scream of rage and aimed his gun at Joseph. The sound of a shot made Joseph blink, thinking his end had come. But it was Gino Gianelli who fell to the floor. Michael shot him again to ensure he was dead. Doing so, he took his eyes off Joseph for a split second. Joseph seized the moment, ran to the open window and jumped down into the garden a few feet below. Michael followed and fired at him.

Despite being hit in the thigh by a bullet, Joseph, high on adrenaline, threw himself up and over the wall.

Guards, on hearing the gunshots, stormed into the house. Running into the room, they were dumbfounded to see the dead bodies.

Michael screamed at them, 'It was the African! He killed Sergio and Gino! Get him! I want him and every African on the streets dead!. Kill them all!'

As they rushed out, Michael looked down at the bodies and smiled. For years, without creating suspicion, he had been tying up the Gianelli money in a way that he could access every penny. Now that Sergio and Gino were out of the way, there was nothing to stop him from taking over. A sleeping psychopath, whose wife thought was better, Michael Rossi was no different from Sergio, Gino or Fredo Sturla.

Joseph, blood oozing from his thigh, stood on the edge of the clearing and ripped off his shirt, revealing a well-muscled but scarred body, damage from the cruelty that life had inflicted on him. He picked up the panga and detonator from the ground and watched as the iron gates swung open.

Armed men appeared at the gates, ready to release the dogs, which were straining on their leashes. The group hesitated at the sight before them. Michael came running out. 'What are you waiting for?' he yelled. His eyes followed theirs to Joseph, who now stood defiantly on the edge of the clearing. All he could see was the panga, which Joseph held aloft. *What the hell?*

'Release the dogs!' he yelled.

Ignorant of the real danger and thinking a man with a knife was an easy target, Michael smiled as he snatched a long-range rifle from a guard and aimed it at the only witness to his murder of Gino.

The snarling dogs were almost upon Joseph when Michael fired, and at the same instant, Joseph pressed the button. The explosives he had planted against the wall, backing onto the armoury, erupted, followed by several enormous blasts from the weapons stored inside. It blew away the walls, half of the house, and Michael Rossi. Frightened by the blast, the dogs disappeared into the trees. The bullet Michael had fired slammed into him, and Joseph dropped to the ground. His mind rushed back to Uganda, where, as a young soldier covered in blood, holding a Kalashnikov in one hand and a panga in the other, he had screamed at the heavens, 'No more!'

'No more,' he uttered before sinking into oblivion.

Hearing the explosion as she drove away, Carla stopped the car. Climbing out, she looked back and saw black smoke billowing into the air, coming from the direction of the compound. Heart thundering in her breast, she got behind the wheel, swung the car around, and drove back. Seeing Joseph inert on the ground and ignoring the carnage of the burning building before her, she got out of the car and ran to him, a desperate prayer on her lips.

Chapter 54

Despite it being a beautiful, cloudless day in Naples, the humidity having been washed away by the autumn rain, a lull hung over the city. Hundreds of people silently lined the Via Duomo all the way to the Duomo di Napoli and its 1,200 metres of religious grandeur. Hard-looking men in dark, expensive suits, lined the cathedral steps: clan bosses, seemingly there to pay their respects to the dead, each with an army of armed thugs protecting them. No one knew who had attacked the two families and killed two powerful dons, or the reason why. They were all on edge, wondering if they would be next. They cared nothing for Sergio, Gino, or Fredo, whose funeral it was today. If they got themselves killed, it wasn't their problem. Every one of them had greedy eyes, plotting and planning. Like hyenas, they watched Marco Falco closely for any sign of weakness.

With the Gianelli Clan disbanded, it left the fake business open to Marco Falco, who moved in swiftly. Shiploads were arriving from China and goods were already being distributed around Europe. The opening of a bank in China was underway. The people in the underground Gianelli factories were still working, no longer making fakes, but still turning out their cheap clothing for the remaining crime families who had shared control of the business. Peace was once again restored to the streets.

The men of the Sturla Clan formed a guard of honour, up the steps to the cathedral entrance, where the bishop stood gowned and mitred. As the hearse passed slowly by, carrying the coffin adorned with a mass of white flowers and religious icons, people crossed themselves and muttered prayers. An outsider would be mistaken to think they were for Fredo's soul.

In the car following the hearse, Carla, dressed in black, sat in the back with Maria. Giancarlo sat in the front with the driver, Mario.

'A grand funeral for a man who has gone to hell. Even the damned bishop is here,' whispered Maria, adjusting the black veil over her face.

'Pious-faced bandit, he should be, considering all the donations Fredo made,'

'Judas money,' said Maria, scowling.

The car drew up behind the hearse in front of the cathedral steps. Carla and Maria, both their faces now covered with black veils, got out. Clutching Gianni tightly by the hand, they stood to one side as six men lifted the coffin from the hearse, then followed them up the steps through the door. Marco Falco and his men walked behind.

As they entered, Carla was thankful that her veil hid the scorn she felt for the saintly show being presented for her monster husband, all organised by Marco to show the clan bosses he had respect – not for Fredo, but for the syndicate and what they stood for. Walking down the aisle, she caught sight of Irina, who gave her a small smile. The voices of choir boys filled the air. The sound of angels singing for a demon.

They endured the service for two hours, listening to false expressions of sentiment. Marco handled it well, Carla thought, as he managed not to show contempt for a man she now realised he had obviously despised.

After the sickening eulogy given by the bishop, they removed the coffin to a nearby crematorium, where they held a short private service before it entered the furnace.

'Thank God that's over,' muttered Carla as they left the building.

'It was a small price to pay,' said Maria as they walked to the car, lifting their veils. 'It was very satisfying seeing him burn. What happens now?'

'Fredo paid vast amounts of money to the church to have his remains interred in the cathedral – they have no room for more coffins, no matter how much you pay, but they have a wall in which you can place the ashes. Of course, he never dreamed he would die so soon.'

Maria frowned. 'Will you honour his wish?'

Carla smiled. 'No chance. He'll go down the sewer where he belongs.'

Maria nodded her head and grinned in approval. 'That's my girl.'

Giancarlo walked a little ahead. 'Will Gianni be okay? Animal that he was, Fredo was his father,' Maria said, pulling off her veil.

Yes, and he gave me the most precious child. But a monster is a monster.

'He'll be fine once we're out of the unhealthy atmosphere, Nonna.'

Marco came hurrying after them, excusing himself to Maria for wanting a word with Carla. Maria huffed, but taking Gianni's hand, she walked ahead to the car.

'What is it, Marco?' asked Carla, feeling slightly irritated.

'I worry. We could still be in danger. I want you to take care.'

'So you still don't know who was responsible?'

'We checked every possibility and came up with nothing.'

'Maybe it was an angel of death,' she teased.

'I doubt it.' He said it with a wry smile. 'But it is strange that with all the informants we have in this city, we never discovered who it was.'

'Why? You want to thank them?'

Marco almost chuckled.

'I've told you before, Marco, I can take care of myself and my boy. Gianni will never be one of you.'

Marco shrugged. 'Most of the city is one of us, Carla. The clans have the biggest workforce in Italy. What would happen if we didn't exist? The politicians would take our place, and it would be no different, except they make the laws and unmake them when it suits them.'

Carla snorted with derision. 'Oh, please. You are the biggest slave drivers and prolific killers with your guns and drugs. That is what you have inherited, Marco. Look at the crowds today. You think they're here to mourn the death of a capo?' she scoffed. 'Of Fredo? They are here to make sure he's gone.'

Marco reflected on this for a moment. 'Things will change. I promise you, Carla.'

'I'd like to think you're different, but only time will tell. I will move out of the penthouse as soon as possible. No doubt you're eager to move in.'

Marco shook his head. 'Not at all. You can stay there as long as you wish. It's your home.'

'My home? You think I would choose to live in that house of horror? Really?'

'Fredo has gone, Carla, but whatever you choose to do, I will support you.'

'Thank you. Just leave me and Giancarlo to get on with our lives. Now, if you will excuse me, I have another funeral to arrange,' she said, walking off.

'If there's ever anything I can do for you…' he called after her.

Carla hesitated and turned to look at him. She walked back, unaware of the crowds all wanting a glimpse of the beautiful widow, watching her every movement.

'Actually, Marco, there is something.' She hesitated. 'But no ties attached?'

Marco shrugged. 'Just say the word. Whose funeral?'

'Someone who deserved better.'

Chapter 55

I feel nothing about my actions. I don't fear a god full of anger, wrath, and revenge. If such a deity exists, it must be beyond those petty human emotions that have entrapped me for all these years, and will not judge my frantic scrabble to survive because I am what he created. My soul felt lost years ago with the death of Ariya and the maelstrom that followed, but it is thanks to Kizza that my heart remains capable of love, and I will never stop loving her.

Joseph and Mussa laid roses on Kizza's grave, together with a sign that read: RIP.

He struggled, trying to dig a little hole in the soil topping Big Moses' grave, which, together with Abdi's, was close by.

'Let me do it, Joseph,' said Carla, standing to one side with Maria, Benjamin, Jacob and Bolo. 'You don't want those wounds to open. Remember what the doctor said. You have to be careful.'

The bullet had missed Joseph's internal organs by a fraction, but the damage required intensive surgery. Carla spared no expense in getting him to an exclusive private hospital, the same one the Pope had used when he was operated on the year before. She wanted the best doctors that Fredo's money could buy, and she got them.

Joseph shook his head and held up a hand. It was something he had to do himself. He buried the Bible in the hole and put a sign on top of the little mound, moving to put another on Abdi's grave.

'What does it mean, Pappy, RIP?' asked Mussa, slipping his hand in Joseph's.

'It means rest…rest in peace,' he answered, the words choking in his throat.

'Has Uncle Moses gone to Jesus?'

'Yes Mussa, Moses has gone to Jesus, and he is happy now.'

'Mamma too?'

Joseph looked at the earnest face of his child. His heart lurched in his chest. Kizza, whom he had loved all his life, was gone. *Maybe she has found peace at last*, he thought. *Maybe there is a God, and she is safe somewhere with all those I lost.*

'Yes, Mussa, Mamma too.'

***

Joseph and Mussa, approached Café Borolo just as Carla was arriving with Giancarlo. Seeing them she smiled, looking bright and happy, a long way from the woman he had first laid eyes on. Mussa ran to Giancarlo, delighted to see his friend, and they disappeared into Maria's café.

Carla handed him a large envelope. 'Courtesy of Marco Falco.'

Joseph was almost afraid to accept it.

'Well, open it. It won't bite,' she said, urging him to read it.

Doing so, he opened it and took out a sheaf of documents. He read the top one, and his face broke into a big smile.

'Work papers…?'

'Yes. Work papers for you and your friends. I wanted it to be a surprise, so I got their names from Mussa. I hope you don't mind.'

Joseph couldn't believe it. No more selling from the pavement. He could get a proper job, maybe in carpentry or construction, hopefully with decent wages, and take good care of Mussa.

' I don't know how to thank you.'

'You already did,'

He suddenly frowned, looking suspicious. 'But, from Marco Falco? Who do I have to kill for this?'

Carla laughed. 'The only thing a capo has ever done without wanting repayment. Maybe things *are* changing. Come into the café. I have some news for you, and Nonna wants to feed us.'

Maria welcomed them with a smile. The smell of bubbling cheese coming from the lasagne, invaded Joseph's senses and made his stomach rumble. While Joseph was recovering, and in Maria's care, the Café had become a second home to Mussa, who, despite the occasional breakdown – crying for his mother and Moses – was beginning to feel secure again now that his father had returned. He was standing next to Giancarlo, who began pleading with his mother to buy him a *pulpo* to set free.

'Nonna, what have you started?' Carla asked, looking perplexed.

'Don't blame me. Blame David Attenborough there,' Maria answered, nodding towards Mussa.

'Joseph, take a seat.'

Maria beamed with pleasure seeing them tuck into the food. When the meal was over and enjoyed by all, especially the walnut and coffee cake that had disappeared before she could blink, Maria looked at Carla and said, 'So, are you ready to go?'

'Yes, Nonna.' She turned to Joseph. 'I wanted us all to enjoy this meal together before we leave. Tomorrow, Gianni and I start a new life in Rome.'

'Rome? So far?' asked Joseph.

'It's two hours away, not a million miles,' huffed Maria. 'But far enough,' she grumbled.

'I've enrolled in a collage of architecture, Joseph. Something I have always wanted to do. We will come back often to see you and Mussa, I promise. And you can both come and see me.'

'And I will come and walk down the Via Veneto, like Sophia Loren,' Maria said, preening a little.

'To look at all the rich women in their finery?' Carla teased.

'No. So they can look at me.'

Carla smiled fondly. 'And so they should, Nonna.'

Joseph looked at Maria properly, realising that, despite her age, she was a beautiful woman.

'Yes, so they should.'

Maria grunted, trying hard not to appear flattered. Her expression changed suddenly when something outside the café caught her attention. She jumped to her feet and went to the door.

A young African was setting up his stuff outside of her café.

'Not on my pavement, you don't! Move it!' she yelled at him, hands on hips.

The youth quickly pulled his blanket away. Grumbling, she returned to the café and winked at Joseph, making him smile. Carla was on her feet, ready to leave.

Maria hugged and kissed her and Giancarlo.

'As soon as we're settled, I'll be in touch,' said Carla, welling up.

'You need to be settled to pick up the phone? Use that pad thing. I want to see how much Giancarlo grows every day. Mussa can show me how.'

'Good idea, Nonna.'

Carla turned to Joseph. 'Take care.' She hugged him. '*Grazie mille*, Joseph.'

'No, Carla. Thank you. *Arrivederci*. Good luck in Rome.' Carla gave him a gentle smile, and bent down to hug and kiss Mussa, who was looking sad that he was losing his friend.

'We will see you soon, Mussa, okay? Giancarlo will be back to visit you, me too.'

Mussa nodded his head. 'Verdaci...' Carla smiled at his attempt to say goodbye in Italian. It brought tears to her eyes.

'*Arrivederci* Mussa.'

She pressed something into his hand. And closed his fingers around it. 'This is a little gift for both of you, because I no longer need it.'

Maria stood on the pavement, wiping away a tear as she waved them off. Yes, it hurt that they had left, but she accepted that in Rome they could start a new life, a good life where they would be safe. And yes, she would see them often; deciding that, at her age, it wouldn't hurt to open the café just three days a week.

'It's for the best, and it's not that far away,' Maria said, as she sat down at the table with Joseph. 'Besides, I have a free pass on the trains. It's the only good thing I get from this damned thieving government.'

Mussa held out his hand. In it was the heart-shaped diamond ring. 'Pappy...?'

Joseph was stunned. It was obviously worth a small fortune. He took it from Mussa.

'Go see Jacob, Mussa.'

Mussa left quickly, delighted to stand on the pavement with Jacob and the other men.

Joseph looked at the ring and the memory of seeing it on Carla's finger after he had killed Fredo flashed through his mind. There had been blood on the stone.

He held the ring out to Maria, shaking his head. 'I can't take this. You must give it back to her.'

'I will not! You want to throw my granddaughter's kindness back in her face? Is that what they do in your country?'

Her outburst took Joseph aback.

'She gave it with a good heart. Accept it with a good heart.'

'It's a lot.'

'What you did was a lot. I don't think she wants to see the damn thing again, and neither do I. The sooner you sell it, the better.'

'It's too much,' he insisted.

Maria shrugged with impatience. 'If it's too much, give it away. But don't give it to anyone who will buy a damn boat to bring in more Africans.'

The same old Maria, but as she spoke, he could see the humour in her eyes, which turned to concern.

'Joseph, you have a child to keep, a life to build here. This is an opportunity.'

Looking through the window, Joseph could see Mussa standing with Jacob. He wanted a good life for his boy, as would Kizza. Proper schooling. An education that would get him a good job away from the streets and the clutches of people like the Messiah and the clans with their way of violence. 'I want to be a 'bologist,' Mussa had told him, mispronouncing the word, 'working with sea creatures.' His son had a dream, and now he had the chance to help it come true. He looked at the ring again and remembered the blood. *Superstition be damned. Fredo Sturla was just one of the crocodiles in my river,* he thought as he nodded at Maria, and slipped the ring in his pocket.

Maria smiled. 'Of course, you'll probably get arrested when you try to sell it,' she said with a twinkle in her eye.

Joseph laughed, knowing she was right. Who would ever

believe that he hadn't stolen it?

'Unless you have this, of course.' She handed him some papers. 'It's verification that the ring is genuine and belongs to you. Carla has signed it.'

Feeling overwhelmed, Joseph took the papers. It took a moment for him to speak. Apart from the gift of Kizza and his son, not in all the years since he was kidnapped from Cobo village, had life shown him any kindness. 'Apart from Kizza, no one has ever done anything for me,' he said.

'No? Well, remember this: it took a Neapolitano. This city has its problems, but there are plenty of good people here, too.'

'I believe it. How can I ever thank you?'

Maria shrugged. 'I need some shelves mending. And I've been thinking, maybe you and Mussa should stay in the apartment.'

'You want us to stay?'

Maria, wiping her hands on her pinafore, shrugged. 'Well, I don't think I'll find another idiot to rent it.'

Joseph roared with laughter, and Maria joined in. His laughter turned to tears. He dropped his head in his hands and cried at last. A tsunami of tears that had been welling since the day the soldiers had burst into his home, killing his family and kidnapping him and Kizza. Maria put a comforting arm around him.

Winning Maria's acceptance was something he once never wanted or thought would ever happen. *But here we are.*

He could hear Kizza's voice in his head, replying, *Yes. Here you are.*

The End.

I can be changed by what has happened to me, but I refuse to be reduced by it.
Maya Angelou

Acknowledgements

As with the dedication, I must acknowledge my son, Karl Jago for his insistence that I write this story. I am deeply grateful for his contribution, unflagging support, and enthusiasm.

My Mother, Harriet Taft Clements, for passing on her creative gene.

To my elder sister, Norah Adams, whose unshakable love and belief in me since childhood, is a beacon of light in my life.

And to my dearly departed sister Lily, whose voice remains forever in my head, telling me to get on with it. Last but not least, to all my family and friends who encouraged me on the way.

You know who you are. Thank you, I love you all.

Barbara

Author's Notes

In my research for this novel, I came across many disturbing facts, which assisted me in forming the following opinions:

The LORDS RESISTANCE ARMY'S principal means of recruiting its forces in Uganda is the abduction of children because they are easier to corrupt and cheaper to maintain. Joseph Rao Kony, the self-appointed 'Messiah' of the LRA, who claims to be sent by God, oversees the rebel group responsible for Africa's longest-running armed conflict. His war of attrition against the government and people of Uganda is a conflict without national vision or unifying social objective, other than a general aim to depose the Ugandan president Yoweri Museveni. Over 25,000 children were kidnapped, forced to strengthen Kony's army, commit atrocities, and fill his brothels.

The intensity of international trade in recent years has made it difficult to confirm the authenticity of manufactured goods and so counterfeiting has become a lucrative market for criminals in Europe. Another factor is the high demand among consumers for counterfeit products. For criminals, the phony wares are cheap to produce – such as those involving forced labourers — and distribution. Counterfeit product sales also serve as a convenient way for OCGs to launder money. Estimates of the global market for counterfeit goods range from $250 billion to $650 billion. In Europe, one study, based on consumer surveys on willingness to buy counterfeit instead of authentic goods, has been estimated at more than $42 billion a year, with Italy having by far the largest illicit market. The U.S. is not far behind.

If you would like to do your own research and more reading into the subjects covered within this novel, please check out the following resources:

https://en.wikipedia.org/wiki/Lampedusa_immigrant_reception_center

https://en.wikipedia.org/wiki/Triangle_of_death_(Italy)

https://borgenproject.org/

https://www.hrw.org/topic/international-justice

https://www.cam.ac.uk/research/features/the-bible-as-a-weapon-of-war

https://invisiblechildren.com/challenge/kony/

https://wwf.panda.org/es/?207485/Konys-LRA-engaged-in-poaching-and-ivory-trade

https://reliefweb.int/report/sudan/human-rights-child-soldiers-uganda

https://globalinitiative.net/analysis/konys-ivory-how-elephant-poaching-in-congo-helps-support-the-lords-resistance-army/

https://www.voanews.com/a/hundreds-of-african-migrants-dead-or-missing-in-mediterranean/1762002.html

https://www.britannica.com/topic/Camorra

https://www.understandingitaly.com/mafia-camorra.html

https://www.thenewhumanitarian.org/ar/node/218178